I0617632

SENIORS
HAVE IT TOUGH

A WALLETECTOMY
HITS THE BIG SCREEN

COMEDY, ROMANCE, AND CLONE
FARM MEDICAL TRANSPLANTS

E. SCOTT SPENCER

Copyright 2008 Thomas M. Dodington
ISBN 978-0-9785587-3-4

Previously published as S.H.I.T. in 2006

Also by E. Scott Spencer:
GYPSY WAVES, 2008
HAUNTED STEEL ADVENTURES, 2007

Published by Horsington Press
Martindale, Texas
www.escottspencer.com

AUTHOR'S NOTE: This book, its characters and actions, are fictitious: locations and names, if real, are used fictitiously.

Warning

This book has not been dumbed-down, sanitized, or edited to make it politically-correct. The End-notes explain the motion picture terminology used in the text.

Seniors Have It Tough

Chapter 1

Opening Night

Bloody, slippery, disgusting flesh squished beneath Keith's feet as the security guards edged him through the angry screaming crowd toward the limo. His handsome athletic fifty-year old body almost fell down in the muck, but Jessica dug her fingers into his arm, her spiked heels giving traction through the slime. Camera strobes blinded them as mangled disconnected arms and legs sailed by, red blurs in photos that hopefully would run in the world's papers tomorrow morning and on TV tonight. Her thin, almost translucent, white slip-like gown was protected from the flying blood by a clear ankle-length raincoat as they neared a guarded platform by the car.

Violent protestors in green medical scrubs and white nursing uniforms screamed as they hurled insults and body parts while waving signs, "Transplant This Movie To Hell", "Doctors Care, Shouldn't You?", "See You In The Operating Room". Among the medical protestors were wrinkled gray old people shouting with other signs, "Tax This!", "Free Parts For Everyone", "I want yours". Left-wing politicians and their lackeys worked the crowd, complaining that the film was un-American: it poked fun at tax collectors and hard-working government employees. They struggled through the crowd to grab face time with the reporters and cameras. Scattered among these identifiable groups were children's rights lawyers, religious nuts, and fringe-group whiners. Searchlights scanned the sky as drunken street-people peered from the filthy shadows of Hollywood Boulevard. Keith, his raincoat dripping red slime, felt himself shaking as he and Jessica joined three friends on a little platform near the long white blood-spattered limo.

Keith Warrington, a quiet serious screen writer at the peak of his career and his group were just outside Grauman's Chinese Theater as one of his films premiered behind the violent protests. Keith was unusually anxious about the success of this particular film because it had been hidden from the public, locked in a vault on Cole Street, for the past twenty-five years. The group had been young, unknown, and more than a bit crazy when they had made SENIORS HAVE IT TOUGH long ago. Back then they had all been nobodies, pinching every penny to breathe life into this film, his first production script. The marquee gave the film's theme, "The ultimate realities, death and taxes, and how Senator Savage almost escaped both". Keith had staged the premier here for nostalgic reasons. Grauman's Chinese had opened more films than any other venue, but the luster and cachet were only memories. He knew that the real domestic box-office would come from suburban multiplex theaters and ten dollar tickets.

Goose bumps and cold sweat rippled across his body as he struggled not to cry. He was remembering the events that had led to the creation of this film, the beautiful life that had been lost, and the part of his heart that had been ripped away. The sudden surge of old memories crushed him almost to the breaking point. Jessica, Keith's wife of twenty-five years, was close beside him, holding him tightly and smiling to the cameras as though nothing was amiss.

To an observer, Jessica at fifty appeared quite beautiful, still retaining the charm of her youth and a mysterious smile that gave a slight hint of the unusual person behind it. Although she appeared composed and in-control of her actions, she was a mass of confusion inside, just barely holding onto reality. From the moment she had seen the medical protesters and the bloody parts flying, old emotions and thoughts had overwhelmed her consciousness. Tonight, she fully believed that in the distant past she had died under the bloody hands of a surgeon whom Keith had subsequently murdered, then she had been reborn as another person through a mystical transformation. These thoughts were unfocused, swimming, appearing then dissolving, though she vividly remembered specific incidents actually happening. On clear days she wondered how much was real and how much she just imagined or dreamed: inside Jessica, reality and dreams were often interwoven. Her emotions, that linked events and thoughts together, that colored their meaning, allowed factual reality and her imagination to switch back and forth. Yet she knew right now when looking at the marquee that the film was real, they had made it together, their names were on the posters. And when she looked through the old photos hidden away in the back of a bedroom drawer, she could see Kristin's smile: that girl had also been real. The razor sharp carving knife was still in its place: Keith had been adamant about keeping it even though it's discovery would have landed him in the gas chamber.

She trembled in her thin gown and whispered in Keith's ear, "You're doing fine, we've just got to hang on for a few minutes more and we'll be out of here." He squeezed her arm in silent reply.

The group of five people gathered on the small platform by the car was dressed for a party, tuxedos and designer gowns, protected from the mess by clear raincoats, and a ring of security guards. Xenon searchlights slowly panned the hazy night sky like ghosts from the past.

In contrast to the seriousness of Keith and Jessica,

David Nosrak, who had directed SENIORS, was nearby, laughing through the noise and mess with Sam Merano, who had played Senator Savage, the leading dirty-old-man in the film. Spunk Spunkbody, rounded out their group. She had played the over-sexed part of Spunky in the film when she was a nubile scantily-clad teen, and had liked the name of the character so much that she had changed her name, and her personality, to match it. Spunk had grown up to become a well-known actress, expertly playing tough girls who scored in bad situations. David and Spunk were almost A-list celebrities, attracting cameras and attention wherever they went. Spunk was having fun catching body parts as they flew by, hurling them back into the crowd trying to hit cameramen, reporters and quacks, as she swore continuously, purposely generating piles of crazy footage for the gossip shows.

Keith could see the exiting audience, mostly young and irreverent, just leaving the first-ever public screening of SENIORS. The viewers were laughing and telling the line of waiting customers that they were in for a great show. Their laughter was in sharp contrast to the shouting voices and waving placards from the protestors, who were separated from the customers by yellow tape and usherettes.

Beside Keith, a TV news crew covered a shouting match between two bloated politicians and David, who was laughing into the camera, explaining that the film was outrageous entertainment, fun for everyone, a belly-laugh, not a serious medical statement. One of the politicians threatened committee hearings, lawsuits and investigations, as David exclaimed, "Look at that line of customers stretching around the block: they're voting for us with their wallets, not for you."

The guards edged Keith and his friends toward the limo. As an ancient protestor tried to swat Sam with a sign,

Spunk yelled, "Up your nose with a rubber hose." David, Spunk and Savage laughed hysterically at this odd rejoinder, leaving a mystified TV crew behind as the limo drove away. The gullible TV reporters would have had a real story to report if they had known that most of the protestors were a hired flash mob, arranged by the film's publicity team, along with look-alike body parts from Stage Specialties and Fake-O-Blood from Delightful Gore. They had been hired to generate publicity, and their antics were being carefully filmed by bogus tourists to flesh-out the DVD release and publicity materials. Everyone knew that over 80% of a film's revenue would come from the sale of ancillary rights and DVDs, while traditional box-office income was a smaller and smaller part of the take.

This strange and implausible film had been waiting a long time for its chance to entertain the world.

Seniors Have It Tough

Chapter 2

Birth Of A Film, 1980

In 1980 Keith was twenty-six and lived alone on Le Conte Street in Westwood, a lovely part of Los Angeles between UCLA and Beverly Hills. Manicured homes, tree-lined streets with Magnolia blossoms and Jacarandas, flowers and fruit trees in every yard, all built by The Janss Development Company in the twenties.

Keith was a Production Sound Mixer, responsible for recording the track on other people's movies. Like many in the business he fantasized about writing a big hit and worked on his dream nights and weekends, aiming for the comedic hit of the century. Purely by good luck, though he might have attributed it to skill and hard work, Keith had managed to sell a screenplay which he had written on spec. At least he thought he had sold it, but now it appeared that he had almost given it away. He was badly shocked when he had a chance to carefully examine the agreement that he, David, and their agent Bernie had signed with a medical investment group, SUPERIOR COMMERCIAL AND MEDICAL Fund, or SCAM-F.

Keith's remuneration came in three parts. The first part, and the only part he might actually receive, was for working sound on the crew. The Production Sound Mixer was the person responsible for the sound track. He might have a Recorder Operator and a Boom man or two working under him on a large project. On this el-cheapo deal, he would probably be running the recorder, mixing the sound from the various mikes during shooting, and schlepping the gear himself, with one loyal Boom man to help with the mikes. He would receive IA scale, which was the minimum that he could be paid. (IATSE, International Alliance of Theatrical and Stage Employees, had a lock on all Hollywood theatrical film production craft jobs, and he was a member of local 695). Keith was good enough that he usually received 20% over scale, but he could live with the discount in return for working on his own film. However, these wages would only be paid during production, which was at least two months after the signing.

For the screenplay, Keith would receive 2% of the gross which the film actually earned. This could be wonderful if the film were a hit, but trivial if it flopped. He was pleased to see that his percentage was 'of the gross', and not 'of the profits', because accountants usually fudged the books so that there were never any profits, even on blockbusters. The third part of his pay was $1000 for each page he re-wrote, but the rewrite fees would not be paid until the film recovered all of its other production costs. Against this potential writing income, was his agreement to be available for consultation and re-write twenty-four hours a day from contract signing until the film was screened for preview. He had signed away six months of his life, in return for a slim payment.

David and Keith were old friends, and had managed a package deal, where David would direct what Keith wrote. David's contract was even worse. In return for his big directing breakthrough, he would also receive 2% of the gross, and DGA scale (Directors Guild of America, which controlled the management of all Hollywood films), but payable only after all other costs, including Keith's, were paid. David wouldn't get a penny until the film was ready for the screen.

As an aside, Keith noted that Bernie had received ten

grand in cash up-front for negotiating the deal. Keith and David might be unknown and exploitable now, but they were determined to send the world into hysterics with their first film.

Before the ink was dry on the contract, David and Keith were headed up Sunset to the pink stucco Beverly Hills Hotel. They were in David's black Porsche 911 because they knew that the valets wouldn't park Keith's old VW. They had a laugh about turning the tables on the snooty valets in their fancy uniforms when the same goofballs showed up for the next casting call. Virtually all parking attendants and waiters from downtown to the beach were unemployed actors waiting for a break.

They walked nervously through the ornate hotel to the poolside café where they were to meet three of the men from SCAM-F. Keith had no idea what the men looked like and whispered to David, "If this were a film and you were casting these guys, what sort of fools would you hire? How would the audience recognize them quickly?"

"I'd get some pale-skinned semi-bald overweight guys with painted-on tans, then dress them in white slacks and the most expensive and inappropriate shirts and shoes I could find on Rodeo Drive."

"And don't forget over-priced Italian dark glasses and a D-cup hooker for each of them."

"That's going too far, at least the hookers. This is supposed to be a business lunch."

"Too bad, cause there're three painted guys with hookers over in the sun to our left. Let's introduce ourselves and see if I'm right."

David hid his laughter just in time as they walked to the table and politely introduced themselves to the men, who indeed turned out to be the financial representatives. These guys were writing the checks so humorous comments about their appearance were suppressed. Keith noticed that in spite of their appearance and the bimbos rubbing against them, all three men had wedding rings and would have easily passed for dull middle-aged accountants in Queens. Their names were Mike Harnschreiber, Herb Schaeffer, and Sy Greenberg. Two nearly-empty bottles of Veuve Cliquot were on the table. The girls smiled their perfect teeth and stretched their tight blouses when the two handsome young men approached. But they realized immediately from the youths' accessories that they didn't have the cash to pay for favors. Neither David nor Keith had European shoes or Rolexes, the two most important clues in the girls' world. Keith's old Patek Philippe watch, which was worth twice the price of most Rolexes, didn't register in their eyes since it wasn't gold.

Waiters quietly brought two chairs, glasses, and another bottle of champagne, as Sy commented, "We've got five films in production: a romantic tear-jerker, a kung-fu chop-em-up, a motorcycle flick that's sure to be a blockbuster, an X-rated porno, and your medical flick."

"Wow, you've really covered the bases," David said. Keith was too surprised at the weird bundle to say anything. He was also furious that artists like David and himself were forced to deal with such fools. He wondered if film was the only art-form that was dominated by bean-counters instead of aesthetics.

"Yea, our docs are looking for fun as much as anything, so they told us to buy five of the screwiest el cheapo scripts we could find," Herb added.

"They've got tons of normal investments, so this is just pocket change for them. If one of these makes it big, it will cover the other four, so we're just playing the odds."

"We are going to be that film, the one that pays for all

the others," Keith added quietly as he burned with desire to make this film outstanding.

"I like your attitude! You've got youth, weirdness, enthusiasm, and inexperience on your side, while the others have track records, hot bodies, foreign locations, sex, and crapola."

"The only thing you five have in common is that each of you is making a theatrical feature for a million bucks total cost."

Somehow David had thought that they had five million, a decent but low, budget, but before he expressed his shock, he realized that he must have misunderstood Bernie. Five was the price for the whole package, not just their film.

"We're anxious to start, to match our ideas to the budget and the script. Have you made any kind of financial plan that you want us to follow," Keith asked quickly before David could react.

"Of course not, we have the big ideas, and expect you to work the details and to report to us weekly, in writing, on your progress. The key rules are that the film must be thirty-five millimeter, color, two hours long, and have a total production cost under a million."

Keith could see that David was almost apoplectic, so he wanted to escape quickly before anything bad happened. If David lost his temper at the wannabes' insensitive comments, their film would be dead. Thousands of other projects were piled on the desks of hacks like Bernie, just waiting for a break like this, so it was time to get busy and make this a success.

"We understand exactly what to do, so if you don't mind, we'd like to skip lunch and start work immediately," Keith said as he rose from his chair and placed a hand on David's arm, signaling him to keep quiet.

"Send your detailed budget here as soon as its ready,

and poke some sex into your script. When I scanned it, I don't remember getting a hard-on anywhere, so goose it up a bit," Sy said as he squeezed the honey who was practically in his lap.

"Take advantage of those nubile young virgin clones. Those hot young bodies should be humping away, making babies as fast as they can to keep the old farts ticking. That could be the best part of your flick." Herb added with a laugh as they walked away.

Keith's screenplay indeed had "nubile young virgin clones" as a key feature. However they were not sex objects, at least not yet. His story centered on a group of extremely old people, average age 150, and their struggle to stay alive. They kept going by replacing their body parts as they wore out: just like keeping an old car running. To ensure a steady supply of parts, they raised perfect young human clones on a secret farm. This all happened at a posh retirement complex, a remote fenced enclave far out in the desert. The film opens with an explosion as a group of teenage clones escapes, and the rest of the film concerns the oldies' bumbling efforts to recapture the perfect young bodies before the I.R.S. discovers what the oldies are doing.

Keith knew this weird plot was gruesome, but he had turned it into a comedy by making the oldies similar to the Marx Brothers, and satirizing the government and doctors; it was all somewhat in the vein of the film A DAY AT THE RACES, with slapstick scenes involving doctors, the oldies, and government workers. The transplant doctors operated in a flashing-lights game-show atmosphere focused on money: their favorite operation was a walletectomy. Keith knew that his most unusual film could be a big hit or a total disaster, depending on how it was perceived. The line between horror and comedy was very thin and most of this film was right on the edge. They also realized that they were dealing with a highly controversial subject and that unless they were careful the film would be unmarketable due to human rights protests.

After a short drive, David and Keith sat in the Westwood Village Hamburger Hamlet pondering burgers and coffee, adjusting to the realities of their situation.

"I still can't believe the package of crap those guys are buying for their clients. How'd we ever get associated with those nitwits?"

"Take it easy David, at least they've given us some money and a free hand on the creative side. With cleverness we can make a dynamite flick with their dough."

"And how'll we do that?"

"As a start, we could shoot it in Techniscope, and cut the film stock and processing budget in half. It would still be thirty-five millimeter."

"Shit, I've never worked on a film that was that cheap; save that option for last."

"OK, it's obvious this isn't going to be seventy-millimeter, or anything fancy given the budget, so let's use normal cameras with anamorphic lenses and be careful about how much we shoot."

"Do you have any practical ideas?"

"We could hire unknown teens for the clones and a bunch of has-been old farts for the leads: both groups will work for scale (the minimum wage, determined by union contracts), so we don't need to spend money on talent (generic term for all actors and actors)."

"That's a good point, and you could re-write to use standing sets and locations we find on the cheap, so we can save a pile in that area too."

"But let's hire great crew people (the workers on a set who are not on-camera), even if we can't afford very many. Neither of us has any tolerance for jerks, so we need to get the

17

work environment right."

"Wait a minute, speaking of crew people, I heard a rumor that Angela Smithson is available and looking for a project. I'll see if she'll do it," said David as he jumped from the table. Keith knew that Angela was one of the most experienced Assistant Directors in the business, but he doubted that they could afford her. As First A.D., she would be responsible for running the set, organizing everything, seeing that people were at the right place at the right time. She was a middle-aged hard-talking volcano, a mean bitch in many people's opinion, but a very smart clever bitch as Keith knew from working with her once. He had been very impressed at the subtle favors she did for him, such as arranging action so that the speaking parts would be close to his microphones. She was always aware of everything going on, and made sure that each crew person gave a 110% effort. There were no slackers on her sets.

David returned with a big smile, "She's ours, and she'll do it for scale."

"How did you arrange that?"

"Old connection, but in reality, she's recovering from time in the hospital, so she'd like to work an easy project, which matches our schedule perfectly. I told her we'd be glad to work pre-production at her house so that she wouldn't have to move around."

"Great, so we don't need to rent an office."

"Well, I told her about the assholes and the hookers and your pledge to make our film the one that pays the rent, then came on with a sob story about how it was our first big break and we needed serious help pulling it off."

"I've worked with her, and can see the look on her face when you described the champagne and the bimbos. I'll bet she swore a blue streak, then jumped at your offer."

"Let's go, she wants to read the script, and give you

suggestions for an immediate re-write. When I told her about their desire for more sex, you know what she said?"

"Let me guess. She said that sex scenes were great because you could shoot them in any seedy motel with a couple of non-speaking illegal aliens, stock music, and two crew people, thereby filling up screen time on the cheap."

"You do know your stuff! We're in for a wild ride, now our only problem is to make all this into an artistic whole, that we'll be proud to put our names on."

Angela's house in Beverly Hills, on Benedict Canyon Road, was a beautiful old wooden white colonial surrounded by gardens and trees, filled with souvenirs from her long career. She had started acting when only four, then transitioned to work behind the camera after college. Not only had she been successfully working in the business for almost forty years, her parents had also been prominent. Her father, Harry Smithson, had been a young cinematographer during the First World War. He had begun as an assistant, but then promoted himself when the rest of his crew was killed by a bomb. As Keith and David talked with her, they began to realize that she knew almost everyone, and could call-in favors and advice from people they would never dream of talking with on their own. Keith became excited, realizing that their first hire on the project had been perfect: the way Angela talked, their film was not only possible given the budget, but it would be dynamite entertainment. She could talk dollars, schedules, cheap locations and actors as easily as he could describe sound equipment.

They made basic schedule and shooting decisions, blocking out the major aspects of the film. Keith could tell that he was already into major re-write as Angela and David trimmed expensive scenes and substituted ones that they could afford. They replaced distant locations and fancy sets with cheap near-by lots, then told Keith to apply his creativity to working-out the details. Keith went home to start rewriting from the pile of notes he had hastily scribbled during the whirlwind afternoon.

As Keith drove home, he was filled with thoughts about the script, but when he walked through his front door, sad memories engulfed him and he started to cry. He walked around the house aimlessly shuffling his feet and wiping his burning eyes. Everything reminded him of Kristin, her charm, her laughs, her tears. Keith and Kristin had been engaged, but she had died just before their marriage: run-over by a huge foreign car that ran a red light at high speed. Eventually he realized that his only relief would come from writing, that somehow the spirit of her beautiful body was looking down on him, counting on him to realize the film he had conceived to cheer her in the hospital before she died.

His immediate problem was how to comply with both Angela's desire for more excitement on the screen while spending less money, and the wannabe's comments on adding sex to the plot. He knew that Kristin would be sorely disappointed if he cheapened their writing, if he turned its scant artistic merit into dreck. As a start, he moved his favorite picture of Kristin, a black and white night shot of her smiling in a low-cut gown, next to the typewriter. Whatever he wrote would have to be acceptable to his memory of what she would have liked.

Keith thought about the old people and their clone farm. How could this lead, to an inexpensive but exciting and funny sex scene? The more he thought about it, the more ideas started to flow. He put himself into the story and looked around at the scenery. Surely the oldies would exercise complete control over the breeding of their replacement parts. Un-planned sexual coupling between clones could lead to wasted energy and useless babies. Therefore, they must have had strong rules against clonal sexual activity, perhaps keeping the sexes completely separated. Probably there were penalties for screwing around and maybe involuntary sterilization for undesirables. Malformed children would be sent to the fertilizer plant at birth, but those who were OK for parts, but not for reproduction, would need to be prevented from procreating. These ideas led eventually to four potential sex scenes, one for every half hour of the film. If each were two or three minutes long, he could cover ten minutes of the flick, one twelfth of the whole film, with sex, at a very low cost per screen-minute, leaving money for the important scenes.

The first idea was to envision two clones who became magnetically attracted to each other's bodies: their desire would build, then explode in an ultra-rapid orgasmic flush of teen-age desire. To make this work, he would need to precede it with explanation of the rules against such activity, and the normal separation of the sexes, so that the clones would be frightened and excited simultaneously. If repressed desire were a theme established early among the clones, then this would make sense as a breakout. And what if this led to pregnancy. How to explain, who was the father, abortion, forced sterilization? The possibilities built quickly. In the end he decided to put a teen clone boy and girl in a bedroom, drudgery, making the beds of the old people, which they did every day. Their hands would touch, they would look into each other's eyes, they would sensually smooth the satin sheets on the bed in close-up, their hands would touch again, as the desire built, they would duck into a linen closet and couple in seconds, pants and knickers around their ankles, pumping with desire while standing, pressed against the piles of sheets. Maybe this happened just as some oldies walked past the closet door. The wannabes would love this, and it would be cheap to shoot, with no speaking parts, low-rent actors, and a simple set. It would be a brief silent movie filled with completely natural orgasmic energy.

21

There could be a follow-on scene where the girl's pregnancy was discovered. The doctors could tell her that there was a reward for the boy involved, the boy who had learned to do this special activity. Eagerly the girl would give his name, then the doctors would cruelly sterilize him to prevent future trouble. Keith realized that almost any discussion or presentation of forced sterilization was almost taboo on-screen, but if taboo, it must be a very strong emotion, and so could create powerful feelings in the audience.

The next idea was already scripted, but poorly. There was a sex scene between Senator Savage and his wife, Mary Maker. (they were the two oldies who had founded and now controlled Senior City) This could be boosted if it were shot with the periscope camera, a snorkel-like device that could roam over their bodies in close-up, gradually-exposing the stitch marks and scar tissue joining all the various multi-colored parts that comprised these two-hundred-year-old people as they screwed away: this would be played for humor and for shocking surprise as the audience discovered the hodge-podge that was their bodies. The key was finding some music that could play against the visual, something that would juxtapose their apparent happiness with the reality of the parts they were exercising. Maybe something like HUMORESQUE (". . . late last evening in the park, while goosing statues in the dark, if General Grant can take it why can't you. . . "). This would be expensive, due to the cost of the make-up and the camera gear, but it could be a great scene.

The third sex scene would be part of genetic engineering among the clones. It would involve unwilling and unknowledgeable participants. This would be a couple that needed to be bred, like animals, to create mathematically-correct offspring. The boy and girl wouldn't have a clue as to what they were supposed to do, so an oldie, perhaps Judge Julie (a 300 pound ancient judicial nightmare, the 'legal system' in Senior City), would explain the needed activity. Cheap to shoot, with JJ doing the talking, mostly in Voice Over, while shooting close-ups of her wrinkled hands leading the kids in exploring and arousing each other's bodies. In a flash, he realized the impact this would have if JJ were played by a transvestite. What a surprise for the audience, as they saw her erection build under her dress! What a hoot! The possibilities for this scene were endless, especially with something like BOLERO playing in the background, while on-screen we saw a clinical setting as the kids slowly disrobed each other under JJ's direction. Crap, this scene alone could take five or ten minutes if this were a porno flick! Looking at Kristin's picture, Keith realized that he had gone too far, and started to tone down the scene, while retaining the central idea of unwelcome sexual activity between two clones who didn't have a clue. JJ's vicarious pleasure as she played with both the girl's and the boy's bodies would ring true as an example of just how bad these oldies had become. Then the awakening desire among the clones as they mated would be a great finish. This scene could have an interesting follow-on, as either the girl or the boy told his/her friends about the strange activity they had just experienced.

Keith placed the fourth scene in the nearby city, where he could have two escaped clones fall in love and into bed, learning all about each other, tasting the forbidden fruit in a candle-lit scene in the dark. Again, a scene with minimal dialog, stock music in the background and trivial cost. A sure-fire winner. The girl would be Spunky, a virginal newly-escaped clone already in the script.

Keith knew that at least one of these scenes would be dropped, but for now he had a way to chop the cost and substantially boost audience excitement for almost ten percent of the running time. His final activity, after midnight, was to

23

tally the number of new pages, eighteen, and to begin a log of the revisions that he had written. Perhaps one day he would collect the re-write fees, so maybe he had just made almost twenty grand. He switched off the light and kissed Kristin's picture good night, wondering what she would have thought of the evening's rewrites.

∾∾∾∾∾

The next day Keith couldn't wait to tell the others about his new scenes and rushed to Angela's house early in the morning. He found her in a thin silk bathrobe, drinking coffee and quarreling on the phone with a producer in London who owed money. Keith was surprised that Angela looked quite attractive with her hair down, no makeup, and a loose robe swinging about her body as she casually walked around shouting into her phone. Even though her face wasn't perfect, her figure was nice, and he wondered why there didn't seem to be a man in her life. Perhaps her acid tongue kept most guys away, but he had already realized that she could be quite soft when she wanted. Angela waved Keith toward the kitchen and told the maid to make him breakfast while she dressed and hit a few more calls. Keith had a brief impression that Angela had seen him appraising her body through her semi-translucent robe and had enjoyed the attention, but he knew that she was perhaps twice his age and would have no interest in him outside of work. As Keith left the room he smiled as he heard Angela start another call: her first words were, "Hey you won't believe the two cute guys I'm spending the day with."

Jessica was on the other end of the line. She had just accepted Angela's offer to do the wardrobe on Keith's film and wanted to clarify dates and responsibilities as well as have a friendly chat.

As their conversation was about to end, Jessica added, "And guess what, Angela, you won't believe it, but they want me to perform on Saturday nights at the Magic Castle, but not as a Magician."

"Really! This I've got to see. When do you start?"

"In a few weeks, I'm working on my costume right now."

"Ooooops, got another call, see you soon, ciao."

Jessica, a very serious young woman of twenty-five, was calling from a portable phone in her parents' old stone house in Hancock Park, adjacent to the Wilshire Country Club. She was in the dry cedar-smelling attic, under the large timbers that had supported the heavy slate roof since the turn of the century: a roof of thin Vermont stones, thick copper flashing, and lead straps, the kind of construction designed to last centuries rather than years. She had a vague memory of a drawing she had made as a child and was searching through her old school papers in a dusty trunk trying to find it. Her mother, or perhaps her mother's maid, had saved everything that Jessica had brought home, even though both parents were often far away. Jessica had been drawing and painting continuously since nursery school and enjoyed an occasional prowl through her early work when an image from those long ago happy days surfaced in her mind. There were recognizable pictures of the beach, the sky, pets, birds, trees, flowers, as well as abstract or unclear works perhaps representing dreams or thoughts.

The painting she sought was from Kindergarten or First Grade when she had seen Peter Pan. As Jessica remembered it, the picture showed Wendy in a lovely white dress sprinkled with Tinkerbell's glittering fairy dust, but perhaps she remembered Wendy rather than her childhood painting. It was easy to become lost in old memories as she held each painting, trying to remember the actual scene she had imagined as she painted. An hour went by in an instant, then she found the picture, and her mind blended what she remembered of Wendy with the painting in her hand. She had remembered correctly: the painting was still sprinkled with bits of sparkling mica snow from a toy Christmas tree. Jessica excitedly kissed the painting, returned everything else to the trunk, and ran downstairs to make a detailed drawing of the dress. Wearing a diaphanous gown like the one in her painting while performing, would be perfect, she just knew it. Her dressmaker was going to be surprised: Jessica had never worn anything like this before!

Back in Angela's kitchen, David had arrived and sat down with Angela and Keith as Keith nervously explained his four new scenes. What had seemed like great ideas last night, appeared simplistic and crude now. Angela sensed his feelings and smiled at him, saying quietly, "It's OK, we know these are fresh ideas that you haven't had time to polish. We want to hear, tell us about them."

Keith felt her warmth and comfort supporting him, encouraging him to explain instead of criticizing his ideas. "The best one involves Judge Julie and two virgin clones who are to be bred, like horses or dogs. The oldies control clonal reproduction, or try to, but of course we also have a scene where two clones manage to screw on the sly, in a closet, but that's not this scene. It's sensual, yet clinical. Julie is in her Judicial robes, and by the way, she's really a transvestite. She's alone in her bedroom leering and rubbing her hands together, and the bed has only sheets. A doctor brings in two perfect teen-age clones, who wear their standard track suits. Doc says, "Here they are, ready for procreation 101, genetically and physically perfectly matched, so go to it Julie." He exits laughing and the clones are mystified, nervous and afraid. Julie tells them that they are going to learn a new game, a special skill, that they can play together, but only with each other and never with anyone else. She gets them to slowly undress each other, helping them run their hands over each other's bodies in the process. We can tell that lecherous Julie is much more excited than the clones. Perhaps BOLERO or something like it is on the track. They slowly learn to excite each other as we see in close-up Julie's hands guiding theirs to the right spots and motions, stroking each other with more and more excitement."

Angela interrupted, "I've got the picture, and David can figure out how much to show to keep this out of X territory: this can be R, but X is the kiss of death. We can milk this for maybe three minutes of screen-time and shoot it in an hour. Great idea! Now how're you going to show that Julie's really a guy?"

"I want to hint broadly at it here, maybe show his erection or wet pants or something, but save the real revelation for the torture scene when Julie in her undies comes out of the bathroom as John is frantically talking on the phone asking for help."

"Can we show a transvestite in a movie? Won't that be censored out," David worried.

"Depends on how you do it, you've got to stay just inside the line, that's the whole secret to putting interesting sex in an R flick." Angela laughed.

Angela turned to Keith, "You could probably write good art-porn, you know, gritty black and white foreign flicks that pretend to be art, but which audiences go to for the sex. I think you've got the knack, so after we finish this, I'll put you in touch with the people who run that business. You think we're doing things on the cheap? They shoot sixteen millimeter blowups on out-of-date stock, and charge the actors for the privilege of being in a flick. Working with them on old European streets is a riot. They don't pay for anything."

"One thing I'm worried about is that the oldies wouldn't allow the kids to screw around because it would lead to genetically unwanted babies that would need extra care. So I figured that the oldies would forcibly sterilize clones who shouldn't reproduce. This could be gruesome, but also make for some really powerful footage, depending on how we did it," Keith suggested.

"It makes me cringe just to think about it", David said.

"Wait, you've got the germ of a good idea. Maybe not castration, but perhaps vasectomy for the guys and having their tubes tied for the girls, but castration would be definitely over the edge: we'd be killed in the press," Angela stated.

"Punishment, or sterilization, or whatever wouldn't have any meaning if the kids didn't fear it, so somehow the oldies need to plant very bad ideas about sex into the clones' brains: get them scared stiff, so that when a couple does it on the sly, they are really afraid of being caught."

"Right, a modern version of THE SCARLET LETTER, maybe with branding or a tattoo or something really painful and ugly to identify the bad ones."

"These clones will have perfect, one hundred percent functional bodies, at the peak of hormonal development, so they're bound to have thoughts and wet dreams. Maybe they want to escape so that they can experience sexual freedom?"

"We've got to watch it or we'll be hit up for pedophilia."

"Hey, we can have the clones watch a sex education video, made by the oldies, telling the clones all sorts of bogus crap about their bodies and what will happen if they taste the forbidden fruit. It could be hilarious, especially when the oldies in the video demonstrate!"

"There's no way that the clones would know that

babies come from sex, because the oldies would keep pregnant girls hidden away in quarantine. However, some clone could discover this and tell his or her friends."

"Stop, I've just rewritten eighteen pages, and you two are redoing all my clone stuff," moaned Keith in jest.

"Actually, on most films, the rewrite continues until the final cut, and you will write the whole thing over and over maybe three or four times, so oil your typewriter, eighteen pages is nothing," Angela told a startled Keith.

They worked all day, then David left Angela and Keith alone. Angela put her hand over Keith's and squeezed it. "What's wrong? All day it's seemed like something's been bothering you, something below the surface."

At first Keith didn't know what Angela was talking about, but then he realized that his worry, his guilt, must be showing. "It's nothing really, just a feeling I had last night that won't go away."

"Come on, tell me about it, maybe I can help."

"I started to write a new scene about two quacks, doctors in Senior City. In this scene they talk to a couple of old people, fresh ones that Savage has just brought in. The docs assure the new people that medical care is wonderful, that people can live forever here, all sorts of medical B.S."

"So, what's wrong with that, sounds perfectly in-character for quacks, who are obviously lying?"

"Well I extended the scene, and after the people go, the two quacks laugh about how ignorant and gullible most people are about medicine. One quack comments that people will believe almost anything a doctor says if the words are big enough and have Latin overtones."

"Sounds like real life to me, so where's the problem?"

"The problem is Kristin's death. When she was in the hospital, I tried to help, to get more information, to bring in outside specialists, but the medical staff stonewalled me and I fell for it. I could have gone around them and done something while she was alive, but I believed those assholes because they were wearing white coats and using big words. They intimidated me, and I backed off instead of using my brains: I know something was wrong, but I didn't investigate, I didn't think."

"Perhaps they were O.K. and just being realistic?"

"No, I was as gullible as the people in my story, but I didn't see it at the time. Dammit, I could have done more, a whole lot more, but I let Kristin down, and now it's too late, the most beautiful girl in the world is a box of gray ashes."

They were alone in the garden, surrounded by high hedges and formal plantings in the late afternoon sunlight. Angela was next to Keith, her hand holding his tightly, as she softly comforted him.

"Keith, you're letting your imagination become your life. Films aren't real, they're make-believe, but when you're creating one it's hard to keep the two separate. Drop the docs for awhile and polish the sex scenes. Have a little fun."

"It's not that easy, I just can't get over how naive I was."

He was about to leave, when he realized that improbable as it seemed, Angela appeared to be sexually interested in him. His perception turned to reality as Angela whispered, "A girlfriend once told me that sex is like arithmetic: twenty-five goes into forty-five at least once, but the reverse is a waste of time."

Her lips were on his and her hands were all over his body before he had made a conscious decision to stay. Angela pulled him onto a nearby chaise and devoured him. At first Keith enjoyed it, but as they continued Keith had a strange idea. All day Angela had been treating him softly, mothering

30

him as his real mother had never seemed to do, paying attention to his feelings and helping him with his writing. Now he was, at least mentally, deep inside her womb, and he recalled the story of Oedipus, and the thought flashed through his mind that he was mating with his mother, returning to her body, doing something very much forbidden.

Afterwards, Angela lay on the couch, her legs apart, her raised skirt crumpled around her waist without a trace of shame or embarrassment, "Don't take it personally Keith, you really turned me on, and I'm feeling so great that I just had to get laid."

Keith dressed quickly, very much confused by his thoughts. "I think I'd better go home and get to work." Looking down at her semi-naked body, Keith could see huge purple scars and long stitch lines from her recent operations but he had no interest in talking further.

"Let yourself out, I'm going to stay here and let the hot sun caress my body, unless you want to try for a double play?"

As Keith drove home he thought over what had just happened, and the emotional upheavals of the past half hour. He was totally consumed with making his film succeed, but had just done something he had never thought he would do. He wondered if Kristin were still alive if he would have given in to Angela's desire, if he would have prostituted himself for the sake of his film, if he would have lied to Kristin to please a woman who was making his career dreams come true. He thought that perhaps prostitute was the wrong word, but realized that no, it was correct, he had been screwed in return for favors and a little bit of motherly attention. There were male prostitutes too.

Keith spent the next month totally rewriting the script, with almost hourly suggestions and comments from David and Angela. They had hired a location scout to find cheap nearby

31

places that looked somewhat like the scenes in the script, then sent Polaroids of the scenes to Keith so that he could adjust the script to fit existing places, instead of the other way around. When he worked with Angela, she was all business, as though the scene in her garden had never happened, but they had a shared secret and were closer now than before.

Keith often called Jim, his lawyer, to ask if there was any news about the car that had run over Kristin, but the police were making no progress, even though the charge would now be murder, or close to it. During one of these sad conversations they talked about Keith's contract with SCAM-F and the amount of rewriting he was doing. Jim admonished him to take the rewrite activity seriously, and to stamp each new page with the date and time, then have it witnessed and signed by either Angela or the Script Supervisor. Jim knew that the only way they would collect the rewrite fees was if they had solid, documented, proof that each page was actually done. In addition, he made Keith mail the signed pages to Jim, as they were written, so that they would be in sealed postmarked envelopes. Jim had dealt with film lawyers before and knew how hard they would try to weasel out of any payments. While they were discussing Keith's contract, Jim mentioned the hospital and asked how much they had charged for Kristin's care, figuring that maybe they could have the bill reduced through legal action. Jim was astounded when Keith told him that the medical care was completely free, and that he had already signed the release papers: it was over. Jim's curiosity was aroused as he had never heard of any hospital or doctor giving free care.

When Angela and David weren't busy finding cheap locations, they started looking for actors to play the various parts in the film, based on their ideas of how the script might evolve.

Angela and David focused first on filling out the parts for the oldies, using has-been actors who might still have name-recognition, but who would work for scale. The fact that the script called for at least a half-dozen golden oldies with speaking parts made this film unusual in Hollywood, where almost all films featured only handsome young actors and actresses, except in big-name-star and ugly parts. Senator Savage, Admiral Right-hand, Orson, Bean-Counter, Judge Julie, and Mary Maker were the main old characters, and each part had excellent dialog and screen-time.

Savage ran Senior City, an old people's community hidden away on the desert, far away from anything else. Mary was his wife, and together they controlled most of what happened at SC. While he often tried to appear polite and sympathetic, she was hard as nails and did little to soften her image. The Admiral commanded the Marines who guarded SC: a totally ineffective group of soldiers. Judge Julie, who weighed at least 300 pounds, ran the judicial system. These four often traveled together, interfering with each other's activities. In the faraway city of Abandoned, Orson ran the I.R.S. which consisted of Suckers, heartless creeps armed with suction machines that could pull the clothes and money from victims. The residents of Abandoned ate their meals at the Canteen, which was administered by Bean Counter, an old shrew.

At the other end of the age spectrum were the clones, actors and actresses who looked teenage, innocent, well-rounded, and healthy. Thousands of actors fitted this description, so it was a process of elimination, finding actors who looked the part, could take direction, remember their lines and behave like grown-ups on the set. There were no stars or bankable actors, as both categories were financially out of the question. Originally Keith had placed children in the cast, and the clones were all ages, from one to twenty-one. Angela had vetoed all school-age parts because these actors would require teachers, portable class-rooms, short working-hours, and the hiring of Welfare Workers. (a California legal requirement: Social Workers whose only job was to see that the children were not exploited or treated harshly.)

Six of the teens had most of the young speaking parts. Poins, a boy, lived in the city and was very bright. He worked with a girl, Jo, who was the essence of 'street smart'. These two scrappy bright kids contrasted sharply with three who had escaped from the clone farm, John, Dawn, and Scott. These beautiful teens could not read or speak properly since they had no schooling or formal brain development. Jo and Poins taught them about life in the city and made a plan to free all the clones. Later the teens rescue another female clone, Spunky, who falls in love with John.

David and Angela's casting activities raised the profile of the project, and led to a small amount of press curiosity. People began to ask questions and to suspect that something unusual was happening. The press knew Angela, and figured that if she were involved, the project was real, and perhaps newsworthy. This led to interviews, explanations, publicity, and then, to protests and pickets. The reporters, who didn't have a clue, portrayed the film as an evil attempt to exploit old and handicapped people, as well as doctors and transplant medicine.

Before long, Keith received an urgent call from Angela, demanding that he come immediately to their casting session at 1330 North Vine Street, to mollify the protestors who were picketing and preventing actors from entering the building.

As Keith approached he saw people with crutches and wheel-chairs surrounding the doorway. He had a brief flash-back, thinking of what would have happened if Kristin had lived, but as a cripple. He might have been one of the wheel-chair pushers himself, protesting against public insensitivity. The protestors had posters and were doing their best to block the entrance. Keith recovered from his sad thoughts and walked up to the leader, who was chanting with a megaphone, and asked, "What's going on, what are you guys doing here?"

"These money-grubbing creeps are exploiting sick old people, and we're going to put a stop to it."

"Where'd you get such a screwy idea? These people are making a film that glorifies old people and medical breakthroughs, you should be cheering and buying tickets for opening night!"

"You're nuts, we saw it all on TV. New York millionaires are exploiting helpless people who can't fight back. Get out of the way! We're gonna sue, we've called our representatives in Sacramento."

"This film is about wonderful old people who have found a way to live forever, it's a beautiful statement, and old people will love to see it." As Keith said these words, he thought about the film's reality, and its cruel treatment of many of the characters. He knew that he had to be careful of what he said to these people: he had never been a spokesman for a film before. He didn't want to hurt them, but he also wanted them out of the way.

The protestors gathered around Keith and the spokesman as they argued. Keith wondered what he could say to defuse the protest, and noticed David with a Sony U-matic cassette video camera, disguised as a tourist, covering his attempt to stop the protests. One of the protestors, in a wheel chair, pulled up to Keith and yanked at his sleeve, "What's your angle, what're you doing here, defending these crooks?"

"I wrote the screenplay, and I believe it's an excellent artistic statement, describing medical realities in the not-too-

35

far-distant future. Someday you'll be able to get a new pair of legs and walk again."

"Bullshit! We're never gonna get well and that's god's truth."

"In our film old people do get well, and live for hundreds of years, but you're right, it hasn't happened yet. Our film is about what the future could be like, it's not about the present."

An old lady in another wheel chair came up to Keith and tugged at him with the hook she had in place of one of her hands, "What're you gonna do about my hand? You youngsters don't have any idea of what it's like to be crippled, to be missing parts of your body, and to know that you will never get them back."

An image of Kristin's mangled body lying in her bed flashed through Keith's eyes as he fought back sudden tears. He turned to the old lady and tenderly held her good hand between both of his, "I do know, I know very well. My fiancée died just before our wedding because much of her body was broken and could not be replaced: she needed far more than a new hand. You're still alive, but she isn't. Maybe she's watching us from Heaven, and if so, I hope she sends her love to you."

This personal touch stopped the protestors, who could say nothing in return. The old lady held onto Keith's hands, looking into his eyes, "You're so young, and so, so sad. Enjoy the gifts you have, and don't mind us, we're just out for an afternoon of fun, causing a bit of trouble. We don't have much to look forward to, but perhaps we'll enjoy your film, and you're right, at least we're still alive and kicking."

The protestors dispersed slightly, and promised to let people through the doorway so that casting could proceed. Keith went inside and visited with Angela, David, and the pretty young actresses who would play Spunky and Dawn.

"Keith, you were great, I captured it all on video for the publicity campaign," David began.

"Please don't use the part about Kristin, it hurts to think about her."

"It's OK Keith, we don't need to involve her in the publicity stuff. We're just taking advantage of anything interesting that happens. Wait 'til we start production and the media comes to see what we're doing," Angela added.

A shapely young actress took Keith's hand. "Hi, I'm Spunky, and I can't wait to battle those doctors and ancient farts from Senior City." Keith liked her cute sly smile and thought of the sex scene in the school that he had written for her. Her body was nice, but he wondered if she knew what her part in the film entailed.

"You look perfect for the part, but have you read the script, especially the night scene in the old school?"

"Oh you mean the candle-lit sex scene where John screws me. It's great. Bet you got excited when you wrote it."

Keith was embarrassed by her frankness and the disconnect between the innocent young girl he saw in front of him and her attitude and language.

"I suppose it's all in a day's work for both of us."

"Don't worry about me, I'm eighteen, and David's already seen footage of me humping in a porno. He almost wet his pants, so that's how I got the part."

The other young actress, playing the part of Dawn, shyly introduced herself. "Hi Keith, I'm Dawn, and I sure am glad that I get to keep my clothes on during the film."

Keith noticed that she looked to be perhaps twelve or thirteen with a slight figure and a beautiful clear child-like face. "Are you old enough, I mean, we can't afford any children on the set."

"I'm nineteen and a sophomore at UCLA, but my

specialty is playing young adolescents. I fooled you, even though you should know better."

"You're perfect. By the way, I live near UCLA and wander about the campus a lot. What are you studying?"

"History and philosophy, but I love acting when I get an interesting part. This film is so different from anything I've ever read or seen. I'd love to learn more about it and why you wrote it this way."

Keith was pleasantly surprised to encounter an attractive actress with brains, and realized that talking with her about his writing would be pleasant. He smiled, "I hope we can get together sometime in the Village and talk about it, but now I'd better get back to work."

After visiting for a few more minutes, Keith drove home, thinking back on his encounter with the protesting old people, people whose medical problems were real. For the first time, he saw their side of life and realized that his film was poking fun at many innocent people. He thought about one of his favorite quotes, "comedy is a man in trouble" (attributed to Jerry Lewis), which implies that cinematic humor is based on people with exaggerated problems; he had filled his pages with such characters. Now Keith wondered how to add tender scenes that showed life from the oldies' viewpoint. These could be juxtaposed against the funny scenes, giving the audience a wider range of emotional experience, and boosting the impact of the humorous parts.

While Keith wrote and rewrote, locations were found and rented, sets were designed and built, actors and crew were located and hired, and props were designed, built and/or rented. There was only one situation which made Angela furious, the selection of the Costume Designer. One of the wannabes, Herb, had announced that his girlfriend Marge would be given that position. When Angela demanded references, union membership, a list of screen-credits and other credentials, Herb was incensed, since Marge's experience extended only to clothes-shopping. He made it clear that his bimbo was now on the payroll, and further that she was already picking out clothes for the cast, even though she hadn't read the current script or talked with David. Marge was in for a major surprise if and when she showed up for work.

Angela normally filled her crews with highly-experienced lead people, helped by a scattering of young, eager, and willing assistants who were learning their craft. In this way everybody was busy all the time, either working, or instructing the junior members of the crew. It made a vibrant work environment as everyone gave full attention and enthusiasm to the project. In the wardrobe department, Angela had hired Jessica, an up-and-coming Assistant Wardrobe Mistress, and was busy talking a well-known Designer into sketching a series of unique, and low-cost, costumes for the cast. This arrangement would give Jessica extra responsibility and allow her to grow into a more complex assignment, while providing artistic unity to the look of the film. When the sketches were done, Jessica would supervise the construction of the costumes, fit them to the actors, and take full responsibility and credit for the wardrobe. Marge was not needed and worse than useless because she would distract Jessica.

Keith heard about the wardrobe problems Sunday night when he and David were invited to Angela's house for dinner with Angela and her father, Harry Smithson. Harry was far into his eighties, but strong. To Angela's horror he was still driving his tomato-soup red 1949 MG T.D. roadster, but only in daylight. Harry laughed at their project and wanted to know where he could get some spare body parts and a general overhaul, or at least a new pelvic section. He had read their script and this was the idea that he enjoyed most.

Seniors Have It Tough

Chapter 3

Exteriors in the City of Abandoned

Before Keith knew what was happening, it was time to start production, which would mean that in addition to his continuous rewrite chores, he would need to work twelve hours a day recording the sound track. The normal union work day for the crew was ten hours, but preparing equipment before work, and taking the day's tape to be transferred after work, meant that twelve hours would elapse, even if shooting were on a nearby stage. Shooting anywhere within fifty miles of downtown Los Angeles was called the 'Studio Zone' by union rules, and travel to and from work inside the zone was not provided or paid except in special circumstances. Given the traffic, this could easily add an extra hour at the beginning and end of each day. In addition, the economics of the business often made it less expensive to work the crew an extra hour or two so that a particular location or actor's part of the picture could be finished without carrying it over to another day. The only positive aspect of this arrangement was that the production would usually pay to have plentiful food delivered to the location so that minimal time would be wasted traveling to meals. (this allowed meal times to be reduced to thirty minutes.)

Early Monday morning, Keith nervously climbed into his faded old VW, swore, went back into the house for his dark glasses, then sputtered down LeConte, arriving on location just before seven.   He was thankful that it was only half an hour from his house in Westwood, and that it didn't involve driving the jammed freeways. The first day of shooting any film was confusing and his stomach churned with worry about the script and its many problems. He looked at the hazy summer sunrise and laughed to himself for a moment: this was the first day in two months for which he would definitely be paid.

Today they would shoot outdoor scenes, exteriors, in a two block stretch of ruined slums, a street which had been trashed during the Watts Riots and never rebuilt. It was even worse now because two other film projects had boosted the mess. Grass grew through cracks in the pavement, trash littered the sidewalks and gutters, and buildings were either burned or gutted and abandoned.   When Keith put on his Engineering hat, he marveled at how cheap this location was to rent, but when he put on his Sound hat, he cringed at the noise from the nearby freeway and the airplanes overhead.   Keith had objected about the acoustic situation to Angela but she had quickly calculated that the cost of replacing any bad dialog on a dubbing stage would be far less than the cost of finding a quiet but appropriately-ruined location.

Keith parked near the equipment trucks and started to wander, looking for the other crew members and to see what the prop people had done to match the ruined street to his script. Angela's rasping voice through a powered megaphone called to him and the others. "Hey everyone, come over here for a minute so David can introduce the project and say a few words. The coffee's hot and there's a pile of donuts."

Keith half-suspected that she was about to announce yet another money-saving change to his plans. Everyone walked to a large truck, where David and Angela stood on the tailgate above the crowd. There were perhaps twenty crew people, and five of the young actors. Friends gathered together in small groups and everyone looked up at Angela.

Angela, who was known by reputation if not by sight to the crew, introduced David, who was unknown to most. It almost looked like a mother and son scene. Angela, forty-five trying to look like thirty in her tight Leviis and dyed hair, was next to David: he was actually twenty-seven but looked younger and he was handsome enough to have played lucrative parts in TV soaps as a teen. Today he was trying to look like the person in charge, someone who would be respected and listened to, but he was apprehensive and had already lost his breakfast. The contrast in self-assurance between David and Angela was obvious.

"Most of you know me, Angela. I'm the First A.D. If you have any problems or suggestions bring them to me pronto. Each of you has been hired because you're the best person for the job, so we're going to have a happy and efficient crew with minimal trouble: each of you knows what to do, and is only waiting for direction as to when to do it."

Anglea moved close to David and put her arm around his shoulders. "David Nosrak is our Director, and a few of you have worked with him on industrials and TV commercials. This is his first feature film and he's scared shitless, so we all need to help him get started and find his way. We've been there before and I know each of you will do whatever he or she can to make this a success for all of us. Before I hand the horn to David I need to mention another virgin on the set, Keith Warrington. Some of you know him as an excellent Sound Mixer. But surprise, he wrote the film we are making, so he will need to constantly jump between writing tasks and the sound track. That's not the way he planned it, but he signed a really awful contract with the money people to do both jobs, so let's cut him a bit of slack if he's slow to move his gear or in the wrong place at the wrong time. This is his first script to reach production, and like David, he's petrified."

Keith couldn't help but laugh with the rest of the crew at this introduction and covered his face with his hands in mock embarrassment. Now that part of the tension had been released, Angela handed the megaphone to David and stepped aside.

"I know I'm at least as worried as Keith. Thank you for being here and for the help I know you will give both of us. My limited experience has shown me how much I don't know about directing, so I'll be glad to have advice. You're an especially experienced crew, so I look forward to learning a great deal as we work together."

To David's surprise, he was interrupted by spontaneous applause from the cast and crew, which dissolved some of his fear and first-day jitters; he smiled for the first time.

"Thank you, thank you all very much. We're about to shoot an unconventional film. Much of it is intended to be funny, though some of the material is gruesome. You've had a chance to read the script, and Angela has copies if any of you would like one. We have almost no budget, and are relying on cleverness rather than hula-dollars to make this picture a hit. There will be much improvisation, and you will each have a chance to use your ingenuity to breathe life into the film. We're all part of the same team, and each of us is a craftsman. Together we can make a great film and have a lot of fun. When we're finished, and our names roll by in the credits, each of us will be able to proudly say, I helped make that film. Now let's have a cup of coffee and take ten to meet each other before Angela starts cracking her whip."

As most headed for the coffee urn, Angela pulled David and Keith to one side. "We're still over-budget, so start thinking of things we can chop or shrink to save dough."

"God, I'll be lucky just to execute the plan we already

have, and I know we need to expand a few scenes." David's mind cleared as the need to work hard to avoid further cheapening the film took over his thoughts.

"Why can't we shoot some of the simple stuff with a short crew? Who'll ever find out?" Keith asked.

"You haven't seen the details of my latest schedule because I don't want it to get out, but I'm already planning on doing the Bloodmobile and Sun City crap with just a few people."

"How few?" winced David.

"I saw the footage you shot on that indie last year David. It was adequate, so you can be the cameraman, and Keith can be everybody else. Now think of some more ways to save money or you two will be completely screwed out of your percentages."

Angela walked away, leaving Keith and David to fight the Hollywood battle, art verses money. From the first day when they had sold their souls money had been their main problem. Their deal had a wonderful, from the financiers' viewpoint, clause: if Keith and David ran over in time or budget, their share of the film proceeds would start shrinking, headed for zero without too much imagination. Their homerun schedule was already based on the assumption that nothing would go wrong and that they would finish exactly on time and budget. That never happened in the real world.

The scenes the crew was filming during this first week showed activities in the City of Abandoned, where the escaped clones were hiding from the oldies.

Keith found the truck which held his sound gear and unloaded it with Jack, the Boom-man with whom he had worked many projects. When they were recording, Jack's main task was to float a microphone above and in front of the speaking actors. The trick was to stay close to the actors

45

Boom Man with strong shoulder muscles shooting on location. Note that he is listening to the resulting sound track through headphones so that he can aim the mike to minimize background noise and maximize the quality of the actress's dialog.

(to please Keith) and yet stay just out of the picture, while avoiding making shadows that fell on the scene.

When Jack was lucky, he would use a Fisher Boom, a counterbalanced mechanical contraption high on a three-wheel dolly that allowed him to move a mike over a scene by turning a crank, to move the mike in and out, and pushing a lever, which rotated the mike. Such a mechanism not only saved his shoulder muscles, but it also allowed him to reach much further and higher than he otherwise could. More than once, Keith had operated a Fisher boom himself, with a heavy recorder hanging from his shoulder, when the project was so poor that it couldn't afford a Boom-man.

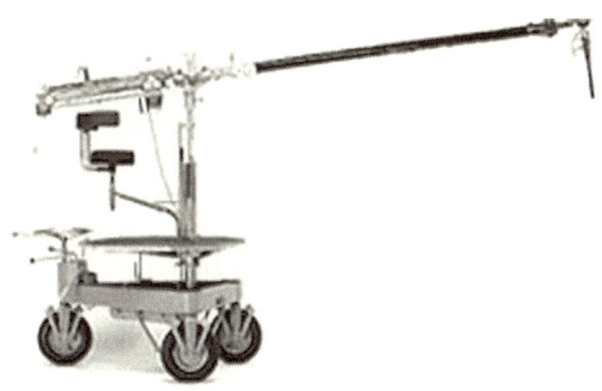

Fisher Boom. The wheel axles can be shortened for transport, and the boom can be lowered to reduce its height. The round cranking drum is operated with the right hand to move the mike away from the operator, while the left hand controls a lever that rotates the mike. A special soft silent mike cable coils and uncoils automatically on pulleys as the boom's length expands and contracts.

    Keith was completely responsible for the sound track during filming. He was paid well, but allowed few mistakes. His judgment was assumed to be perfect, and if it wasn't they would hire someone else immediately. During filming the normal process was that the AD or Director would shout "Roll em", then the Sound Mixer would reply "Speed" when his recorder was functioning. The camera would also start. As soon as "Speed" was heard, an Assistant Cameraman would clap a slate to provide both the film and sound with a brief loud and clear mark. Then the Director would start the scene moving with "Action".

    At the end of a shot, if the Director liked the way it had worked, he would turn to the Director of Photography and ask, "OK for you?", and then to Keith with the same question. In both cases it was an aesthetic decision based on experience and practical considerations. If both said yes, the Director might move on to a completely different scene, scrapping the current set-up. Re-staging the scene on another day for a re-shoot was expensive, and sometimes impossible, so the Director and A.D. relied on both the camera and sound teams to ensure good results. Although embarrassing, it was acceptable for either team to answer "No", with a brief explanation. This might infuriate the Director and perhaps the actors, but the Director would usually run the scene again if possible. It was far better for the crew to admit a mistake at this point than to sit through it the next day during dailies. A mistake in judgment could trash a reputation and send you out the door: in a free-lance world, there was always someone waiting to take your place.

When the sound or picture was borderline, and the crew was running late, there was a strong temptation to shade the truth and accept the shot, in hopes that it wouldn't look too bad on the screen. Marginal sound could always be looped later, at considerable expense, but if the picture was out of focus or a microphone shadow moved across the hero's face, there was no way out except to cut away. More than once Keith had had to request another take because he had misadjusted the gain controls. Everyone working on a set knew that thousands of dollars were flowing every hour, so delays of any kind, especially those caused by imperfect craft, were frowned upon. When a person goofed, the question "Why don't we hire someone who knows what he's doing?" passed through many minds. The money people knew nothing of the difficulties of operation, they only watched clocks and budgets, continually pushing everyone. In this atmosphere it was especially hard to say "I made a mistake, please shoot it again." To lessen the pain, Keith, or the Camera Operator might say to the Director, "I could do a little better also if we run it again," when the other team screwed up. Helping each other through difficulties was an unwritten rule in this tight world.

As Keith and Jack moved their gear and began to set-up on a wheeled cart, Keith noticed Angela talking earnestly to an unusual young woman whom he did not know, but he was far too busy to introduce himself.

Keith frequently referred to a Xeroxed schedule which Angela revised daily. It showed which scenes were to be shot and had no relation to the script: it was designed to extract the most value from each day's activity. This was called 'shooting out of sequence' and was the norm on most films. An outsider watching the set wouldn't have a clue as to how the pieces would finally fit together unless she happened to read the screenplay. Often the crew didn't know or care how the film would be assembled either: they just wanted to know enough about the schedule to do their jobs.

Today, while the camera and sound crews worked on a close shot of the escaped teenage clones climbing into and out of a man-hole in the middle of the grubby street, most of the grips, prop people, and gaffers (electricians) were preparing for a long trucking shot of the entire two block area. From Keith's perspective, the manhole was a simple scene since the actors had just a few lines and Jack could easily hold a mike nearby. They were going to use one man-hole, shot from two different angles, to represent two different locations. The only prop was a balsawood manhole cover which would be easy to lift. Grips had already placed Apple-boxes in the hole so that the actors would be at the right height as they emerged.

One of the clones, John, had a shaved head with a big 'X' painted on top. In the screenplay, it develops that he illegally had sex with another clone, and the punishment was that all his hair was removed so that his head could be tattooed to mark him as trouble.

Angela, David, and three teen clones, Spunky, Poins and John walked to the manhole. The actors were in grubby tattered clothes, with dirty hands and faces. Spunky, as a partially-clad young girl, wore a torn dress, purposefully revealing bits of flesh and underwear as she walked. She looked fifteen and innocent. Keith heard Angela shouting, "Where the hell's Jessica?", then saw the young woman he had seen earlier come running with a bit of cloth and a scissors. He deduced that Jessica was the wardrobe person he had heard about as she deftly applied pins in different places while David described the scene to the actors. Jessica had dark hair hidden under an old scarf and wore an old sweatshirt under an unbuttoned faded blue chambray work shirt, its pockets stuffed with pencils and tools. She was all business, working rapidly with concentration and skill.

Keith and the camera team had already practiced the shot using one of the grips as a stand-in, so they were ready to let David and the actors take the set. Although neither the sound nor the camera crews were needed while David rehearsed the talent, both quietly sat or walked nearby, carefully observing the movement of the actors and listening to David's instructions for hints of possible technical problems. The camera team was watching for shadows, highlights, inappropriate backgrounds, and focus shifts, while Keith and Jack were scoping out the best placements for mikes as the actors practiced their lines.

A breeze had come up, blowing dust and trash. While this added gritty authenticity to the picture, wind could ruin the sound from a mike as it blew across the sensitive diaphragm. Jack placed a foam cover over the ultra-directional Sennheiser 815 shotgun mike which they were using to minimize wind rumble and tried different angles to find the best way to avoid both wind and background noises.

In the first shot, the manhole cover would lift slightly

Part of a Film crew working on a street with child actors in Hollywood. The Cinematographer is pondering the lighting, while the Boom Man watches traffic. The Director stands next to the Script Girl, and the sound gear is in the foreground

and the clones would peek out, from under the edge. Then "when the coast was clear", they would lift it all the way and climb out of the hole quickly. Their only trick was to act as though the phony wooden manhole cover was heavy.

Close-ups of the worried faces peering out from the man-hole were part of Keith's low-cost plan. He had peppered his script heavily with tight emotion-revealing close-ups. His reasoning was simple. They couldn't afford giant fully-dressed and populated sets and locations, so they would rely much more than an average film on close shots which could be made in small, inexpensive, settings. A manhole on a deserted street was the first of many such scenes.

Soon they were rolling, covering the action from different angles. Everyone was glad to be shooting instead of rehearsing. Things were going well until just in the middle of a take, a gust of wind knocked the light manhole cover from the clone's hands, sending it rolling down the street on edge. David groaned, "Cut" and turned away, but George, the Director of Photography, yelled "Keep Rolling". Poins and the others had sworn liberally at the wind and had run off down the street in pursuit of the wooden disc, as George zoomed and panned to follow their chase. A moment when having a very experienced Assistant Cameraman paid dividends. Without a pause, Stubby, the Assistant, estimated the focus distance as the kids ran and adjusted the lens accordingly. The shot would be well-composed and focused, as though it had been carefully rehearsed.

David watched then yelled at Poins, "Run back and look scared as hell!"

As Poins returned panting and swearing with the disc and the other clones, George was beside himself with laughter. "You should have seen it through the lens, it was the funniest piece of film I've shot in ages: what a fuckup. Keith, wait 'til you see the dailies, there's gotta be some way for you to write this into the film. Maybe they know it's a fake manhole and it's the only one they can lift?"

Keith played back his recording for everyone to hear, laughing at the unscripted swearing and confusion, and realized that all he had to do was to add a voice-over line, perhaps for Spunky, something like "Poins, I told you to be careful or the cover would blow away: it's the only light one we have." They were all laughing as George told the actors how funny the shot had turned out, and Keith voiced his suggestions. Angela pointed out that although there were probably a few crew people walking in the background during the unplanned shot, an audience would assume that they were just other inhabitants of the city. David and Keith huddled to quickly devise a few close-ups that would match the new footage and story angle, and everyone went to work. The script supervisor, responsible for continuity, was writing furiously, making notes both for the Editor as well as to herself so that she could ensure that the scenes before and after this meshed.

The crew was dressed for long, hard, physical outdoor work in the sun and wind. Leviis, long sleeve work shirts, tee shirts, work boots and sneakers, were the most common basic garments for male and female alike. Practicality and comfort were the over-riding considerations. Into their midst walked a woman in heels, designer jeans (with a crease), and a too-clean white blouse which revealed an impractical amount of cleavage. Keith recognized her as one of the hookers, Marge, from his meeting with the New York financiers at the Beverly Hills Hotel.

As soon as Angela saw Marge coming, she turned and stared at her, like a hawk watching a mouse. Everyone sensed that something was up and waited with curiosity as Marge approached Angela, who growled, "Where the fuck have you been all morning? The call was seven, on location, having had. You think we're running a fucking country club out here?" The phrase 'having had' made it clear that the person was expected to have already had a meal and be ready for work.

Most people thought Marge must be an actress, but one who didn't seem to match any of the parts in the script. Only Keith, David, and Angela knew the truth: she was the unwelcome Head Wardrobe Mistress. Most women would have cringed at Angela's words, but not Marge, "Cut the crap Angela, I'll get here when I want to, and there isn't a fucking thing you can do about it. Now where's my trailer and my crew: I need to show them what to do."

"You already missed the first sequence, and the extras for the suction scenes aren't due until after lunch, so why don't you rest your tits somewhere, or heaven forbid, you might finish sewing details onto costumes, that is, if you know how to sew."

Angela walked away swearing and mumbling to herself. David tried to defuse the confrontation by walking over to Marge and announcing to the crew, "Marge is working on wardrobe issues, and as she is new to the business, please help her fit in. Welcome aboard Marge, we're short-handed so we can use your help."

Keith walked over and shook her hand, "Wish you had been here earlier, we just shot a really funny scene quite by accident, and now we need to do some close-ups to fit it into the script."

As they worked to quickly develop a few alternate shots which explained the balsa wood manhole cover, Marge poured herself a cup of coffee and walked away, showing little interest in the busy crew.

When the manhole shots were done, Keith went for a cup of coffee and while standing at the urn, Jessica approached. "Hi Keith, I'm Jessica, the Assistant Wardrobe Mistress and I see that you already know Marge. Wish I could have met her during prep since she's supposed to be my boss. What's she like? Are you two good friends?"

"God no, David and I only saw her once, and she was sitting in the lap of one of the guys who is financing this flick. He gave her the job no questions asked, which pissed Angela as you can imagine. Maybe you can put her to work and teach her something, but I wouldn't count on her to actually do anything. She knows where the big money is, and it isn't on this set. For us, she's the boss's secretary, so it's wise to be nice."

"Thanks for the info, and by the way, I like your script. We're going to have a blast converting it into a film."

Keith smiled and as Jessica turned to leave he saw an unusual painting on the back of her faded light blue work shirt. He couldn't resist asking, "Jessica, what's, what's that on the back of your shirt? Where did you get it?"

"Oh, it's just for fun, I painted it to wear while working on your film. Do you like it?"

"It's really different, but what is it?"

"It's a new Tarot card in honor of the medical complex in Senior City, it's the Three Of Quacks."

"What did you call it? I don't know about Tarot: what's it supposed to mean?"

"Three of Quacks. It shows three crazy doctors, somewhat stylized, and they represent money, Latin words, and golf scores. It fits your script perfectly."

"I love it! Maybe you can spruce-up the quacks' costumes, though Tarot isn't part of the story, at least not yet."

"You aren't serious, are you?"

Keith laughed and chuckled to himself as they parted. He realized that he hadn't smiled in a long time as he thought for a moment about Jessica. He was flattered that she liked his script and realized that she might be a lot of fun. She spoke with a kind of cultured accent that he couldn't place, and had bright blue eyes, a slightly narrow face, a nice athletic figure, and smiled like she really meant it. Something about the way she talked was uncommonly friendly and engaging. But if Keith had quickly turned around and looked back, he would have seen Jessica staring at him for a few moments with a peculiar and confused expression.

For an instant, Jessica had been frozen, slightly shaking,

as she stared at Keith's receding figure. Although the duration measured on a clock was only seconds, in that brief time a blur of visions had rushed through her consciousness. Everything was out of focus, moving rapidly, and smeared across her view. Perhaps she saw the rest of her life pass by, and in it she saw Keith crying, she saw him leaning over her, children of different sizes and ages ran past in confusion, playing, emotions both happy and sad. Nothing made any sense and it proved impossible to sharpen the focus or see images more clearly. Abruptly the visions stopped as reality intruded. Jessica watched as Dawn walked over to Keith. As they greeted casually she felt a sharp pain like an ice pick going through her heart.

Jessica turned away and stamped a foot on the ground. What the hell was going on? She knew that logically she should have zero interest in Keith, a neophyte writer of a most silly film: not someone from her usual circle of friends. Besides, she wouldn't even have been here if she hadn't agreed to Angela to do this film over a month ago. Just last week she had made her first big sale, unloading two of her large paintings onto a Japanese collector for more money than she had earned in a year. She should be in her studio cranking out more in the same style and perhaps traveling to Osaka, to accept the lady's invitation to view the rest of her collection.

Jessica struggled both with the vision that had gone through her mind and also with her reaction to seeing Dawn and Keith together. Neither made any sense. The vision implied that Keith could be, or maybe was already predestined to be, part of her future, and her reaction to Dawn, a young struggling actress with little to recommend her but her body, was one of jealousy. Damn, Jessica knew that the last thing she needed was an emotional entanglement with a young man. But as she walked away she also knew that it wasn't over, it was just the beginning of something important that would start to materialize in the coming months.   A new branch of her complex life was budding out: she could sense it quite clearly and although she was afraid of what it might bring, she smiled and began to look forward to the adventure.

Back in the film world, three important scenes comprised their work for the rest of the week: a gas station scene, a huge two-block wide shot, and a group of Day-for-Night scenes with the clones creeping down dark streets. This trucking wide shot later in the week would reveal the city of "Abandoned", where half of the film's action took place, as the oldies chased the escaped clones.

They shot the gas station first, while the crew continued to work on track and props for the two-block-long trucking shot of the whole street. In the "gas station scene" the clones steal cans of gas to power an old garbage truck that they have borrowed. To divert the owners of the gas station, the clones have arranged an IRS raid on the station.

Visually, the gas station was just a tattered billboard showing Arabs selling 'Sheik' gasoline as oil-wells squirt on sand dunes. In front of the billboard several disheveled Arabs wearing dirty robes and burnouses are gathered around red five-gallon cans of fuel, dispensing small amounts to customers while looking over their shoulders. All at once there is a big commotion as IRS tax-collectors, 'Suckers', rush into the scene. Each Sucker wears a tank-type vacuum cleaner on his back, and carries a hand-held hose. Lights flash on the suction machines and sparks snap from the business-end of each suction hose. Sucking people dry, taking their money and maybe even their clothes, is the current method of collecting taxes. The suckers ignore the clones because their tattered clothing shows that they don't have anything worth taxing. Pandemonium is the general idea. To emphasize the barren and impoverished nature of the street, a wind machine blows trash and dust across the scene.

Keith noticed that Dawn was one of the clones in the truck. He waved to her and they had a moment to talk while David rehearsed the Arabs. She looked even younger than when they had met weeks ago: a perfect young body from the clone farm. Keith walked over to the truck, "Hi, you guys look perfect, just like I envisioned when I wrote this."

Dawn replied, "Thanks. This truck smells terrible. It's a real garbage truck isn't it?"

"Yes, and a word of advice, when they start the wind machine you want to be wearing dark glasses or something as the dust's going to make a hell of a mess."

"Thanks, somehow this scene's a bit different than I remember. Has the script changed?"

"Oh yes, every day, usually to make it less expensive to shoot. We'll get a chance to talk about it sometime. Good luck!"

Keith walked back to his gear as they continued to rehearse carefully. Just before they started to shoot, Marge walked over to David, "Hey, you were supposed to pull all that Arab crap from this scene. What gives?"

David was surprised, "What do you mean, we've always had Arabs in the script?"

"Herb sent you an order, telling you to cut that stuff because it would offend financially-important people."

"News to me. Where did he send this order, and when?" David and Keith had assumed that as long that they stayed within budget the financial people would ignore them.

"Beats me, but I heard him talking about it a few days ago."

Angela was nearby listening to the conversation. "It's time to roll, if some guy named Herb doesn't like it, he can get his ass down here before we build the sets and dress the talent."

Marge turned and walked away, leaving a worried David to recover his concentration and begin shooting. Angela put her arm across his shoulders and gave him a tight hug. "Welcome to the real world David, now let's focus on putting a great scene in the can before anything else comes up."

The crew started to shoot, beginning with a wide shot to show the entire sequence from two simultaneous camera angles. This scene in the script contained no dialog, so the actors were free to improvise in pseudo-Arabic and English. Normally, cutting together shots with random dialog would be a nightmare, but the final sound track for this sequence would be exaggerated vacuum-cleaner sound effects from the suction machines pulsating against loud driving music, so almost any nonsense dialog was OK. Keith planned to record the scene, even though the noise from the wind machine's engine would make the dialog almost unintelligible. The recording would help the Editor with a first pass and enliven the dailies.

After their adventures with the manhole cover, the crew was on the lookout for interesting disasters, and they didn't have long to wait. During rehearsals, they hadn't used the wind machine because the noise from its four cylinder gas engine would have made it difficult for David to communicate with the actors and crew. Now, as they started to roll, the giant wind machine's speed governor jammed and it ran flat out, its powerful six-foot-diameter airplane propeller immediately blowing the fake beard off one Arab. His breakaway clothes, which were supposed to be "sucked" into a suction hose, by pulling on a piece of monofilament tied to them, blew down the street instead, leading to much laughter among the actors as they played-out the scene. One of the suction machines fell off an actor who swore at it as he tried to put it back on. As another IRS Sucker helped him lift it, a naked Arab grabbed the

Cinematographer using Arriflex 35mm camera mounted on Chapman crane. Although the Arri is much smaller and lighter than huge silenced 'blimped' sound cameras, the lens quality and, for most purposes, the resulting film quality, are identical. Note that the Key Grip is holding the end of the crane, which he can move in any direction since it is counterbalanced and floats on very smooth bearings.

machine's hose and goosed the tax-collector with it, knocking him to the ground as he grabbed his butt in surprise. The clones stole the fuel, but their old truck wouldn't start, so the Suckers and the Arabs attacked the clones and the captured fuel. Finally the truck started with a cloud of billowing diesel smoke and the clones drove away. Everyone was laughing as the cameras ran out of film and the naked actors looked for their wind-blown clothes: for the purpose of making a funny film, it had been a great master shot. In spite of Marge's implied command, they loved it so much that they continued the Arab theme, shooting matching close-ups and medium shots of the Arabs, Suckers, and clones.

That night, an exhausted Keith went home with a copy of the script supervisor's notes, bewildered and delighted with the day's activities. To his surprise, Angela insisted that he follow union rules and send the day's tapes to Ryder Sound with a Teamster instead of taking them himself. She wanted him to spend the hour that he would save rewriting tomorrow's scenes so that they matched today's adventures.

❧❧❧❧

Most of the next day involved working with a large Chapman Crane, a heavy truck-based camera crane that would slowly drive the length of the two-block-long "city", revealing its features in a long continuous shot. The crane contained a massive battery bank, and could drive slowly and silently on electric motors if desired. However, it could also run full speed on its diesel engine when sound wasn't an issue, or when running shots were required, as in a car chase.

Coordinated with the crane's slow movement down the street were frightened actors peering around corners and running between buildings, fires burning in ruins, and fog which added aesthetic value and hid undesirable features. At several places, teams of IRS suckers would run in front of the camera with their machines buzzing. The plan was to start late in the morning, rehearse all day, then shoot at dusk and into the twilight, when the fires and fog would be most visually effective, but when there was still enough light for a decent exposure. In order to get as much as possible from the crane's slow drive down the street, the grips had built a small platform off the side of its chassis, with an extra camera and crew on it.

Keith had a free day from a sound perspective, since the only recording needed would be a guide track made from the main camera position. The fidelity would be poor, but the sound would only be used by the editor, to let him know what was happening in general terms and give him initial clues about the placement of sound effects. David would be shouting directions to the actors and crew during the long camera move: the goal was to get the visual perfect, then add music and sound effects later. Keith spent most of the day in a Winnebago, typing and reviewing his notes. Jack, his Boom man, worked with the grips to prepare track so that the crane would move smoothly through the shot. Although union rules said that he didn't have to do this, and actually forbade it because he was 'taking a job' from the grips' local, he was an old experienced hand and couldn't imagine sitting still while his friends worked.

Every crew member brought his own tools and whatever else he needed. For an Electrician, this might be just gloves, a wrench, and a pair of pliers. However, the Key Grip always had his personal wheeled trunk-sized box filled with tools and useful spare parts. On a big location shoot like this, the grips would have at least one large truck filled with equipment. It was split between things to modify light (e.g. reflectors, scrims, flags, and stands to hold them) and things for moving and supporting the camera during shots (e.g. track, plywood sheets, wedges, apple boxes, furniture pads). Good Grips could fix or build almost anything quickly, and would try to do it before it was requested. Their boss was the Director of Photography, but on a friendly team like Angela had assembled, everyone worked together doing whatever was needed. The standard line was "It all pays the same". There was a firm though unwritten rule that nobody used another's tools without asking permission, or in an emergency, asking

Chapman Crane ready for a boom shot. The Key Grip is holding a rope, to pull the boom down, while his Best Boy is holding the weight bucket to steady the movement. Note that the crane's cab, which protects the driver from wind and rain while motoring, has been re-moved. The fake oil well, 3/4 scale, is squirting nigazine into the air: this is a harmless black liquid made with 'secret ingredients'

forgiveness afterwards. These were all craftsmen (or women) and their personal tools were a part of their skill-set.

The rehearsal of the crane shots went well, but just before shooting began, everyone was astonished to see Marge leave to catch a plane for dinner in Las Vegas. This left Jessica and a few helpers to finish dressing the dozens of extras and actors who populated the scene, just as it was time to shoot. Keith saw her predicament and started helping. They all knew that the sun was going down and that it was time to roll.

George held up his hand toward the setting sun, squinted, and proclaimed, "Sixteen minutes to sunset." He knew that when the sun was near the horizon in mid-latitudes, it moves roughly one finger width in eight minutes, measured when a person holds his arm straight out toward the sun.

Keith told Jessica to concentrate on the people closest to the camera, while he helped those in less-visible positions. Jessica finished pinning the last actor's clothes just as the crane reached his position on the first take: close but it worked.

When they wrapped at eight Jessica sought-out Keith and thanked him for pitching-in. They were both furious at Marge and hoped that she would stay in Vegas where she belonged. Keith smiled nervously: he hadn't had a real date in weeks, and hesitatingly asked, "Want to go somewhere for a quick dinner?"

"Thanks, thanks for asking, but I'm a wreck. Any chance you're free late Saturday night?"

Keith was startled, "Sure, I mean yes I don't have anything planned."

"Would you like to see something special?" Jessica asked coyly.

"More tarot cards?"

"Not exactly, but you'll be surprised when you see me in action. Do you have a proper dark suit and tie?"

"Sure. Are we going to church?"

"No, but you need to wear your best clothes because they have a strict dress code, so do put on your suit, white shirt, and tie, and meet me at The Magic Castle at nine. I'll be just inside the front door."

"Thank you. I can't wait. This sounds mysterious."

Keith was delighted at the turn of events and helped Jessica carry laundry bags full of wardrobe to her car. As they walked across the street he was surprised to see that she was driving a new black Mercedes sedan. It was uncommonly formal and didn't seem to match her appearance. Keith wondered what she would think of his old beetle. Maybe she was rich, or had a rich boyfriend? What a pain, just when Keith thought that perhaps he had met someone like him who might become a good friend. Jessica drove away, to drop the laundry at an overnight specialty cleaner on Melrose. She would collect it on her way back to work in the morning.

As Jessica drove, she wondered to herself what had just happened: and in particular why had she invited Keith to her performance when she could have just as easily turned him away. She had only met him a few days ago, yet on the spur of the moment she had asked him into her personal space, to see a part of her life that had nothing to do with the film world. Jessica thought first that perhaps her motivation was to outshine all the pretty but shallow movie girls, like Dawn and Spunky: to show Keith that she, Jessica, had much more to offer than a body. But Jessica knew that this was not the real answer, the prime motivation behind her actions. Oddly enough she was beginning to like Keith: he was creeping into her thoughts just a little.

The rest of the week was normal for the actors and sound crew, but complex for the camera team. These were all night scenes, with the clones creeping around the "city". Keith had placed these exterior scenes in the dark because shadowy exteriors are much cheaper to arrange than fully-lighted scenes. Anything that didn't fit the scene, like modern cars or billboards, could be in black shadow so that the audience didn't see it. While this was easy to write and act, it was not easy to shoot.

Everything would be day-for-night (DFN), which meant that the crew would be working in normal daylight, but the film would look like it had been shot at night. Actual night shooting was expensive, with overtime rates being paid, and it was difficult since most people wouldn't get sufficient sleep in the daytime to compensate. Night-for-night was only used on special occasions, for example on city street scenes with lots of traffic and store lights. George was going to make a bright sunny day look like moonlight.

For each shot David described what was supposed to happen in terms of action, then George determined the camera angle relative to the sun that would make the best DFN effect. The idea was to have the sun slightly behind the actors, enough so that the background would be dark with shadows falling toward the camera. The front of the actors would be in contrasty partial shadow. Dark backgrounds and actors with lighter clothing were preferred whenever practical. George underexposed the film two stops and filtered to give it a bluish tint. He shot from a high angle or against backgrounds so that the bright sky never appeared in the frame. A small amount of tungsten cross-lighting, with straw-colored gels over the lamps, was aimed at the actors, to warm their skin tones against the blue-tinted scenes. Front-lighting was avoided because the idea was to have as much contrast, with deep black shadows, as possible. When it matched the script, the actors used bright flashlights or walked past fires, or other night-time effects to help the audience think this was night. Cricket noises and other night-sounds like owls hooting would be added later to enhance the effect.

The grips had a busy day, using flags to block light completely and scrims, to partially block and soften the light. They darkened backgrounds, and used reflectors to enhance the contrasty cross-lighting as the sun moved constantly.

At the start of each roll, George shot a standard Kodak color chart with normal lighting and exposure to cue the lab. Overnight dailies are normally one-light prints. This means that the Printer, in the lab, looks at the first scene on a roll, in this case a color chart, then adjusts his equipment so that this scene prints correctly. Then the circled takes on the entire roll are printed immediately without further adjustment. After the film is edited, the color balance of each piece of film is carefully adjusted to match the adjacent pieces: this is expensive and careful work which is not needed for dailies. Stubby marked the log sheet for each roll in big letters, "DFN, print for color chart". This would ensure that the print shown tomorrow morning to the editor in the screening room had George's night effects baked in.

Seniors Have It Tough

Chapter 4

A Magic Night

The Magic Castle, in Hollywood.

On Saturday night Keith wore his best dark navy blue suit, white shirt and tie, and arrived at the entrance to The Magic Castle precisely at nine, filled with anticipation. The large Victorian house, with pointed turrets and slightly illuminated glowing windows looked like a film set for a Halloween horror movie, but he could hear happy music coming from inside. Much to his surprise a polite young Valet parked his low-status car without question. He thought that this must be one of the few places in L.A. where "you are what you drive" was not in effect. Keith had heard of this place before, but had never been inside and was most curious. The intricate old wooden door creaked open by itself, revealing Jessica in the small library-like lobby. He had never seen her wearing anything but grubby film clothes and was speechless at the vision standing before him. Jessica was wearing a floor-length gown that seemed to be composed of dozens of layers of soft blue and white gauze, with glittering metal reflective flecks in the top layers. It covered one shoulder but the other was soft and bare: the composition was topped by her flowing black hair, a sparkling tiara and a glittering necklace. She twirled around once and laughed at his surprise, enjoying the effect her costume had on him.

"Well Keith, you clean-up nicely. How do you like my weekend work clothes?"

"They're fantastic, you look like an angel who has drifted down from the clouds to visit mortals on the ground."

As Keith said this casually, he was suddenly gripped by intense sadness as the words resonated with Kristin's final breath. Tears came to his eyes then flowed down his face as Jessica stood silently by, not knowing what to make of his instantaneous mood change. Instinctively, she took his hand as he turned away to brush his tears aside.

"I'm sorry Keith, let me take you to a quiet room," she said softly. With a nod to the doorman, a bookcase swung away and Jessica led Keith inside to the main bar. Instead of stopping to explain the ornate Victorian surroundings, she led him up several flights of stairs, then through a hidden door into the members' private library.

Keith had stopped crying but the vision of Kristin watching him from Heaven still burned his eyes as they sat at a small table in the deserted library. Jessica opened a cabinet and poured two glasses of scotch, then started on one as she asked "Do you want to tell me what happened? I can feel your pain, but I don't know what causes it."

"It's so simple, but so sad, and so clear in my eyes. My fiancée Kristin was killed, run over by a car while she was jogging, in August. Her last. . ." Keith started crying again and couldn't continue.

Jessica held his hand silently and waited for him to recover. After a few minutes he began again, "She helped write our medical screenplay while she was in the hospital. Almost her last words were that she would be watching me from Heaven, and laughing with me as our silly story became a film. Then, she smiled and stopped breathing."

"And when you saw me tonight, and said that I came from a cloud, it all rushed back into your heart. Oh, I wish I had worn my black outfit tonight instead, it's scary, not nice."

"You couldn't be scary. You'd look great in any color, it's just me. I'll be all right now. Let's have some fun. Tell me about this crazy place." Keith worked to regain his composure, to be upbeat, to recover his interest in Jessica. He thought that she must think him a basket case, crying the moment he saw her on their first date.

"I wish I didn't have to do a show at midnight. This is a time to talk quietly, not fool around acting."

71

"No, we'd better have some laughs, so I don't ruin your evening with my old memories. What do you do here? Why the beautiful dress?"

"I know you'll find this hard to believe, so please don't worry about it now.   I'm a medium, a psychic. All the other members here are magicians, but they asked me to join because none of them could figure out how I work. They said that I was either the greatest magician alive, or a genuine psychic, and in either case, I could help them have lots of fun."

Keith was silent in amazement as he thought of the contrast between the description she painted and the busy wardrobe person he knew on location. Then he tentatively asked, "I had no idea, I mean, it's hard to believe, fortune telling and all that stuff, do you really do it?"

Jessica looked into his eyes, perhaps seeing a little into his thoughts. "Don't worry, you'll get to see for yourself later on. Now, are you sure you're going to be OK? You could see my show some other night, you don't have to stay, I'll understand, I can feel how deeply you hurt inside."

"I don't want to interfere with your performance, so if you'd rather, I can go, but I'd really like to see what you do, and wander around this old place with you."

Jessica jumped up, "Then Let's get busy. We can grab a snack quickly in the kitchen, then hit the bar and you can meet Irma."

"Who?"

"She's everyone's favorite, you'll see, come on, it's too hard to explain with words." Jessica's enthusiasm was contagious, and Keith rushed to follow her. He was surprised at how quickly and gracefully she could move in spite of her large dress.

Jessica led him down a narrow back staircase and into a corner of the kitchen where a small buffet was set for members who didn't want to eat in the dining rooms. As they ate sandwiches and snacks, she explained: "This is a private club, and there are two kinds of members, Magicians, and Friends. I'm a magician member, though I don't know any magic. The Friends pay dues and high initiation fees because Magicians are mostly impoverished and can't afford this. What makes the place click financially is that the Friends bring lots of expense account guests here. We have a rule that all guests must eat dinner whenever they come, and chef Howard makes fancy meals and charges them a fortune. We also make a killing in the bars: they're seven bars scattered around, and we also charge the guests for special shows and table magic. Guests usually ask the waiter to have a magician join them after dinner and he, or she, will do a bunch of clever card tricks right under their noses for fifty bucks. Visiting clients love it."

"So, in other words, you and the Magicians have a nice club that the expense account guests pay for."

"Right, everyone's happy and has a good time. These are some of the best magicians in the world, and lots of visiting magicians pass through and perform as well. The guests are seeing some of the best magic available anywhere. We keep expanding and adding rooms and fun events, and people are always donating historic magic stuff and Victorian bits and pieces. The library we were sitting in has an outstanding collection of magic books."

Keith asked "Who's Irma?", but Jessica laughed in reply and led him from the kitchen into the main dining room, then down the formal staircase into the first floor bar. As they walked down the stairs an adjacent statue of an owl with glowing red eyes hooted at Keith, startling him. Everywhere he looked were Victorian artifacts and dark wood paneling. As Jessica had mentioned, there was a strict dress code and everyone was properly attired, with quite a few in tuxedos. Some people stared at Jessica, as none of the other women wore anything resembling her ethereal costume. She smiled and greeted many by name, and Keith began to recognize differences between guests and members. Among the members, Jessica was something of a celebrity, or at least a notoriety, an unusual decoration that added to the atmosphere. He discovered that her stage name was 'Divine One' as members greeted her. Keith overheard a member explaining to a woman, ". . she's a real medium, not a Magician like the rest of us. . ."

As they approached the long bar, Jessica whispered in Keith's ear, "Don't sit on the middle stools, they slowly collapse after awhile and you wind up with your chin on the bar as everyone laughs."

Behind the bar was a grand piano playing by itself. On top of the piano was an empty bird cage containing nothing but a swing that moved back and forth by itself. Keith was surprised as the bartender placed a glass of whiskey on the piano, which stopped playing and drank it mysteriously. Then the piano notes slurred and segwayed into "Happy Days Are Here Again" to a big round of applause from the people gathered at the bar. People stuffed money into the bars of the cage.

Jessica called out to the piano, "Irma, would you play "We're In The Money" for me?"

The piano keys tinkled, almost as though they were laughing, then played a gay rendition of the requested old song from the nineteen thirties. Jessica knew this song was part of a hilarious sequence in their film, and saw Keith smile when he heard it.

Keith asked, "How does it work, where are the strings that move the piano keys?"

"That is a secret, and actually the only secret that members aren't allowed to tell. Irma's knowledge of music is incredible and wait 'til you see this. Watch that guy, he's Peter Isacson, a famous pianist who comes here sometimes just to visit Irma."

A patron in black tie had risen and walked to the piano. With no introduction, he sat down at the keyboard and started to play one part of Motzart's "Sonata For Keyboard Duet in C". Without missing a beat, the piano itself accompanied him through the intricate music. Half way through, the pianist slid down the piano bench and started to play the other half of the duet without missing a note: Irma switched parts without hesitation to the amazement of all. The applause at the end was stupendous, as the pianist bowed and Irma pounded her keys triumphantly.

Jessica glanced at her watch, "Let's go, we can just catch a show before I need to get ready." She led him down a small secret spiral staircase onto the stage of a little theater on the floor below. They walked from the stage into vacant seats at the side, to the surprise of the people who were already seated in the audience. It was a little theater, seating perhaps fifty people, and everyone had a great view of the nearby stage.

Keith asked, "Where are we, what's about to happen?"

"They're four theaters here, all different sizes, and you're about to see one of the funniest acts I've ever watched. Don't volunteer whatever you do. Magicians perform in these theaters and it's always a hoot. Here, you're performing for your friends and their guests, so you can try new things and make a few mistakes. It's so different from performing in front of thousands in Reno and Vegas, where if you goof, you're fired. Of course, those places pay real money, so there's some compensation."

As Keith sat in the theater, he realized that he was having a great time, the most fun that he had had in weeks or months. He smiled to himself and relaxed. Tonight was going well and he hadn't even seen Jessica's performance. He had never seen a psychic perform and was very curious to see what she did on stage, though he was sure that it didn't really involve spirits.

A magician walked onto the stage and introduced himself as Fandango The Slippery, direct from the streets of New York. He called for a volunteer and walked into the audience, selecting a somewhat inebriated visiting salesman who made the mistake of raising his hand. The victim's friends cheered him as he was led to the stage. Fandango pushed and shoved the volunteer, helping him up the steps onto the stage, giving a stream of contradictory instructions to the hapless person. From the audience Keith could see Fandango remove the victim's belt, his wallet, and then his tie, as he rotated the victim, pointing him first one way then another. The audience started laughing, as Fandango and his pretty assistant directed the victim to stand first in one place then another. As they made him raise his arms, Fandango removed his coat to the audience's amazement. The shapely assistant distracted the victim as the audience roared.   Finally Fandango asked the victim if he could borrow a few dollars for a magic trick. The victim reached in his pocket, but found his wallet missing. Then Fandango asked if he could borrow his watch, and the victim found that missing too. As the audience howled, the victim began to realize how many of his personal possessions were missing. Jessica led Keith away through an exit. "Time to go upstairs."

It was eleven-thirty as they arrived outside a room containing twelve people having a private dinner at a large round table. Jessica whispered, "This is where I perform. I'm going to put you in a little room up above which has a one-way mirror. Clifford, a magician, runs the effects from there and he'll fill you in. I need to prepare for awhile, but you'll see the whole thing."

She opened a door behind a dark velvet drape, "Go up there and watch: I'll meet you here after the show."

Keith climbed the steep narrow stairs and found himself in a little room with a young magician, Clifford. He whispered, "Hi, I'm Keith, a friend of Jessica's, or should I say Divine One?"

"I'm Clifford, did she tell you anything about this show?"

"I don't have a clue."

"It's a séance, and a group of twelve people have to sign up for it. They come into the room down there and have a special dinner, prepared by a chef right in the room. Loads of fancy food and wine, package deal, very profitable for us. See, they're thirteen chairs at the round table, but only twelve people. They're just finishing desert. Every other night of the week, a magician does the séance, which is faked, but they have lots of fun. I run the effects, rocking the table, sending spirits through the air and that sort of stuff. On Saturday night, if we're lucky, Jessica does the show and it's a lot different, because she's real. Some of those people around the table are magicians, because they know how good she is. The public almost never gets to see her perform. We time the dinner so that they're on brandy at the stroke of midnight."

"What happens then?"

"Normally a magician enters as the clock strikes twelve, and he tries to bring Houdini back to life as I work the special effects. It's harmless fun, though some people mistakenly think it's a real séance and get bent out of shape. After all, this is a magic room, not a psychic tent. But with Jessica anything can happen."

Keith thought of how he had misjudged Jessica's

performance. He had expected Jessica to perform on a stage, like the Magician that they had just seen, and that it would be faked. The way Clifford talked, and he seemed to be sincere, Jessica was a genuine psychic who might conjure spirits from the dead or who knew what. Keith, having a scientific and engineering background, knew that this was impossible, and Jessica seemed like a normal and uncommonly nice young woman. She didn't look like a witch or a gypsy with a crystal ball. He began to realize that the Jessica that he had seen was perhaps nothing like the real person about to appear down below. He sensed Clifford's anticipation, and realized that if a professional didn't know what would happen, this could be a very unusual performance. The thought caused goose-bumps to briefly travel down his back, and he shuddered involuntarily as he shook them off.

Keith watched through the mirror as the twelve people below finished eating and the dishes were cleared away. As the sound of a clock began to strike midnight the only items on the table were twelve brandy snifters. As Clifford worked the controls, the lights faded and Jessica seemed to float down from the ceiling in a cloud of luminous fog. What an entrance.

She sat in the thirteenth chair, "Greetings. I am the Divine One, and I will help you try an experiment tonight. Normally a magician puts on a fake séance in this room, but not this evening. We do have some clever effects."

Clifford made the table rock back and forth slowly. ". . . as you can see, and I'll use them now and then to add to the fun. Each of you has latent psychic powers and I am going to try to activate and coordinate all of them to see if together we really can contact Houdini tonight. As you know, on his death bed he said that he would try very hard to reach the living world if there was any way to do it from the other side. Oh, before we start, I can feel that one of you is going to faint in the next hour, but I won't embarrass you by giving your name. You're among friends, so don't worry when it happens. And I see that Francine is here. Francine, I feel that your cat has been locked in the neighbor's garage all day, so don't cry anymore, she isn't lost, and she misses you. Try the neighbor to the left side of your house, that feels stronger to me. And Max, stop worrying about your business deal on Monday morning. They'll all sign and you'll make a fortune. Spend it wisely."

As Jessica casually gave these predictions and bits of personal information, the twelve murmured and shuffled in their chairs with anticipation. The lights slowly faded to complete darkness. Although the Fire Department would have been annoyed if it knew, there wasn't even an illuminated EXIT sign in the pitch-black room.

Jessica talked quietly as she slowly went into a trance, holding hands with the others in a ring of thirteen. Things happened and Keith couldn't be sure how much was Jessica and how much was Clifford as he subtly worked various levers and controls. Glowing spirits shimmered across the room, odd sounds came from the table and corners of the room. Suddenly Jessica commanded, "Clifford, stop rocking the table and fooling around. Everyone concentrate: he's really coming through!" A garbled male, foreign, perhaps Hungarian, voice seemed to come from beneath the table, and then from all around the room.

Clifford whispered to Keith, "My god, we don't have any vocal effects: that's the real thing."

The voice struggled to make itself understood. It moved around the room, as Jessica tried to communicate in English and in French. She tried so hard to make it understand and the voice in turn was struggling in pain and difficulty to come through. The agony lasted perhaps half an hour, then the voice slowly faded, becoming weaker and weaker and sounding further away, as though it was reluctantly going back to whence it came. Jessica whispered in the silence, "It's over, but he was so close, I could feel him in the room with us. I wish I understood Hungarian." As the lights came back on slowly, everyone noticed that one man had passed out, and worked to gently revive him. Jessica had disappeared. A woman named Francine was anxious to rescue her cat from the neighbor's garage.

Keith was completely bewildered. The performance seemed so real, so genuine, yet how could it be. When he asked Clifford how she did it, he smiled and said that Jessica was their mystery: none of the magicians could figure out how she did anything, but they loved watching her. Keith thought that he knew that spirits didn't come back from the dead and talk to the living. He went down the stairs and found Jessica, who was wrapped in a floor-length black woolen cape. Without her necklace and tiara, and covered by the hooded cape, she looked like a different person. They went into a small bar and sat in soft old wing chairs in a dark corner. Jessica was shivering with cold and fading nervous energy. She kicked off her shoes and curled up in her chair with her legs folded on the seat under her cape. She could have been a cat, curled up tightly for warmth. A waiter brought a dusty bottle of port and two glasses, "A present from Max, our best bottle. They say it was a divine performance."

"Thanks Kurt, it really was the best show I've ever done. I'm as amazed as anyone, and please thank Max for me."

"Everyone's talking about it, you're wonderful."

After the waiter left, Keith turned to Jessica. "You were terrific, I've never seen or heard anything like that. How did you do it, and how did you know about that lady's cat or know that guy's business deal would go through?"

"Oh, the cat was nothing. Before the show, I sit

outside the room and try to sort of listen-in on their feelings. Sometimes I can tune into something specific, and if so, I put it in words to help people. I can see the future a little bit, sometimes, and Max is always worrying, but he's a very nice guy. If you asked me to foretell a specific event I couldn't do it. The feelings about the future flow into me randomly, but no matter how I try, I can't make predictions of specific things on request. You can imagine how many times business people have asked for concrete information on stocks and economic stuff. If I could really tell the future, I'd be the richest girl in the world, and I wouldn't be schlepping around your movie set. As psychics go, I'm very young and inexperienced, but I have the gift. If I live a long time, I'll become much better as I learn to control the power. But right now, I just try to get into the mood and see what happens. The big deal tonight was Houdini, I've never come that close to him before. I'm going to find a Hungarian translator before I try to contact him again. This was so fantastic, I don't know how to tell you what I feel."

"Clifford said that the strange voice was real, that he didn't fake it, how could that be? How could you do that? Before tonight, I would have thought it impossible."

"You're so logical. I don't know how it works, and it's not consistent, sometimes it's much better than others, and you were very lucky to be here tonight. Those twelve people wanted something to happen, they weren't skeptics, there was no negative energy, very receptive, very clear ring of kindred spirits, so maybe it was Houdini. I tried so hard to make it happen for them, I strained each muscle in my body, all the pores on my skin opened, I gave it everything I had, and now I'm really pooped, but I'm so excited that it worked."

"You're shivering, can I get you something, a blanket or I don't know what?" Keith reached over and gently massaged

Jessica's shoulder as she smiled at him. He noticed that she had already drained one glass of the thick strong port and was well into another.

"I'm fine, just wiped out. Have you ever been on stage? Do you know what the rush is like when you really communicate with the audience? It's like being inside them, part of them, and yet leading them. I'm just slowly coming down, and I'm soaking wet from perspiration."

"Would you like me to drive you home? You don't look like a safe driver."

"Thanks, but then I'd need to come back here in the morning to pick up my car."

"I'll drive you home, and return in the morning to bring you back. It's the least I can do in return for such a spectacular night."

"I'd like that, but first let's just sit here a little while longer and get to know each other, and finish this lovely bottle of port. Then you can drive me home."

They talked about how each of them had fallen into the film business. Neither had studied cinema in school. Keith was an Electrical Engineer and Jessica had studied art since childhood. She loved to draw and was talented, but her paintings were unusual, far from the mainstream art hanging in museums and galleries. Jessica remarked that she could make more in a month working on films than many painters made in a year, so she blended her avocation and vocation, switching back and forth as opportunities arose. She loved to paint imaginary people in unusual clothing, and explained that the white gown she was wearing had been made from one of her childhood paintings. Her psychic talents led occasionally to unusual dreams and visions, which she tried to express in paint. For both of them, their conversation was on the surface, guarded, with many strong emotions and thoughts hidden below, unvoiced.

Keith drove her home, but Jessica didn't even let him walk her to the front door. She jumped from the car with a quick "Thanks, see you in the morning," and was into the house before he could follow or hope for a good night kiss.

Jessica was in a hurry for at least three reasons. The most pressing was a sudden need to recycle the booze that flowed through her body, as she dumped her fancy gown on the floor and ran for the bathroom. The next order of business was to grab sketch pads, pencils, and a full bottle of scotch then head for her favorite chair where she curled up under a blanket and began to draw rapidly, page after page in the dim light. The interaction with Houdini had been the strongest psychic experience she had ever had and capturing her feelings and the visions that she had seen on paper would take the rest of the night. The third activity was mulling over Keith and what he might or might not mean for her future. He was so sad, so wrapped up in Kristin and her death. Jessica began to realize that if she were interested in Keith, she would need to outshine his memory of Kristin, rather than a few bimbos scattered about their film sets.

As Jessica worked, she saw in her sketches echoes of some of the thousands of paintings she had studied in school: she had been an outstanding art history student, earning her Phd when only twenty-three, the youngest ever to do so at The Sorbonne. However she sometimes thought now that she had crammed too much into too short a time: three years for Marlborough in Los Angeles, three years for college, and three years of grad school in Paris left too little time for what was called "growing up": her excessive brainpower and voracious appetite for study had robbed her of a normal transition into adulthood, but tonight it didn't matter as drawings poured from her hands. Many of the sketches reminded her of "The

Scream" by Edvard Munch. Somehow Houdini's efforts to come through from the other side seemed as painful as the melted face in Edvard's famous painting. Jessica was smart enough to realize that tonight's contact with Houdini could have been a case of mass hypnosis, with herself as the instigator, but that didn't stop her hand flowing across the pages: damn, she knew that at this very moment she had enough new creative material to keep her painting continuously for months if she could pull the visions from her mind and get them onto paper.

Jessica also mulled over Keith and Houdini and their possible interrelationships. Sometimes both were in a sketch together, almost by accident: both in pain they could not control.

Then she chanced to think of Max and The Magic Castle. She had been a member for a few months, and had given only a few proper performances with Clifford's help. Normally not much happened, though her simple predictions usually came true and she could put on a better show than the magicians. Tonight had been very special and she sensed that everyone knew it. Much to her surprise she had instantly become a star, albeit in a small world, and now a worry began to emerge: what would happen at her next performance. How could she ever repeat tonight's show? Everybody would be talking about it and trying to get in to see what happened next. Perhaps it was time to quit on a high point. Her psychic world was totally unpredictable and she now realized that a great performance was almost more of a problem than a reward. The psychic arena was so unlike any other field in life where steady advancement was based on practice and study: in this game it was almost as though she was the ball, rather than a player.

The moonlight that shone through a window onto Jessica also, miles away, illuminated Keith's road home along Sunset to Westwood. He chanced to look up at the stars and wondered if perhaps Kristin had sent Jessica down to earth to comfort him. He had just discovered that many things were possible that hours ago he would have thought ridiculous. Kristin might actually be up there somewhere watching him. He smiled and thought that perhaps there was a connection between the two wonderful young women.

ɔɛɔɛɔɛɔ

Daybreak found Keith drinking black coffee and re-writing to match the week's changes in scenes: he hoped to finish work before eleven, then drive to Jessica's. Only one week into production and he had completely re-done the script almost twice, at least in terms of page-count. However, some pages had been re-hashed over and over. He was growing tired of the continual editing and hoped that his lawyer was right, that he stood a chance of being paid for all the work.

A Magic Castle valet called at ten and told him that Jessica had talked him into delivering her car, so Keith needn't bother driving over to collect it: he passed a message that Jessica was looking forward to seeing him Monday, but she was sleeping today. Keith had been looking forward to seeing Jessica, but apparently that wasn't in the cards. Disappointed, he went for a long walk around Westwood, then napped until it was time for dinner. He missed Jessica, even though he hardly knew her, and he was fascinated by her talents. Tomorrow and the following days would be fun, working with her and learning more. Then in a moment of panic, he thought that someone so special must have a boy-friend, or lover, and many admirers. Maybe one lived in the house where he had dropped her. What to do? What would the weeks ahead bring?

When Keith awoke from his nap he drove to Angela's house, where he and David were to have dinner with Angela

Cinematographer with an old Mitchell in 1973, not too different from ones that Harry used in the twenties. The main improvement here is an electric motor mounted on the right side, to replace the crank.

and her father, Harry. Keith looked forward to talking with Harry about his experiences in the teens and twenties. On a previous visit, Harry had given Keith very useful advice when they had discussed the creative differences between silent films and today's productions. Harry had told how the writing of silent films had been much harder because the whole story was told though the lens. The writer couldn't give clues to the audience with sly dialog and tense violins. The story had to come through pictures, which meant lots of close-ups. Shots like hands touching, eyes blinking, and a smile could tell a thousand different things, depending on the actress and the situation. Keith had realized that these intimate emotion-revealing close-ups were also very inexpensive to shoot so he had used them whenever appropriate in his film, to save money as well as to impart additional emotional impact.

Tonight Keith hoped to learn more about the equipment used in the old days, equipment which was still scattered about Hollywood and in-use because it was so rugged. He began by asking Harry if he would tell them about the old equipment and the differences he had seen when sound entered the business.

Harry began to reminisce. "I remember when they moved the crank from the rear of the camera to the right side. I was lucky because I had a steady hand, though of course I would over-crank when we wanted a slow-mo effect, and under-crank when we wanted the actors to appear to move quickly. There weren't any tachometers, you just judged the speed by feel, and if you did it well, you were hired to do another film. The Mitchell rack-over cameras with four-claw pull-down and dual registration pins that we used are rock-solid precision machines: you still use them today, with a motor instead of a crank. Of course they weigh a ton, but we could hire coolies to move them around, and we had time, plenty of time to wait for the right sunset, or the right lighting on a scene, at least when shooting background plates."

"But you asked about differences between then and now, and to me there were several big ones. A key change came when film became uniform and exposure meters were developed, both around the mid-twenties. Before that, the cameraman was responsible not only for the shot, but also for the lab work to develop the film. I had tables and notes, and memories of what had worked before, but I was never really sure of either the light or the film, so I covered myself with bracketed exposures whenever possible. I remember some guy who said that if he had to put on dark glasses, the exposure was F-eight. He was a big hit, so it worked for him, at least outdoors. On the stage however, life was different, because the lights could be too dim and you'd never know it because there was nothing to compare the brightness to. We covered our asses by using strong rim light on all the key actors and props. That way, no matter what the exposure was, you would see a white rimmed shadow, or if you were lucky, an actor, moving across the set."

Keith added, "Right, and some so-called experts think those old dark films with rim-lit actors were an artistic effect, not a necessity."

"And you should have seen the sets in the silent days. They were all sorts of colors because we used ortho film, which is sensitive to blue and green, but not red. So if we wanted something to look dark, we painted it red, and if it should look bright, it was green or blue. Makeup was weird for the same reason. Most actors hated it, but the good ones took it all in stride. The talent, and probably the painters, loved the introduction of panchromatic film."

"But you're a sound man, and I haven't answered your question. In fact the main difference was that you had to be quiet on the set. A big fart could ruin a scene, so you had to be careful what you ate for lunch once sound came in: no chili dogs from Pinks! But in practical terms, we adjusted easily. The gear was always changing in small ways, but the basics stayed the same. We had to tell the story in the most effective way possible, and put something that worked in the can (film is stored in steel cans) no matter what happened. I remember working with a grouchy actress who was worried that her wrinkles were beginning to show. Her fear was messing up her performance and we were short of time. I took a dim twenty-five watt bulb and put it on the front of the camera, right against the side of the lens, for her close-ups. You couldn't see a change in the exposure with a meter, but it was just enough light to fill-in the dark shadows in her wrinkles: made her look years younger. What a change in her performance, she became so happy, and we finished the film on time."

Angela smiled, "And dad worked every one of her films after that. But I think some of his best stories are about the years he spent shooting background plates all over the world. What a life for a young man."

"I was strong and had proven that I could reliably operate a camera under difficult conditions. When I pulled into Veracruz, or Tokyo, or Rio, there would be a big box of film and whatever equipment I had requested from my last stop. Then there would be a detailed list of shots they wanted us to get. I almost never saw the developed film, but just shipped the exposed cans back to Hollywood and prayed. I hoped that at the next stop I would find more film instead of my final check. Sometimes, the first time I saw my footage was in foreign theaters. It was a riot to see a film with some posh actors sitting in a car, which I knew was on a Hollywood stage, while some of my footage of Paris or New Delhi rolled behind them. I once saw a newsreel that used my stuff, even though the reporters had never left home."

"You kids should go back and study the great silents from the twenties, like METROPOLIS, to see what was possible when creativity was unbounded but the equipment was primitive. They had around thirty-seven thousand people in the cast, and great special effects long before color and modern tricks. I knew one of the Mitchell guys who went over to Germany with a couple of cameras to help make that film, same basic cameras you have today. They used all sorts of tricks, and lots of first-surface mirrors. Sometimes they would scrape just enough silver off a mirror so that the camera could see one scene reflected in the mirror, and another scene through the clear area in the glass. To the eye it blended perfectly. There's one scene of the city with hundreds of cars moving. They shot it frame by frame, and moved every car model by hand after each frame: thousands of frames were shot this way. Somewhere, I think in the moving around the city montage, there's footage that they double-exposed in the camera over thirty times, each time carefully re-winding the film then shooting again from another angle."

Keith and David encouraged Harry, and let him talk late into the night. It was a living history lesson that they felt very fortunate to hear first hand.

Chapter 5

On Stage 9

Monday morning found Keith and his weekend rewrites headed for stage nine at Paramount on the Gower Street lot, an old dusty stage which Angela had wangled on the cheap. Keith wondered if Harry had been around when it had been built and perhaps used it when it was clean and new. However, time to get to work instead of thinking about the past. Keith's first task was to find the truck which held his boxes of sound gear, then help Jack schlep it onto the stage through the huge door. Every stage had a door big enough to drive trucks and large sets through. These doors were easily twenty feet high and at least as wide. They were also sound proof, so they were thick as well. The doors were hung on tracks and slid sideways to open. Each usually had a chain-hoist so that its bulk could be raised and lowered a few inches. After the door was slid closed, it was lowered, to form a sound-proof joint with the ground.

All of these old stages had wooden floors. The studios which had been rich when their stages were built had solid parquet floors, made with six-inch end-grain hardwood two-by-fours: these floors would outlast the buildings. However, Keith was working on a less-deluxe stage, which he noted as he stubbed his shoe on a large splinter. The advantage of wood was simple, anything could be temporarily nailed in place anywhere. Zillions of double-head nails had been in and out of these floors over the years. In most cases the floors were strong enough to support trucks, fork-lifts, and camera cranes which were at least as heavy. However, one stage, built over an unused swimming pool dating back to the days of Ester Williams, had collapsed under a heavy load to the truck driver's surprise.

Today, they had a simple set dressed to represent a dormitory at the clone farm. Cheap single beds, minimal furniture, and heavy bars on the windows. Four physically-perfect teenage boy clones were in the dorm practicing their dialog and action with David while the crew worked quietly on lighting and camera angles. The clones, both boys and girls, wore identical skimpy track suits in all the clone farm scenes. This saved money, both for the production, and for the oldies who were raising them in the story, and it showed much of their perfect bodies to the audience. In this scene the clones talk about a sex-education film they have just seen. From their dialog it is clear that they are being brain-washed with a completely bogus description of the purposes of and uses for male erections. There was no mention of reproduction or girls.

Two of the actors were having an increasingly hostile argument with David. "Who the fuck wrote this stuff?" demanded a clone.

David looked around and saw Keith walking toward the set. "Keith, come over here, we need to talk."

"I've been listening and I don't see what's wrong."

"You're making fun of gays, with this homosexual dialog, that's what's wrong buster," said another clone.

"It's part of the story: the oldies don't want any genetically-unplanned reproduction, so they keep the sexes separate, encouraging the clones to play with themselves instead of with the opposite sex," explained Keith.

"Yea, what's wrong with that, they're being trained to

be queer," added Marge who was nearby.

The clone turned sharply to Marge, "You make it sound like homosexual relationships are weird, and only happen because some old turds make the clones watch phony sex films."

"They are weird, aren't they, I mean normal guys would like to do it with girls, not boys," Keith replied.

Jessica had been working on one of the clones' costumes and interrupted, turning to Keith and David, "God, how can you two be so insensitive to other people's feelings?"

"We're making a movie, not a P.B.S. documentary," said David.

"So people's feelings don't count, is that it?", replied Jessica.

"We can't change this scene without screwing up the plot. These guys, and the girls, are supposed to be ignorant about reproduction, and the sex video they watch is a riot, with the oldies trying to demonstrate with each other." , David explained.

"But you could at least be polite on the set, and consider the actors' sexual orientation.", Jessica answered, growing slightly irritated.

Marge laughed at Jessica, "What would you know about sex? God, the way you dress I bet you never get laid, but maybe you're into girls?" Jessica quickly turned from the group and walked away.

Keith cringed at the rude comment and wanted to follow, to comfort Jessica in some way, but Angela marched up to the group, her eyes shooting daggers in all directions. She took out her stop watch, and glared at the actors. "You were hired to play a scene in this movie. Either follow David's direction exactly or get the fuck off my stage. In one minute I'm going to call for replacements. Actors like you are a dime a dozen in any parking lot." Angela started her stopwatch with a loud click and waited for a reply on the dead silent stage.

"You just wait 'til this hits the screen: the protests will shut it down over night," glared one clone as he walked off the set, leaving three others behind.

"Give his lines to these other guys and get moving. I hope he does picket the film, the publicity will boost revenue."

They shot the scene without further trouble, then redressed the set and made a similar scene with girl clones. The remaining actors and actresses knew how hard it was to land any part in a film and cooperated fully, regardless of their personal feelings. As they worked, Keith thought over Marge's rude comment to Jessica and wondered if it was true that she didn't have boy friends or sexual relationships. What a thing to say in public, right in front of everyone. How could Jessica take it, she must be furious inside.

At noon, after five hours of non-stop work, Keith picked up a box lunch and looked around for Jessica, hoping that he could say something to make her feel better, something to compensate for the pain and embarrassment Marge must have caused, but she was not in sight. David walked up to Keith, "Man, Marge has a mean tongue doesn't she."

"Wish we could get rid of her somehow, or send her back to Vegas or the hotel."

"She's just a hooker, focused on money and sex. Let's get back to work and hope it doesn't happen again."

They separated, as David went off to study his notes and Keith prepared for the afternoon's scenes.

After awhile Keith spotted Jessica in a corner by herself and walked over. He didn't know what to say but knew instinctively that he must express his feelings. "I'm sorry about this morning: I should have been more sensitive to that actor's feelings. And Marge, I wish she'd drop dead. I felt so badly for you: it was like a slap in the face, but I didn't know what to say."

"Thanks for caring. I'll get over it: she's full of shit, but as you said, she's the boss's secretary."

Keith really wanted to ask about the accuracy of Marge's comments but didn't see any way to do it.

Jessica brightened, "At least something good happened to compensate for the crap from Marge. Guess what a messenger just brought me?"

"It must be something special since you're smiling. What is it?"

"Here, read the note first."

She handed him a handwritten note which read, *"thanks, I negotiated from strength, doubling my price, since I knew in advance that they all would sign!"* Keith was puzzled at first, but then remembered her prediction regarding Max's Monday morning business deal.

"Now, look at this!" Jessica produced a small distinctive light blue box from Tiffany's and opened it. Keith saw a beautiful gold diamond-encrusted watch.

"Jessica, it's, it's as you might say, divine, but it must have cost Max a fortune."

"Max owns half of Wilshire Boulevard to hear him tell it. I'm so glad that my prediction worked for him. It's nice to be able to help someone you like."

Keith felt a twinge of jealousy, and realized how far out of his league he was playing. He couldn't begin to imagine giving someone a watch that cost more than a new car just to say thanks. Jessica smiled at Keith, "Don't look so glum. Max is seventy-six years old and very happily married to Francine, so you've no reason to feel jealous. I'll introduce you next time we're at the Castle, and by the way, her cat is fine if you're

95

wondering, though I told her the wrong garage."

Before Keith could reply, Angela interrupted the conversation as she rushed to Jessica with news of a costume change. Keith turned to face Angela, who smiled as she looked at Keith and Jessica standing close together, "I love you both, but we're here to make a film, so let's move."

As Jessica ran to the dressing rooms, Keith watched after her, struck by the contrast between her menial on-set work appearance and her fancy watch, rich friends, and psychic abilities. He realized that he knew nothing about her private life or financial and romantic situations. He had driven her home Saturday night to a nice street, Starlight Terrace, in Los Feliz. Her house was small, but in perfect condition in a manicured yard. To compound the puzzle, her fancy car was casually crammed with art supplies, costumes and bits of clothing. He wondered if the car had been another thank-you present.

Marge walked up to him. "Why are you chasing up my gofer's skirt? I would have thought a handsome guy like you could do a whole lot better?"

"You haven't the foggiest idea who she really is, do you Marge?"

Keith walked away quickly, leaving a puzzled and pissed Marge standing alone on the busy stage. As Keith walked to the restroom, he almost kicked himself with regret. Why had he said that to Marge. The last thing he needed was interference from the financial people, and pissing-off Marge was sure to backfire. He had only been out once with Jessica, and although she was unusual, there were plenty of attractive young women, such as Dawn, in the film business. Jessica wasn't his girl-friend or anything serious. After the film was done he would have time to look around, but now it was time to work to the limit of his ability. He knew what to do, and did it, in spite of his feelings of revulsion.

He returned to the stage and sought out Marge. "I'm sorry I was rude to you a few minutes ago. Jessica has a lot of talents that she doesn't use here, but that's no reason for me to make stupid comments to you."

Marge was quite surprised and pleased at the prompt apology, "Hey, don't mention it. It's none of my business if you like her, but there're lots of better-looking girls with much nicer bodies just waiting for you. I could fix you up with a warm honey anytime you want."

Keith reached out and shook Marge's hand, "Friends?" She smiled in return, then he rushed to his equipment: he had done enough thinking about girls for one day.

თთთ

The next day they worked on an adjacent stage, where a set belonging to another project was temporarily available. Most sets were made from re-useable panels, four or two feet wide, and ten feet high. The frame of each panel was made from pine one-by-fours, and the surface was quarter-inch plywood. These were called "flats", and good ones were sealed with varnish or shellac so that wallpaper could be easily stripped as soon as it was no longer needed. Special wallpaper glue, peel-paste, was supposed to be used, but sometimes it wasn't, causing much swearing in the paint department. The flats were supported from the rear by diagonal two-by-twos nailed into the floor. Walking between sets or behind them in the dark shadows was often an adventure, bumping into the diagonals as well as the maze of lighting cables scattered about.

The scene to be filmed involved Orson's Office. In the script, Orson is the head of the IRS in a plush magisterial office: he gives a speech to invigorate dozens of his IRS employees.

The scene was supposed to be like this:

```
ORSON'S OFFICE--ABANDONED CITY
        ORSON; large, mean, bombastic, and
the head of the IRS, sits on a jeweled
throne at one end of a richly-appointed
treasure-filled room puffing a large ci-
gar. Standing to one side of the throne is
the HEAD THUG, wearing a yellow tee shirt
emblazoned with "GOVERNMENT TAX SERVICE"
and carrying a sparking electric cattle
prod. Standing on the other side is the
HEAD COLLECTOR, in a black suit and elec-
tric bowtie. A chrome tank-like tax col-
lection machine is strapped to his back.
A bulging sack of collections hangs from
its bottom: a high-suction 2" diameter
hose extends from the top. He holds the
end of the hose carefully, with respect
for its sucking power.

        The scene opens on Orson's heavily-
jeweled hands as he passes a stack of
gold coins back and forth between them.
Then, as a blast of cigar smoke covers the
frame, we move to a close shot of Orson's
mean face as he yells at the assembled,
but unseen, Tax Collectors.

        [Orson gives a bizarre motivational
speech, then]

        Cheers go up and we hear a loud
roar, sounding like the switching-on of
a thousand vacuum cleaners. The Head
Collector fumbles as he turns-on his
collection machine and electric bowtie.
Orson's speech has so excited him that
he looses control of the suction pipe,
which cavorts wildly, drawing in Or-
```

son's gold coins, cigar, and tie. The
Head Thug inadvertently jabs Orson with
his sparking electric cattle prod as he
tries to help Orson restrain the runaway
tax collection device.

Keith had heard something about the set being not-quite-right, since they were re-using one left by another production to save money. He stared in amazement: the set had no relationship to his screenplay's description of Orson's office. This set was someone's bedroom, with pink flowery wallpaper. True, it had walls and a door, but that was the only match to the script. The prop crew had brought in a raised throne for Orson to use during his speech, and the walls were decorated with posters showing stacks of money and paperwork. Keith walked alone around the distant corners of the huge dark stage, fighting his frustration at having to make so many compromises with his vision for the film. Angela joined him and shared his disappointment. Keith was almost in tears.

"It won't look so bad on film, don't worry: we'll hang some drapes behind Orson so his shots will have a good background," Angela said as she gave him a hug.

"I know you're right, but shit, every day we cut corners and cheapen the whole effect."

"Hey, we're working in a business, not playing in film school; you must have realized that by now."

Keith took Angela's hand in his, remembering their brief intimacy a month ago. "I wish there were some way we could get the money to do this right."

She squeezed his hand, and pressed her body against his for a moment, then eased back, "It'll take more than a few rolls in the hay to get that kind of dough. You need to be clever, to be full of fresh ideas every day, that's the key to moving up

Experimental 16mm Art film, being shot with borrowed gear and left-over short-ends: however three of these "students" eventually made their names in the world of feature films.

when you don't have any money."

Keith bumped into an ancient lightning machine which had been left on the stage. "Angela, can we use this? It's here. Who would know if we borrowed it?"

"What's your thought?"

"Let's flash it while Orson gives his speech, adding foreboding visual fire to the scene, and I'll add thunder later. We could even blow those silly window curtains to simulate a storm outside and give the whole room moody dark lighting so that the wallpaper doesn't show."

"You're on! David and George will scream, but it will be a great boost to the shots."

An arc lightning machine is a big steel box, four feet on a side, painted white inside, and mounted on a tall hydraulic column to raise it over the sides of the sets. The open side of the box is covered with fireproof safety glass. Inside the box is a most peculiar arc light. Each of the two electrical poles is a handful of big carbons: perhaps a dozen on each side. (a carbon is a black rod about a foot long and three-quarters of an inch in diameter. A single pair of carbons is used in a normal arc light.) In a lightning machine the bunches of carbons are pushed toward each other by a gaffer pulling a long lever from a safe distance.   When the carbons hit each other, there are huge violent sparks. The light is extremely bright and blue-tinted, and it flickers randomly very much like real lightning. It's so powerful that the flashes are strong enough to work an outdoor scene. Inside the box bits of white hot carbon fly from the electrodes. Smoke pours out a chimney on top of the box, so this can't be done for very long indoors or the stage will fill with haze. Nobody looks directly at any arc light since it can be as bright as sunlight and can cause lasting eye damage. (normal arc lamps are only used outdoors, usually for night scenes.) Running such machines takes a huge amount of electricity, with peak draws of perhaps five hundred amps DC: enough to run several homes with everything turned on.   As the Gaffer pulses the lightning, the distant generator operator will hear the lightning flashes as his generator takes the strain from the heavy current pulses.

During the morning, George worked with the electricians to light the set, keeping the flowery walls in deep shadow as much as he could. Normally a film set is lit so that the actors will stand-out from the background slightly. The ratio between the dark shadows and the brightest spots is chosen for artistic reasons, to match the mood of the scene. There is usually one camera, and its position is carefully rehearsed.

Similarly, actors move between marks, small pieces of white or black one-inch tape on the floor. Since the positions of the camera and actors are carefully controlled, the lighting for each scene can be adjusted for maximum aesthetic effect. Given sufficient time, each shot can be as carefully composed as a fine painting or photograph.

This is in sharp contrast to "television lighting". TV studios are lit by Engineers, who make sure that each set is lit evenly from side to side, so that the exposure for the cameras will be technically-correct in all directions. In addition, TV is normally shot with multiple cameras, so the lighting must work from all angles. One reason for this is that TV shows are run by a director who is cutting among the cameras as the scene is shot. He also tells the cameramen, through headphones, where and when to move. Lighting and camera aesthetics in television are sacrificed for cost and technical considerations. TV crews are in an entirely-different and lower-status union, NABET.

An hour before lunch, the set was ready. Orson, a big fat loud actor totally dressed in black, had been rehearsing his speech with David all morning, and was ready to go. Jessica and the prop crew had been extremely busy fitting twenty-five Suckers with I.R.S. uniforms and suction machines. The lightning machine was loaded with fresh carbons and an electric fan had been tested on the window curtains. Keith and Jack were ready to record, with a mike high overhead on a Fisher boom.

As the lightning flashed through the windows, Orson's speech to the cheering Suckers was impressive. The start-up of twenty-five closely-spaced suction machines was hilarious. The suction hoses grabbed costumes from adjacent Suckers, some machines reversed, shooting-out wads of money and old clothes, and Orson screamed for more and more money:

Camera Operator laughing between takes with a huge 35mm silent Mitchell Reflex camera mounted on a gear head. Rugged precision equipment like this runs for decades: some Mitchell cameras have pulled millions of feet of film.

collections were falling behind!

After three takes of the full-length master shot, the stage was filled with smoke from the lightning machine, so it was time to open all the doors, turn on the roof-top fans, and eat lunch. George, David, and even Keith were pleased with the scene. They would spend the afternoon in tight shots, without much more lightning.

ೞೞೞ

Wednesday they started to film the first scene involving the transplant doctors who made the oldies extraordinary long life possible. In the story, the transplants are facilitated by a special purple gas that fills the operating room. It neutralizes any incompatibility between donors and recipients and encourages re-growth between the freshly-attached parts. The gas is also an anesthetic, so the docs wear masks connected to overhead breathing hoses while they are in the operating room. Since the gas briefly stains skin purple, the docs wear protective gowns to keep the gas away from their own bodies. Many docs wear their masks loosely around their necks even when away from the operating room, so Keith and David often referred to them as hosedoctors.

The scene they were about to film was in the vestibule outside an operating room, O.R. This was where doctors put on and removed protective clothing before entering the O.R. The walls were institutional green and old gym lockers, towels and benches were scattered about. A battered double swinging door led into the O.R. Purple gas leaked from under it, and billowed briefly into the vestibule when the door was opened. Two hosedocs were just starting to rehearse with David.

The scene was supposed to be:

```
A clean hosedoctor, rushes into the
scene from behind camera as another hosed-
octor, covered with blood, comes through
the swinging doors, into the vestibule.
The bloody hosedoc is connected to a ceil-
ing hose. He uncouples from the ceiling
hose and passes it to the clean hosedoc,
who connects his hose to it. They greet
with gusto and move quickly.

CLEAN DOC: "How's it going?"

BLOODY DOC:  "Hypodermic! Got two new
cars, forty grand, and a Nobel Prize."
```

```
CLEAN DOC:  "Since I left! Card-i-o-graph-
ic!"

BLOODY DOC:  "Time is money!"

     Clean doc rushes through the doors
as Bloody exits behind camera.
```

David was unhappy as he watched this brief scene, and called to Keith. "This seemed so funny when we wrote it, but now it just falls flat when I see them play it. What can we do?"

"Let's give them more dialog so they can explain the gas and why they're wearing masks and hoses," suggested Keith.

"No, that's too dull, I want action, I want them to maybe entangle their hoses and fall down, or breathe some gas and puke or do something exciting."

"We can't make the whole film slap-stick action. Somewhere we need to explain things to the audience."

David saw a grip working with a Milwaukee Sawzall, a powerful electric reciprocating saw, strong enough to buzz through steel pipe or large boards. He borrowed the saw and began to smile.

"Look at this gizmo, we'll give it to the incoming hoser, and he can tell the other doc it just arrived with a surgical steel blade. We can do a closeup of him gunning it to demonstrate. Then by accident he cuts the other doc as they entangle their hoses."

Keith was unimpressed by the saw. "Why don't we put the stuff about the medical computer crash back into the script. It was cool the way they were using obsolete software while operating on real people, then bitching about the money the crash cost them instead of about the patient's life."

"That's too dull, lets cut this doc and squirt some fake blood around. That's what people want to see in flicks."

Jessica had been working on the hosedocs' costumes, and turned to David, "You're wrong, but you're the director, so it'll probably be blood and guts all the way."

Keith looked at Jessica, "Please, just let us work this out ourselves. The scene has to fit the rest of the film."

David plugged-in the saw and watched the blade going back and forth vigorously. "Tell you what Keith, let's do the saw and bloody hose mix-up here for violence and comedy, then you can add the computer crash scene when we're inside the O.R. next to a smoking blackened computer."

"Deal, let's get moving. We can call this thing a surgical wallet-remover in their dialog."

Keith ignored Jessica and went to work to change the dialog while David moved the two actors around, showing them how he wanted to use the saw and their hoses. The prop man brought a catsup squirter loaded with fake blood. No one bothered to consider the extra work the new scene required for Jessica, who had to provide clean costumes for the docs before each take. Blood flew everywhere when it hit the jerking saw blade, but the scene gradually turned into a very funny piece of film as the doctors fought over who would be first to use the new saw.

༄ఌఌ༄

The next day the crew started their first scenes on stage with the four oldies who run Senior City. The President of the old peoples' paradise was Senator Savage, who almost always wore a white suit, a dark tan, and crew-cut gray hair. The visible parts of his body were healthy but not young: perhaps those of a fifty-year old athletic man. His wife, Mary Maker, was in charge of social activities. She too looked normal when fully-dressed, with dyed blue-gray hair. Admiral Righthand, who had two right hands due to a medical mistake, was in charge of security and a detachment of inept ancient Marines. He wore a World War One naval uniform, a bushy moustache, and a hat. He was often vigorously day-dreaming, re-living naval battles and submarine attacks. The fourth was Judge Julie, in charge of all legal matters. She was a mess, in wrinkled black judicial robes stained with food. Her hair was straggly black growing in all directions, she had several facial warts with long black hairs, and must have weighed 500 pounds, though she moved like a tank. She was mean with a capital 'M'.

David started to rehearse the first scene, which takes place in the Admiral's control room. This was the electronic heart of Senior City, where instructional videos were produced and where surveillance cameras were monitored. None of the equipment was new, and everything had a nautical flavor. Large transparent maps were attended by ancient Marines who constantly marked new positions and erased others, while tripping over each other. The grey-painted room, the rotating green Navy radarscopes, glowing red lights, and television monitors gave something of the atmosphere of a shipboard Combat Information Center.

This scene was part of a sequence where Judge Julie attempts to screw a young male clone who they have re-captured. The idea is to frighten him so badly that he telephones to his friends back in the city. Admiral's men plan to trace the call and discover where the other escaped clones are hiding.

```
        Admiral  Righthand  is  seated  at  a
plotting  board  studying  a  chart.  In  the
finished  sound-track  we  hear  SONAR  PINGS
and  naval  sounds.   The  television  moni-
```

tors in the room show naked clones in the showers.

An old Marine, wearing a Navy telephone headset, is sitting at a large telephone switchboard. He yells:

MARINE: "Quick! ... he's dialing the phone!"

ADMIRAL: "Man the battle stations!"

Other Marines with headsets run to switchboards and start plugging into various jacks, trying to trace the phone call. "Aye Aye Sir!"

Admiral is wearing headphones and plugging too.

ADMIRAL: "We've lost contact: what happened?"

MARINE: "It went down without a trace."

ADMIRAL: (furious) "That leaky old tanker, couldn't she wait!"

MARINE: "Maybe we can get him to dial again, sir."

ADMIRAL: "After Julie's through with him?"

MARINE: "Yes sir ... well, maybe in a few weeks, sir?"

ADMIRAL: "We haven't got a few weeks! Senator Savage is steaming up my bilges right now!"

While most of the crew prepared to shoot this scene, Marge and a very pretty dark-haired twenty-something woman walked over to Keith. Unlike Marge, this young woman was dressed appropriately, smiled as she walked, and had a confident air as she crossed the set. Marge began, "Keith I'd like you to meet a friend of mine, Carrie. She's a graduate student with an interest in writing and technology."

Keith was surprised and immediately suspected that Marge was trying to find a new girl for him, someone other than Jessica. What a pain! He would need to be cautious with both of these women. "Glad to meet you Carrie. How can I help you?"

Marge wandered off, leaving Carrie with Keith. "My dad's one of the docs financing this film, so I've read the scripts of the five projects those fools put his money into. Yours is the only one with even a resemblance of artistic merit, so I thought I'd visit the set while in town."

Keith was most glad that he had been polite, and pleased at the comment, but didn't know what else to say, "Sorry I'm a bit short on conversation, my head's so full of detail on what we're doing and well, we're really short handed, but I'm sure you can watch all you want."

"Don't worry Keith, you don't need to chat with me: I can take care of myself."

"Oh, I mean, I didn't mean to be rude, I'm just buried here." Then he had a smart idea. "You see we're trying really hard to put as much of your father's money as possible onto the screen: we try not to waste a penny on incidentals that people won't see."

"I gather you not only wrote this but are recording the track too. How can you do so much and keep it all straight?"

Keith laughed, here was someone who at least understood his situation. "It doesn't leave much time to get into trouble, that's for sure."

"Where's the Director, your partner David?"

As Keith looked around the set for David, he saw Jessica looking at Carrie, and wondered what she thought. Then he turned and pointed, "That's him over there with the black shirt."

"He looks young enough to be one of the clones! Has he ever directed anything before this?"

Keith laughed, "You're not the first to ask. He's done several long documentaries and he received an award in Europe for one of them last year, but this is his first feature, and my first too. You're watching us struggle with our big break, as people call it."

"What's he doing with that wooden box and those guys?"

"Remember in the script, the Operating Room, with the money-grubbing computers? When that box is painted and covered with blinking lights, it'll be one of the computers. David is trying to see if a guy can fit inside and make the computer dance. We'd love to have the computers dance around the O.R. in the purple fog as the track plays "We're In The Money.""

"That'd be hilarious: everyone knows computers can't dance, but this is so crude, why don't you have motors and a robot or something to move the computer?"

"Money, time, and we just had the idea. The dance won't be on the screen long, because if people looked carefully they'd figure it out, but before they do, we'll cut to closeups. Then later we'll fake-in computer screen stuff in the lab."

"You weren't kidding about saving money. I know you all work long hours and need any sleep you can snatch, so I'm not going to try to take you and David out to dinner, but maybe we could sit around at lunch and talk a bit?"

"We can do that. Now let me introduce you to David and to Angela. She's the most important person here, at least in the money-saving department."

❦❦❦❦

The week passed in a blur of activity as they filmed another scene in Orson's Office (where Senator Savage begs to avoid an audit as Orson laughs), then started on the scenes in the Canteen. The Canteen was a big grubby cafeteria in the ruined city where old and poor people came for free food, but only if their paperwork was in order.   On Friday morning, Keith was surprised to see Jessica arrive late for work. Angela and Marge were not happy as this was a very busy day with many actors and costumes. They would film the fight between Bean-counter (a mean female accountant who admitted people to the canteen) and her customers. The scene Keith had written begins:

```
CANTEEN--ABANDONED CITY

        In a wide shot we see the inside of
the canteen. Scott is working at a long
steam table. His only helper is Dawn, who
is serving mugs of black liquid to the
line of old people. As each old person
reaches the food, he surrenders a long
paper form. Neither Scott nor Dawn look
at the forms. In the background is a sea
of tables and chairs, mostly occupied by
other old people. Around the perimeter of
the room are desks manned by bureaucrats;
many of the desks are empty.

        A loud bell rings and Scott and Dawn
stop work.
```

111

DAWN: (to Scott) "Nine-forty-three... time to mop."

They grab mops and head toward the sea of tables, leaving the old people standing in line waiting for food.

We cut to the front of the canteen, near the main door. Behind a single massive desk, sits BEAN COUNTER. A shrewish, middle-aged female government bureaucrat. Her desk is at the end of a long line of old people which extends out the front door and onto the street. Each old person in the line must have his, or her, forms approved by the Bean Counter before being admitted to the canteen. After people have their forms approved, they move to one of three lines inside the room. At the start of the lines are signs, "FOOD LINE", "MEDICAL LINE", CLOTHES LINE".

BEAN COUNTER eats candy incessantly, while processing the starving old people.

[Bean counter argues with old people, angering many]

We cut to the middle of the vast room, where Scott and Dawn are mopping the floor. A motorized bucket follows them about. It is old and grey, and occasionally forgets to move when required. It squeaks and groans. It is the electromechanical equivalent of a tired old person on his last legs.

The Canteen was dressed with rusty junked restaurant equipment and department store display cabinets from a scrap yard. The mop bucket was supposed to be robotic, splashing around the room as the clones washed the floor. In this cheap realization, it was pulled by monofilament lines instead of fancy motors. Keith would improve the effect by recording beeps and squeaks for the sound track in his spare time. This was a cheap set in every sense.

The action involved six actors with speaking parts and dozens of extras. This was one of the most complex days for the sound team and Keith had no free time for anything else. He placed radio mikes on each of the six actors, planted two mikes behind props on stage, and hoped that Jack and the Fisher Boom could cover at least some of the action. This meant that nine mikes would be active during the wide master shots. Keith's task was to turn up the gain on the mike nearest to the person speaking, while keeping the volume on the other mikes low, so as to avoid extraneous noise and inter-mike phasing problems. The job was difficult since the scene was a gigantic argument that disintegrates into a food fight, followed by the arrival of police who arrest the fighters. Escaped Clones, who work in the canteen, watch the scene and whisper additional dialog among themselves.

In film work, neither the mikes or cameras are ever visible, whereas in television it is normal to pin mikes openly on people's shirts and place them on tables. Hiding a mike on a person is more art than science. Keith's favorite on-person hidden mike was a Sony ECM-50, which is about three-quarters of an inch long and a quarter of an inch in diameter. Normally he placed it on the actor's chest, hidden in folds of his or her shirt, or clipped to a bra or chest strap. The main problem is clothing noise. As the actor moves, the clothing can rub against the sensitive mike, making terrible sounds. To combat this, the mike can be wrapped in different kinds of foam rubber and tape. Even if the actor stands perfectly still the fidelity is poor because of the unfavorable mike placement. The higher frequencies from an actor's voice project outwards, missing the mike on his chest. (The ideal and most natural-sounding mike location is slightly above and in front of an actor, if the actor is looking straight ahead.) Each radio mike had a transmitter, about the size of a pack of cigarettes. This was placed in a pocket or on the actor's back, under his/her shirt. Each transmitter had a battery which could die at the wrong moment, as well as an on-off switch and a volume control that had to be set during rehearsals.

Today Keith's sound gear had a mixer that could handle twelve mikes, an extra recorder, and six radio receivers, each on a different frequency. Each receiver also had a battery, but these were good for a day's work without trouble, assuming that he had charged them all the night before. Lighting cables seemed to run everywhere, and Keith tried to keep his cables apart from them to avoid any chance of hum pickup.

To add to the confusion, Sy and Herb picked this day to visit the set and watch for a few hours. They didn't like the Bean-counter character, a mean female accountant who won't let a starving guy eat because his paperwork is not in order (she says that he has misspelled his own name.) Sy and Herb wanted the starving people to tear her clothes off during the food fight to add both sex and revenge to the scene. The actress playing Bean-counter had not agreed to take her clothes off, so there was a big argument among David, Angela, Sy, Herb, and the actress. In the end they agreed to pay her triple-scale, and her blouse was replaced with a breakaway that the old people could destroy. A flunky was sent to Fredericks Of Hollywood to buy her a sexy black bra as Jessica worked furiously to make a breakaway blouse. Keith removed the actress's radio mike

Sound Mixer preparing for Multitrack Recording. The stack of equipment to his right are part of a 4-track tape recorder, and his trusty Nagra-IV recorder is further to the right. This mixing console will process up to twelve mikes, with four outputs

and wondered how to record her half of the confrontation.

Early in the day, while discussing radio mikes with Angela, she had encouraged him to do his absolute best to record each actor clearly. She reminded him that it would cost a thousand dollars minimum to loop just one actor's dialog if Keith didn't get it right today. Keith knew how tricky his task was, so for insurance, he started recording the rehearsals. There was always a chance that a piece of dialog from the rehearsals would work in place of sound that was garbled, and tape was very cheap.

It was a complex long day and although Angela pushed as hard as she dared, they ran into two hours of overtime. She had to finish the scenes today or hire all the actors and the stage

115

again for another day. Tempers were short, but everyone knew the financial score. In the midst of this, Keith was startled to overhear a conversation in the women's dressing room. He normally didn't listen to the radio mikes when the actors were off-set because he felt it was impolite and unfair to the people involved. However, this was an accident. Through one of the actress's mikes he heard Marge bitching to Angela that Jessica was drinking and screwing-up the costumes because she couldn't see straight, and furthermore, that she was already a bit high when she had arrived late for work that morning. Angela was furious, but not surprised. She promised that if it happened again, Jessica would be fired immediately. Keith instinctively worried about Jessica and wanted to help her. He wanted to run to her and to offer aid, to do something, but he needed to focus on the difficult recording task at hand. Jessica's problems would have to wait until later, but he was worried. Then he remembered the amount of port that he had seen Jessica consume, and as he thought about last Saturday night, he realized that she had quite a few drinks before her midnight show as well.

After work, Keith waited for Jessica in the dark by her car, wondering what he could say to comfort her. When she arrived he could tell that she was unstable and furious. He guessed that Angela had reamed her out and threatened to can her.

"Hi, I just wanted to say goodnight and see if we could get together this weekend."

"Not now Keith, I'm outta here."

He noticed that her words were slurred and her movements unsteady. "Jessica, you're too wonderful to let booze get the better of you. Let me help you somehow."

"What the fuck are you talking about. I don't have any problem, now get out of my way, I've got a hot date tonight and I need to move."

Keith blocked her path to the car and held her hands as she struggled to break free. "Listen you fool, you're in trouble and everyone can see it. Maybe you can see the future, but I can see you now, and you're drunk. I'm not letting you drive until you sober-up."

"Let go or I'll start screaming rape or god knows what."

Keith released her hands but leaned against the car door, blocking it. She slapped him hard, "Move outta my way dammit!"

Jessica started crying with frustration and the effects of alcohol, sobbing, "Please Keith let me go."

"Jessica, I'll drive your car, then take a cab back here. Where do you want to go?"

"Home, or anywhere, I need a drink."

"Let's go." He led her around to the passenger door and helped her inside, then started to drive. He felt his face burning from her powerful slap and when he glanced in the rear view mirror, he saw a cut, but it had stopped bleeding. Keith didn't have a plan or know what to do next, but he realized that more alcohol was not the answer. Instinctively, he drove west on Santa Monica Boulevard, past Barney's Beanery, thinking that they would go far away where Jessica could recover.

They rode in silence for several minutes, then she asked, "Where are you taking me?"

"To the beach. We're going for a long walk in the fresh air until you feel better, then I'll bring you home or to a restaurant."

Keith was surprised that she didn't object and fight to go to a bar or home. Instead, Jessica curled up in her seat and cried softly in pain until they reached the deserted beach in Santa Monica. They walked hand in hand along the surf

117

line in the moonlight for hours saying hardly a word. Jessica cried sometimes and shuddered against the cold and damp. Keith put his coat over her shoulders. He didn't dare take her to a restaurant that served wine or hard liquor and they both looked a mess. He began to realize that right now, this very night, was a critical moment in their relationship. She was vulnerable, her body was asking for help, and yet he hardly knew what to do. He could take her home, where she would probably drink herself to sleep, or he could think of something better. There was no half-step possible, he had to make his best effort tonight. As they walked, an idea began to form.

Jessica was lost in her own thoughts. She had spent endless days at the beach as a child, with fond memories of lying on the sand, playing with the water, and feeling gentle breezes wash over her body as it soaked in the rays. With an effort she could put herself back into that time and almost feel the warm sun. The blue sky, the sea gulls flying against it, boats and ships passing by, the waves crashing on the shore after their long journey from far away places, found their way into her childhood sketches and paintings. She remembered seeing the gray whales pass as they squirted water in the air. That had been a very happy time and she longed to return to it. Something had gone terribly wrong between then and now, but thinking clearly about it was hard tonight: everything hurt emotionally and when she tried to think instead of to feel, she wasn't quite sure why she was here or what she was doing as they returned to the car.

Keith drove them away from the beach, back along the Santa Monica freeway towards town. Jessica was nervous and asked questions, but Keith didn't answer clearly. Finally he stopped in front of a house.

"Where are we? Whose house is this?"

"It's mine. I have a spare bedroom, and plenty of food.

You're going to be OK Jessica."

At first she was so surprised that she didn't say anything, then she began to tune into the psychic sense of the house: the way the environment felt, perhaps in reality a combination of decoration, furniture, smells, paintings, books, views. Her first vague impression was that the house felt warm and friendly, but there was something else. Then she shook herself slightly and looked at Keith. "I feel terrible, and I look hideous. Where's the bathroom, and what happened to your face?"

After a long shower, Jessica was wrapped in PJs and a robe as they ate microwaved Tortellini and salad in the kitchen. Keith had poured his wine down the drain and thrown away the bottles.

"I'm sorry Keith, I'm such a jerk sometimes, I don't know what comes over me. Maybe you saved my life tonight."

"You're going to move into that bedroom and let me watch over you until we're done with this film. No booze, no bottles of port, no nothing, just lean on me when the desire gets too strong."

"I can't do that, you have your own life to live. I'll be OK now."

"No you won't. I know all about the struggle and sometime I'll tell you a horror story about how bad it can get: at least you're still alive. I want to keep you right here where I can see you."

"You're not my boss, or husband, or father or someone who can push me around."

"Want to bet? I'm not going to loose you; you're too wonderful to wind up in the gutter."

"You're nice, but awfully naïve. I'll stay here tonight, but not because you're ordering me to. Want to know why I'll stay a little while?"

"Why?"

"Because I found a dress in Kristin's bedroom closet that exactly matches one that I have: same size too. It's a sign or a warning, and I need to think about what it means."

"It means you belong here, it's that simple Jessica." She walked to Keith, gave him a light good-night kiss on his forehead, then went to her bedroom and closed the door with a click.

She walked around the bedroom slowly and carefully in bare feet, feeling the texture with her toes, smelling each piece of clothing, looking in closets and drawers, running her hands over the material, pressing it to her face and feeling, sensing, smelling her surroundings, the invisible textures. As her hands slowly explored Kristin's most intimate clothes Jessica could almost feel Kristin's soft warm body inside them and wondered if she could talk with Kristin and ask her about the other side. How strange it was, as though Kristin were here, or not very far away. Just a hovering presence, not good or bad or threatening, but everywhere. Jessica realized that she had never been in a similar situation, in such close contact with the other world. Contacting Houdini had been a big conscious effort, but this was so easy, like walking into a fog, or vapors, or smelling the evanescent perfume of someone who has just walked by. There were artistic possibilities as well, soft, ethereal, paintings in faint fleeting pastel colors, almost invisible shapes, like a ghost drifting away into fog: she could almost see entire scenes waiting for her brush to bring them to life.

And what to make of Keith and her present situation in his house and his attempt at a cold-turkey cure. Jessica had been drinking hard almost since childhood: one of the advantages of being raised by rich parents who were always on the move, away from home and its problems. She had avoided drugs and pot, but booze was a constant companion, part of every day, but usually confined to the dark hours. Already she felt the need for a drink, and her hands trembled slightly with the thought. Perhaps one way to make it through the night was to focus on psychic perceptions, using the concentration to keep her mind away from her craving.

Keith washed the dishes, turned out the lights and went to his own room, separated from Jessica by only a few layers of old plaster and wooden studs. He noticed that he still had the car keys in his pocket: at least she wouldn't go driving off for a drink without waking him. Keith had his own reasons for trying to cure Jessica's drinking problem: his parents, who had bought this lovely house in 1938, had both died in a terrible crash as they returned very drunk from a party in Malibu. Helping Jessica fight the disease in their house would not bring them back to life, but it seemed like an excellent idea in a vague, balanced, holistic way.

ɔɛɔɛɔ

Saturday morning Keith made breakfast and carried it to Jessica, who was still asleep in bed. With laughter she teased him that as long as he brought her breakfast in bed, did the dishes, went to the store, and washed the clothes, she would stay. Later they drove to Jessica's house to pick up a few clothes and art supplies. As Keith looked around her house, he realized that every room was jammed with paintings, and that she had created most of them. "Jessica, you're really good, I had no idea of your talent."

"This is nothing. Come see my second and third bedrooms, they're crammed with art. I paint or draw almost every day."

As they walked through the house, Jessica collected sketch pads, a paint-spattered briefcase filled with paints, brushes, pencils, supplies. As Keith carried her things, she opened a small suitcase and quickly filled it with clothes as Keith waited. "Jessica, you can have any of Kristin's clothes that you want. There are drawers and closets full of stuff. I haven't had the nerve to go through and take it to charity."

"I took a peek last night, she had lovely things. Leave it all alone for awhile and let your pain subside. There's no rush. Maybe I'll wear a few of her clothes eventually."

"Now that you have your art gear, why don't we grab some food and drive up to Leo Carrillo Beach and have a picnic and check-out the view."

"If you're game, I'd like to go further up the Coast, to the beaches north of Ventura, like Emma Wood. I want to sketch the old train track there next to the beach, and maybe wait for fog to roll in and hide the waves and the old trestle."

The weekend passed quickly as Jessica painted and sketched while Keith worked on re-writes for the coming week. Sunday morning they went to the non-alcoholic Family Brunch at the Magic Castle. This was the only time that people under twenty-one years old were allowed inside: a safe time for Jessica to visit her friends. Keith thought that much to his surprise, his improvised cold-turkey cure was working for Jessica, and it was wonderful having her living in his house. Just hearing her moving about was a warm pleasant feeling. He hadn't realized how lonely his life had become since Kristin's death, and how many simple pleasures could be gained just by having another person to share the day's activities.

Chapter 6

Shooting in a School

Angela's Location Scout had found an abandoned school in San Pedro. It was to be torn down, so they could do whatever they wanted, as long as they paid a nominal rent. Although it seemed safe inside, it didn't meet current earthquake construction standards, so the students who had been studying here were now bussed ten miles every day to a crowded school in a crummy neighborhood. Keith marveled at the waste of school money, and at the messy condition of the building. Several film companies had already used it, and by the looks of things the last crew had been making a prison movie.

All of the scenes they needed to film in the school happened at night, so the relevant windows had been covered with black paper, since they would be working during daytime. The main action involved a group of freshly-escaped clones meeting city kids who had escaped earlier. They would make plans to free the other clones and discuss their adventures. There was one big scene where a team of two-hundred-year-old Marines from Senior City attacked the school and captured most of the escaped clones at night, stuffing them into laundry bags. Two of Keith's el cheapo sex scenes would be filmed here with a small crew after the main work was done.

David was surprised as Keith and Jessica both arrived in her car for an early morning call on Monday. For the first time at work, she was wearing a splash of color, a bright red scarf around her waist. "Are you two traveling together?"

"David and I are old friends, with few secrets Jessica. We've survived and caused a lot of trouble together," Keith said as he smiled at her.

"Don't get excited David, this is just a temporary arrangement while I recover from something," she added quickly.

"I hope temporary means forever. Keith needs you. I haven't seen him this happy in months."

They went their separate ways, starting a busy day of hard work. Keith and Jack moved the sound equipment into the school, wrestling it around stacks of lights and grip equipment that was also entering through the narrow doors. Jessica unboxed costumes and arranged them in portable dressing rooms for the talent. Families and close friends were a part of life in the business, and it was not uncommon to find a father and son working together, or brothers, or cousins. Similarly boyfriends occasionally worked on the same set with girlfriends, and husband-and-wife teams could be effective in some situations. However, the unwritten rule was that both crew and talent left their personal lives at the door. Everyone was expected to deliver an honest day's work for an honest day's pay, without emotional complications. Keith and Jessica might have lunch together, if neither of them had work to do while eating, but otherwise they would be busy in their respective crafts all day.

Keith knew what his first task was, as he glanced around the school. The interiors didn't match the script well, so he needed to rewrite to match the main features and discover what props had been rented to dress-out the school. He hoped that they had at least rented the maps that he had described in the script because they made an important point, namely that clones had no schooling and couldn't read. Angela joined him as he wandered through the abandoned classrooms carrying his notes and a script. "David tells me that you're hanging-out with Jessica. Did she tell you much about what happened Friday?"

"I know about Friday, but I don't know what sent her off the deep end Thursday night. I'm trying to dry her out and turn her around. She's worth saving, at least to me."

"She's a really strange girl Keith, so be careful. I met her a few years ago when my father introduced us at a wild party. She seems to know a lot of old and important people, but no one her own age. It's as though she prefers being with her grandparents' contemporaries."

"I watched her do a séance at the Magic Castle, so I have some idea of what you mean about strange, and now that you mention it, I think most of that audience was old people. I hope she isn't offended by the way we're portraying Seniors in this flick."

"I'm sure she'd tell you if that was a problem. You care for her, so I'll do what I can to help. But you know my rules about drugs and booze on the set. I'll can her if she messes up again. You do know that this isn't the first time she's been in trouble with booze, don't you?"

"No, I hardly know anything about her background. I'm trying not to pry, I want to win her trust, to become her friend, maybe more."

"She has loads of talent and I've been trying to channel it into a wardrobe career. She'd also be great as a set designer, but she isn't going anywhere while she's in the bottle. Bet you don't know that she has a PhD in Art History, and with high honors at that. You're in for surprises, but be careful, and don't forget to focus on the film we're making. This is going to be your big break."

Keith shook himself and went to work. He knew that Angela was right about the film being important to his career, but Jessica was sneaking into his life a little more each day. His immediate task was finding a way to fudge the dialog to make this into an abandoned detention-school, so that they could get some mileage from the ruined jail cells in the hallways. With hi-contrast lighting the messes in the shadows wouldn't show much.

Keith walked into an old classroom which propmen were aging-down with a cobweb machine. This was an electric drill with a fan blade attached. A can of rubber cement was attached to the drill so that the cement dribbled into the air flow. When operated skillfully, the fan blew thin strands of rubber cement all over the room. Another propman lightly sprayed talcum powder onto the rubber cement cobwebs. With slight back-lighting the effect was excellent, but rather messy to clean up.

As he thought about the school, he walked the interior, scanning it from top to bottom for ideas. In the basement he found the remains of the cafeteria. This would work fine for the scene where the clones eat brown futuristic glop, which would really be chocolate pudding with a bit of dark coloring. The place was a mess, which was perfect for his purposes. The electricians were also in the basement, attaching a pole pig (a large heavy electric transformer, the kind that is usually mounted on top of utility poles) to the building's incoming high-voltage wiring. The pig would power all the lights, which would be incandescent since they were shooting indoors, in small rooms. The electricians were working hot, which meant that the wires they were connecting were live, so Keith didn't get too close.

The scenes with the clones talking about their adventures went well. The action mostly involved   small groups of actors and actresses talking among themselves at night. High-contrast lighting, black shadows, close shots, easy sound recording and photography. The big scene, where the Marines broke into the school and chased the clones all over the building was much more complex, making maximum use of the long shadowy hallways, the bathrooms, and every hiding place for the clones imaginable. They had hilarious disasters where the ancient Marines and their inappropriate tactics and gear were upstaged by improvised actions by the young clones.

The only real problem occurred when Marge stepped on an old cord connected to a 10,000 watt lamp. The rotten insulation shorted at the plug's metal strain-relief, vaporizing the cord and killing the lamp. The danger wasn't electrocution, at least this time, rather it came from the sparks and the spray of molten copper which flew in all directions from the intense short-circuit. Keith knew that arc welders, the kind that men in fire-proof clothing and hoods use, throw-off piles of dangerous sparks, even though they run at only a few hundred amps. The wiring that Marge had shorted could burn at a thousand amps, making a very dangerous mess. The high power had vaporized the cord instantly, leaving the end smoking on the floor, while the plug was still in the socket. Fortunately she was wearing boots, and had been looking away from the floor when it happened. The burn marks from the molten copper on her shirt and pants reminded everyone to be a bit more careful. No fuses blew, and the cable was replaced with another in minutes. The power was not even turned off, but Keith noticed new cords on several lights the next morning.

On a more positive note, an agent from a huge agency, William Franz, visited the school on Wednesday to talk quietly with Angela and David. Much to their surprise, he had seen the footage of Senator Savage arguing with Orson and had

Cables and Lights illuminating a scene. These are mostly 1K and 2K lamps cross-lighting different parts of the scene. Quite a trick to navigate when the lights are OFF.

an excellent part for Savage in a big picture if their shooting schedule could be juggled slightly. David and Angela knew that the agent had the power to do them a nice favor in return someday, so they fudged the breakdown board to accommodate Savage and the agent. As word spread, everyone was happy. The actor playing Savage had once been a star, but hadn't done much for five years, so he was on their film at scale. He was very easy to work with, always helped the other actors and actresses, and was a pleasure to be around. In the words of the Key Grip, he had paid his dues, and deserved a lucky break. Lucky breaks were a major part of the 'Hollywood Dream'. If you happened to be in the right place at the right time, success could strike. It kept people going in day-jobs and menial tasks.

Another part of the 'dream' was hard work when you did finally land a spot on a film. Every crew member, actor, and actress worked one film at a time, and they all knew the wisdom of the old saying, "you're only as good as your last picture." Each was waiting for the phone to ring, to be hired for the next film. More than in most professions, you had to know the right people and make a good impression on them. Sloppy work, a bad attitude, or laziness was the kiss of death, and word traveled quickly around the small community doing the hiring.

On Friday, the Marines and most of the clones were done so it was time for the two sex scenes, one involving two lovers in the school, and another involving two clones in a bedroom and a closet. During the actual filming, the set was cleared down to the minimum crew size possible: David, George, Stubby and Keith.

The bed-making scene with two non-speaking clones was simple to light. A few soft lights simulated diffused daylight as the clones smoothed the satin sheets in tight shots. When they went into the closet, hard light simulated darkness, with dense shadows, as their clothes fell to their ankles. The whole business was over in two hours. The sound track was mostly heavy breathing caught by a fixed mike.

The gentle night-time love scene on the floor by candlelight in the old school was much trickier. Real candles would give almost enough light for a facial close-up, with a Canon f/0.95 lens, which was the most sensitive lens then available. However to cover the length of their naked bodies

Behind the flats, showing how a window in another set was lit by low light, from 5Ks, through gels which are waved by a fan and fake smoke: from inside the set, it appears that a bright fire is burning outside the window.

would require many candles, which would look odd. Real candles, with much dripping wax, were placed on the floor near their heads. The rest of the scene was lit with soft light, filtered through yellow gels (which are made from real gelatin, not plastic, because gelatin can take the heat). Loose strips of gauze were hung in front of the lamps, and gently moved by a small fan, to amplify the effect of flickering soft candle light. The light was brighter near the candles, and less at their feet. The surroundings faded to blackness quickly, as though the light really was coming from just the candles. Using the sensitive lens meant critical focusing due to its limited depth of field. In addition, the camera would need to move if a change in coverage angle was required during a shot as there was no zoom lens faster than f/4 available. George and David decided to use several fixed camera positions and slow pans along the squirming bodies, blended by very long dissolves, instead of working out elaborate camera moves coordinated with the action. The details of the scene were diffused by a soft filter on the lens, to add to the romantic effect.

The actor and actress for this scene were Spunky and John. Although Spunky was actually eighteen, she looked years younger, with a thin athletic almost juvenile figure. David had cast her for several reasons: first, she had done an X-rated sex scene in another film and the footage was excellent, second, she had a real-life boy-friend who was a good enough actor to play the part of John so the scene would be natural, and third, David loved her casual attitude as well as her appearance and hoped to have fun with her off-stage. John was also eighteen, and he was hired as soon as David met Spunky, almost sight-unseen.

While waiting for the lighting to be finished, neither Keith nor Jessica had much to do: there wasn't any wardrobe to worry about. They sat together in a dark corner, chatting quietly. "How can you write scenes like this, I mean, doesn't it feel odd?"

"Of course, but well, you paint pictures of girls and boys in suggestive poses, I've seen some of them in your house."

131

"But they're make believe, just daydreams. Here, you're looking at people doing it right in front of the camera and you, Keith, are telling them what to do, describing their fornication in detail."

"It's not that much detail, I mean, the reader knows what happens without me spelling it out. When we shoot the scene, it's not real, the actors still have their knickers on, at least most of the time. This is R-rated stuff, not porn."

"Doesn't it make you embarrassed or horny or something to sit here watching?"

"I have to watch the sound-level meter and the tape on my recorder."

"Not all the time I'll bet."

"I've worked sex scenes before, at least the sound portions, but not, well, not with you around. I mean, we have separate bedrooms and bathrooms, and a more or less platonic relationship, but well, I do fantasize about you. You're beautiful and you have a nice body and you know how to make a guy feel hot and bothered, to use an old phrase."

"What's that have to do with this?"

"I don't know, but it certainly ups the embarrassment factor, especially knowing that you've read my writing, and that I care for and respect you. We say goodnight and go our separate ways, but you know I've written this stuff so you must be wondering what I'm really thinking. The whole thing's confusing, so I'd rather not talk about it."

"Would you tell me about your fantasies involving me, not now, but sometime when we're alone?"

"I'd rather not, or well, I wish we weren't on the wagon, but yes, if you'll tell me your dreams too."

"Angela's coming, it's time to clear the set. Afterwards I want to know what really happened."

"In what way?"

"I want you to tell me all about it, what you saw, what they did, if they were hot and bothered as you say, if there was penetration, or just acting."

"Good grief Jessica, I thought I was embarrassed before."

"Girls like to have fun too, Keith. I want all the details so pay attention." Keith couldn't tell if she was serious or just playing with him, but he was enjoying her company more and more. He marveled at the casual and sexy chat they had just had. Physically, the closest they had come to body contact was holding hands and a few kisses on the cheek. He realized that he hadn't even hugged her once, even in a friendly way, and yet here she was expressing interest in his most private thoughts about her and in the details of a faked sex scene. At home he never saw her partially-clothed or loosely-dressed. Although she wore her clothes in an attractive way, they were never overtly sexy. The correct buttons were always fastened. Telling her about the nuances of this sex scene was going to be an interesting conversation. Perhaps she was ready for a major change in their relationship and was looking for a way to make it happen?

This had been a long and busy week, but the combination of hard work that produced good results and the occasional sight of Jessica working nearby made the time fly. When they drove home together Friday night they were surprised to find a car in Keith's driveway. He knew it belonged to Jim, his lawyer, and was apprehensive when he saw it. As Keith and Jessica walked to the front door, Jim joined them in a somber mood.

Jessica started to go toward the kitchen. "Do you two want to talk legal stuff? I can go fix dinner if you don't want me to hear?"

"Please stay Jessica, Jim rarely brings good news,

especially at night, so I might need to cry on your shoulder, or at least let you talk some sense into me."

"Hey, I'm your lawyer, not your shrink. I don't know if this is good or bad news, but let's sit down and have a drink while I tell you about it."

As Jim mentioned having a drink, Keith could almost feel the tension jump in Jessica, so he diffused it quickly. "Sorry Jim, we're out of wine, but would coffee or tea do?"

"No, or whatever you want, let's get on with this. Please sit down. I'll be brief and to the point. Are you ready?"

"Sure. What brings you here at nine at night?"

"A car, a very specific car, a large new expensive Rolls with real gold trim, lots of it, maybe three hundred grand worth, and the DNA from the old blood on its bumper matches Kristin's perfectly."

"What? Whose? Where is it?" Keith nearly fainted as he whispered the words. Jessica froze beside him.

"Let me finish, OK? It has been locked in a Valet Parking garage at the airport all this time. The owner paid the garage five thousand bucks to keep it for him until his return, but I'll bet he's never coming back. The car has diplomatic plates so the guy's probably immune, and he's a dune coon from Libya, so we can't extradite. The case is dead as far as prosecution is concerned. The good news is that I can get the car for you easily in a civil suit if you want me to try."

Keith's hands were cold with sweat, his throat constrained, his breath coming in short shallow puffs. He didn't know what to say. Jessica answered Jim quietly.

"The car's useless to Keith, but why don't you grab it then sell it to someone far away. The money from the sale could do something in her memory, but please don't hurt Keith with this any more."

Keith nodded affirmatively but couldn't speak, he was

so wrapped in his thoughts of that morning, months ago.

As Jim was leaving he asked if Kristin's hospital had sent any further paperwork. He thought it very strange that they hadn't billed for thousands of dollars, and when he called the hospital for information, they had been evasive, saying that her records were sealed and that there was no outstanding balance. Jim didn't know what to make of the hospital situation, but he had never heard of anything like it and had a suspicion that there was something fishy.

Jessica sent Jim away, then wrapped her arms around Keith, rubbing his back, helping him to eventually fall asleep.

Around two in the morning Keith awoke and found Jessica sitting on the couch looking down at him. His head was in her lap and a blanket covered his body. He turned his head slightly and felt her soft sweater-covered stomach against his cheek, then looked up past her breasts at her moonlit face. So peaceful in the faint light. "What are you thinking Jessica?"

"Just daydreaming far away, watching you sleep, caressing your hair."

"You talked with Houdini the other night, you brought him back from the other side. Could you reach Kristin for me?"

Jessica looked away. Eventually she replied quietly, "I knew that you would ask me that, but no, I won't do it."

"I'm sorry, it was stupid of me to ask."

"Why? It's perfectly natural to want to reach the woman you love."

"It was stupid for me to ask you that, with another medium it would be different."

"Not if you love Kristin, it's the way that you feel, it's your heart."

"She's my past, but perhaps you're in my future, I don't want to talk about her if it hurts you, if it makes you jealous."

"Jealous, me? Of what? A dead girl with a size six body?"

Keith knew by the tone of her voice that he had said the wrong thing again. "Please Jessica, help me get over it, I don't want to stay in the past, I want to move forward, to make you happy, but I don't know what to say or do. Maybe my aura's messed up and needs psychic repair?"

"You've been reading the wrong books. Your aura is fine, it's your heart that needs repair."

"What were you daydreaming about while I slept?"

"Oh lots of things, past, present and future. I haven't been that peaceful in a long time."

"Sorry I messed-up your mood with my stupid request."

After a long pause she asked, "Can you talk about Kristin? What happened? What Jim said about the car and the hospital?"

"Maybe, maybe I can tell you a little. It's so hard to put my feelings into words, to convey how badly I hurt inside."

"I've been there too. Someday, years from now, perhaps I'll tell you about it, but not until then."

Keith wondered about what she had just said, about what might be bothering Jessica as he had seen nothing painful in her life other than alcohol. She continued to run her fingers through his hair as he looked up into her eyes, then began.

"It was a beautiful morning, we were up early, around six, and I started to write as Kristin went out for a lap around the neighborhood. She was a fitness instructor, an athlete in fantastic condition and ran almost every morning. She was the star of her volleyball team in college. After two hours she hadn't called and I began to wonder. I figured she'd bumped into some friends and was having coffee with the girls while I waited to have breakfast with her. Then the phone rang, and it wasn't the coffee shop, it was UCLA hospital: she'd been run over by a huge car that ran a red light at Beverly Glen and Wilshire at high speed. I didn't dare drive, I just slowly bicycled over in a daze: it was almost like living in a slow motion scene. At the hospital I sat in an old plastic chair in the waiting room, staring at the linoleum for hours. They didn't tell me anything except that she was near death and they were working hard to save her."

"You can stop if you want, you don't need to tell me if you don't want to."

"Late that night a nurse let me into her room. It was dark and smelled of medicine and ammonia. She was under a tent and tubes and machines were everywhere. The nurse said I could sit beside her awhile, that she might die at any moment: there was no hope. I stared into her sleeping face all night: it was like being mesmerized. In the morning a doctor came in and glanced at the machines, then noticed me. I asked if she was still alive and maybe he looked a bit surprised. Maybe he didn't, but I had a feeling that he was startled to see me in the room. Pretty soon they made me leave and gave me a number to call to check on her situation. There was a bit of scurrying around and doctors talking quietly to each other."

"I walked all over the campus and called every few hours, but nothing changed. This went on for three days, then they called me, and told me to hurry over because she had awakened and might be able to say a few words. She was almost incoherent, really doped up, but so happy to see me. I held her hand and we talked and talked. It was hard for her to say much but I could tell that she was getting better every day, though she stayed in intensive care, in a special room. I wanted to cheer her up, so I started writing our film, satirizing the doctors and the hospital: She could read OK, and whispered changes and comments to me. Her breathing was very difficult: her whole body had been crushed."

"So that's how our film began, as a joke to cheer Kristin?"

"Yes, and one day near the end I showed the script to David and he was so excited that he took it to his agent, Bernie, who sold it to the New York doctors you've heard about. Our supposed big break."

"Kristin had tons of ideas, and pushing them into shape kept me busy so that I didn't have a chance to be sad. It was our secret and we didn't tell anyone at the hospital. Most of the staff didn't talk with us, but there was one old doctor, Doctor Mueller, who often came in while I was there. I couldn't tell exactly, but it seemed to me sometimes that he wanted to tell us more about her condition and prospects, but whenever we asked he changed the subject."

"This went on for eighteen days, then she took a turn for the worse and her pain increased dramatically. She could hardly talk. Doctor Mueller put his hand on my shoulder and told me that he could feel her pain and that he would do something special to make her better. He took a little bottle from his pocket, filled a syringe, then injected it into her I.V. drip. Kristin smiled and began to feel better almost immediately. She was like a new person and held my hands so tightly and smiled. I asked him what he had given her and it was so strange, he just smiled and said quietly that I didn't want to know, it wasn't medicine, it was habit-forming and illegal, but the right thing to do, to make her feel better. Then he left us alone together."

Jessica could see that Keith had begun to cry, "Oh Keith, I can almost see the room, see you two together." She hugged his head against her body, sharing his painful memories.

"We talked a little about the screenplay, then, then, she said that she would watch from heaven as I turned it into a film, that she would always be with me, she knew she was going, then closed her eyes and stopped breathing."

For a long time neither Keith or Jessica spoke, they just stayed together thinking shared thoughts. Eventually Keith broke the silence, "Now you know everything. I'm sorry to have made you feel sad too."

"That's all right. I'd rather hear your true feelings than have you cover them up. Let's have no secrets between us, even if they hurt, OK?"

"OK, no secrets."

Keith smiled and sat up, thinking that it was probably time to go to bed. He stretched and smiled as Jessica startled him by asking, "Let's shake off our sadness and have some fun. Tell me all about the clones on the mattress in the school by candlelight. What happened? Was it all acting? How far did they go? What did the rest of the crew do?"

"You'll be surprised. I made a duplicate tape of the sound track and David's directions to them on my backup recorder just for you. Don't tell a soul. Want to hear it? Bet you wet your pants."

"Keith!"

He loaded the tape onto his old Nagra III, and started to play it in the dark room. Jessica sat beside him as he explained what was happening. They heard Spunky telling David that she wanted to do the scene in sequence, the same way as it would be in real life. She and John would hug and kiss and remove their clothes, becoming more and more excited. They could stop and do close-ups and alternate angles during the foreplay as much as David wanted. It was clear from the tape that David was excited as he asked Spunky how far they would go. Spunky answered that they would do everything, it would be real but the ending would only happen once. David had to figure out how much he dared show on camera and the correct angle from which to shoot the climax.

As they listened, Jessica's body was beside him, their legs touching.   Keith thought that she must be vicariously living the scene with the actors. He became excited and decided that through her nearness Jessica was asking him to join her, to couple with her now. He put his arms around her, drawing her body to his and kissed her passionately. What could be more natural? Jessica turned away gently, but didn't move. She ran her fingers across his face, then smiled. "Not tonight Keith, but I'm glad you want me."

When the tape finished, she thanked him for the trouble he had taken. Keith was bewildered, first by the contrast between her interest in the sexy tape and her asexual response to his kiss, and second by the wording of her comment. He wondered if perhaps she was having a difficult period or another problem that put her off physical contact, but didn't think it appropriate to ask. She hadn't rejected him, but hadn't accepted either.

❧❧❧❧

Jessica awoke with the dawn Sunday morning and smiled to herself: one advantage of no booze was waking up early and with a clear head. Yesterday Angela had left a message asking them both to come to a meeting at her house Sunday afternoon, a meeting with legal advisors. She had just received papers which demanded that they stop work on the film immediately or face prosecution.

Jessica began to think about the coming meeting with Angela and the opportunity it presented to try an experiment, to see if she could become Kristin for an afternoon. Kristin's presence was very strong in the house and Jessica wondered if it would object to or encourage her entry into its clothes, in the rooms it had chosen to inhabit after death. She didn't dare put the clothes on alone for fear of what the spirit might do to her if it objected. However, it would be easy to maneuver Keith into the room while she dressed. His presence might ease the transition: she knew none of this was logical, but if you believed in the spirit world, many things happened that were not normal.

After lunch Keith found Jessica carefully looking through Kristin's clothes: she had already laid a complete outfit on the bed. "What about this camel wool skirt, Hermes scarf, and cream-colored Channel blouse? I want to look just right for those lawyers, and you've some lovely things here."

"You don't have to dress up for them, just be comfortable, I mean we're paying them, not the other way around."

"But I like to play roles, wear costumes, fool people a bit. First impressions are critical in our business."

"Then be sure to wear your new watch and let it sparkle in the sunlight. You'll knock them dead."

"Do you have a gold ring I can wear with this scarf, to loop the corners through: I need a man's size."

Keith hesitated, "I have the wedding ring I was going to wear."

"That would be special, very special. If you're willing I'd like to wear it."

When he handed the ring to Jessica, she held his hand and softly said, "Keith, I'm about to wear her clothes on purpose, to help her memory fade away gently, to take the edge off your pain, to blend present and past. I'm her and I'm not her, she's here but she isn't. Now close your eyes and help me button up the back of the blouse when I'm ready."

He could hear the sound of wool sliding across nylon and silk as Jessica changed a few feet away, but he didn't look.

He had no idea that perhaps Kristin was watching them both. "OK Keith, open your eyes, time to do me up." Fastening the many small buttons on the rear of the soft silk blouse was something he had done with Kristin, and the touch of Jessica's soft warm flesh under them was so tempting. If he didn't watch out, he would be trying to do more than just button her, but then he began to wonder if perhaps she was playing a game, getting him excited then pushing him away, like a cat playing with a half-dead mouse. Fun, but not something to waste sleep over.

Jessica was very pleased with herself and her experiment. Kristin's spirit had done nothing to object or to approve for that matter: it was neutral, perhaps waiting to see what developed between Keith and Jessica, if anything.

Keith had to look twice when he saw Jessica fully dressed, with her hair down in a soft irregular flip, simple matching jewels, and serious smile. As she stood beside her black Mercedes, he was struck by a flashback. "I saw a photo somewhere in the past year. A beautiful woman was wearing what seems like identical clothes, standing beside a black car. The resemblance is uncanny."

"Where was the photo? What was she doing?"

"It was a Swiss bank ad: there were briefcases and serious guys in the background in front of an ancient stone building. A self-assured beautiful woman entering her car was the foreground. I can't get over how close this is. You're not a fashion model are you?"

"No, but the picture made a strong impression on you, so there's a deeper meaning. It could be déjà vu, but perhaps the picture reveals your subconscious feelings, something you are seeking or dreaming about."

"I'll try to track the photo down and show it to you."

Soon they were seated in Angela's formal garden with

glasses of ice tea, accompanied by David and three legal experts. The lawyers were a bit surprised when Angela introduced Jessica as an influential friend who happened to be working on the film in a minor capacity. David was astounded since he had never seen Jessica in her other world. He could hardly take his eyes off her, thinking of the difference between her normal appearance and the sight in front of him. The fancy lawyers assumed that she was a rich smart young woman, the kind of person they interacted with daily on an equal basis. Keith looked at the nearby couch which he and Angela had once used, and caught a touch of laughter in Angela's eyes as she saw him glance at it.

A group called Preserve Our Beautiful Old Bodies(POBOB) had filed papers seeking an Injunction to block their film. The papers claimed that they were making a movie that would mislead the public and cause irreparable moral harm if it were shown to gullible people. Their paperwork contained piles of crap from psychologists and research studies which purported to show that films like this could cause mental illness. An old copy of the screenplay was included as evidence. They demanded that the film be stopped until it could be analyzed and researched properly. Apparently the fact that the film was pure fiction did not matter from a legal standpoint.

They discussed strategy, the filing of counter-suits, and other delaying tactics, until Jessica asked, "I have a funny feeling. Who is hearing the case? What's the judge's name?"

"It's an old fart, Judge Weyburn, why do you ask?"

"Do you have his phone number handy?"

"Yes, as a matter of fact, I do."

"Would it be legal for me to talk with him? He's not so bad. I held his hand and told his fortune at a party last year, so he might listen to me. Keith and I could drive over to his house this evening and give it a try."

The senior attorney stared at Jessica. "That's highly irregular. He's not supposed to be subject to influence, but what a coup if it worked! We'd flatten those clowns from POBOB."

Angela added, "Jessica's a real psychic, so I'm sure the judge was impressed with his fortune. And Keith will be there, so he can explain that this is just entertainment, not a moral statement."

David was speechless.

Chapter 7

Shooting on the Desert

Monday was scheduled to be their first day on the desert, but instead, they were back in the ruined city, with the garbage truck, but no clones or IRS Suckers. Sy and Herb had convinced David and Angela that they would pull their money from the film unless the Arabs were removed from the gas-up-the-truck scene. David had been sorely disappointed since a quick rough-cut of the existing scene was hilarious, with the beards blowing away and clothes flying off while everything went wrong.

Keith had salvaged the scene, at least on paper, and today they were going to shoot replacement pieces of film which hopefully would remove all of the Arabic influence. Keith and David wanted to keep as much of the original footage as possible, but who else would be wearing beards and desert robes? Keith's answer was Hassidic Jews. Angela had a new billboard painted over the weekend. It showed a huge blue Star-of-David, surrounded by a ring of gas cans. Two giant blinking electrified Menoras were nailed onto the billboard. In front of the billboard were men in the identical robes which had been used in the original scene (the same actors, actually), but now they had even bigger black beards and they wore the distinctive black flat-brimmed hats worn by Hassidic Jewish men. The first sequence involved a wide shot of the men in front of the new billboard, then close shots

Small crew filming on El Mirage Dry Lake. It's flat enough for a Moviola crab dolly, on which the Key Grip is resting his foot. Note the small airplane which the Director flew to the location, so that he didn't need to ride the bus

of them counting shekels and selling gas, as they stood under a Hoopa from a Jewish wedding. These shots would open the scene, establishing that these men were definitely not Arabs. After clearly identifying the men, wind would come up, blow their hats away, and with just one or two more shots, the old footage would mesh perfectly. They were done with the new scenes by noon and couldn't wait to see a fresh edit.

Tuesday they would start the desert shots, using El Mirage Dry Lake and its access road for their locations. This is a remarkably flat dry alkaline lake bed about ninety minutes north of Los Angeles. Most of the year it is dust-dry and so hard that anything can drive on it. (A similar lake bed north of it is part of Edwards Air Force Base, and it's ten mile length

146

is used for experimental aircraft.) El Mirage is miles long and wide and it is often used for photographing car commercials when a clean background is needed. There is no vegetation on the surface, though scrub brush and cactus grow on the perimeter. There are no buildings or trees to interfere with the endless view toward the surrounding mountains.

The prop people had built a special vehicle for the desert scenes, a lemon-yellow limousine. An old limo had been found, then spray-painted bright yellow, including windows, chrome, and tires. Then the windshield and side windows had been covered with a bewildering array of travel stickers, totally obstructing visibility. A large round hole had been cut into the windshield so that the driver could see (he wore goggles). The back seat had been removed and replaced with a swivel chair. The occupant of the chair could see in all directions by rotating the chair and looking through a periscope which protruded through the roof several feet. Behind the periscope was a three-foot-high mast from which a three-by-eight foot flag blew in the wind. The Senior City flag was white, with a big mean gray panther covering its length. Yellow tassels flew from the rear edge of the flag as the limo drove across the desert. Under the hood, its engine was freshly tuned and powerful. The tires were bald and over-inflated, so that they could easily slide sideways when the stunt driver wanted to do a flat spin on the smooth lakebed. Lights mounted on the vehicle blinked randomly. There were nautical red and green lights on port and starboard sides.

At lunchtime Tuesday, Keith studied the shooting schedule which Angela had just Xeroxed for everyone. It showed the latest version of her plan to finish on-budget and many scenes had been re-arranged yet again. Keith noticed immediately that a whole block of scenes was missing, that it had been dropped without even asking his advice. He found

147

Angela alone in a Winnebago, eating while reading the script for her next film.

"Angela, what happened to all the nice scenes with the old people in Senior City? Where the hell are the shots of Savage and Mary taking care of the old lady after she fell down?"

Angela stood close in front of him as they talked. "I dropped that stuff: it's the dullest part of the film and we're running out of money. The plot works fine without it."

"But those scenes are critical to the mood, to the atmosphere. They show that the oldies have a nice side, that they're good people, that they care for others."

"So? Your audience wants action, humor, fun. It doesn't want to see some old farts puttering around a retirement home." As she said this, Angela took Keith's hands in hers and moved closer.

"These scenes counterbalance the funny scenes, they contrast against them, which makes the humor more effective."

"Look, they're expensive to do in terms of time: what would you cut instead? Name one remaining sequence that you don't care just as much about."

"Shit!"

Angela put her arms around Keith rubbing her body tightly against his, "Don't get sore, it's just another day in the business. You'll feel better after a quickie. C'mon, we've just got time and there's a soft bed in back."

Keith pushed her away and walked to the door, "Forget it. Go play with someone your own age." He knew she would be pissed but he was too mad to care.

On the desert, the crew needed to cover three major scenes. The easiest involved a clone on a lonely road, his broken down motorcycle, and his discovery and arrest by old Marines from Senior City. Another scene involved a bus-load of oldies, (those arrested at the Canteen), and their arrival at the city limits. They would met by oldies from Senior City in the limo. The most complex scene involved the discovery of some clones in a garbage truck. There would be an intricate chase as the limo and a marine motorcycle tried to catch the garbage truck while the clones in the rear of the truck dumped barrels of glop out the back onto their pursuers.

The first scene to cover was the arrival of the bus-load of oldies from the canteen at the city limits. David and a small crew covered the oldies inside the bus, who were all supposed to be pedaling to make the bus move. The driver shouted instructions and the bus moved slowly. (It was being pushed by a truck). The Makeup man sprayed a mixture of glycerin and water on the oldies' faces to simulate heavy perspiration. To save money, only a few sets of pedals were provided, so they moved the actors around and it appeared that all were working hard in close-ups. George covered most of the action with a hand-held camera as Keith recorded their ad-lib comments. They slowly pedaled the bus down the seemingly-endless access road to the lake.

When the bus reached the edge of the lake, it encountered an old sign, "Abandoned City Limits". They filmed the arrival of the bus, and the people being shoved out onto the desert. After they were all out, the bus's engine started with a huge cloud of diesel smoke, and it drove away.

The people stood alone at the edge of the desert. They saw a large bush in the distance. It moved then stopped, then moved again a few times. Suddenly the limo lurched out from behind the bush and rushed toward them, sliding to a stop in a three-sixty-degree flat spin that sent dust flying in all directions. For fun, the crew had mounted a camera on the front of the limo, and switched it on just before the drive-up. It would cover the blur of the flat spin, perhaps without too much dust obscuring the lens. George had positioned the wide-angle lens inches above the ground, under the front bumper, so the footage would be exciting if it worked.

To do this, the grips had first attached a soft wood stick to the front bumper with a C-clamp, then watched the stunt driver drive and spin the limo. A few efforts of this sort led to a quick determination as to how low they could safely hang the camera from the front bumper. Ten minutes after they started work, a metal platform consisting of a quarter-inch-thick aluminum plate full of pre-drilled holes, some EMT tubing, and nuts and bolts, was solidly mounted to the front structure of the limo. The camera, on a flat-bed adapter, was bolted to the platform, and the battery was duct-taped to the EMT. It was impossible for George to look through the camera to see where it was aimed, so he set it using a small level, then taped the focus and f-stop adjustments in place. With much luck the spin would stop with the camera facing the stranded people. The Arriflex 35mm camera had four hundred feet of film, so it could run for over four minutes from the time it was switched-on to the time that someone reached the switch and killed it.

The main danger in any shot involving stationary people and a stunt driver is that the car overshoots its final mark, hitting the people. For this reason they rehearsed carefully, with no people. The rehearsals were filmed with pass-by shots, buried camera-shots (where the limo carefully and slowly drove over a buried camera with a wide angle lens pointed straight up (the camera was under-cranked so that the shot would appear to be at high speed.) Finally they did the master shot of the limo approach. The arrival of the limo was filmed from the crowd perspective with a long lens to make it appear closer to the people than it really was. Keith planted a radio mike on one of the people, hoping to catch the sound of the approaching vehicle. He already had many takes of the limo driving by and rumbling down the road. He had even ridden in it a few times to record the actual interior noises that it made.

Once the limo stopped in position, normal film work with actors and dialog began. The stunt driver climbed out, and Senator Savage in a white "Colonel Sanders" linen suit moved to the driver's seat. Admiral RightHand rode the swivel seat in an ancient nautical uniform, continuously rotating and scanning the horizon for trouble. Mary Maker, Savage's wife in a thirties-modern dress, was beside Savage, trying to see out the hole in the windshield. Judge Julie, a mean lascivious woman in black judicial robes, was on the right front seat. When they were riding in the car, they all argued constantly.

Jessica was very busy, keeping their outfits in a proper state of disrepair as they worked in the dusty surroundings. The Makeup man had applied stitch-marks and had painted parts of their exposed skin different colors to show that their bodies were a patchwork of parts. Both makeup and wardrobes were Polaroided by the Script Girl so that the appearance of the main actors could be maintained consistently from day to day.

(As an aside, it is interesting to note that filming in India used to follow a completely different approach. There, one entire thousand-foot reel, eleven minutes of the final film, was shot, edited, and finished before the next was started. The reason was that the financiers reserved the right to stop production if they didn't like the look of a completed reel. Much time elapsed between shooting sessions, so actors aged, grew beards, became tanned, fat, thin, and the weather and seasons changed. No attempt was made to erase these variations, and audiences enjoyed seeing their favorite stars

Camera Rigging: a 35mm Arriflex on an O'Conner fluid head, rigged on a car for a snow-tire commercial. The cinematographer is adjusting the camera, but won't ride the rig during the shot. The light is powered by a 120-volt box of batteries in the trunk

with different features. Labor was so cheap that a person was designated as the Clapper: his only job was to clap the slate. Film stock however was relatively expensive, so the camera was started just an instant before the Clapper hit the slate.)

On the desert, after the limo spun to a stop, it appeared, to a film audience, that the Savage and his friends emerged from the limo immediately. Between the stunt driver's work, and the emergence of the fearsome foursome, there was a close-up of Savage's multi-colored hand opening the door, to cover the change in drivers.

Keith needed to record dialog among the four actors from Senior City, as they interacted with the group from the bus. The dialog was supposed to be funny, as the city people were stunned by the strange arrival from outside the city limits. They had never heard of Senior City, or the limo, or its odd occupants. David worked to achieve the correct nuances in facial expressions and inflection, to convey their shock. The plot of the scene was that the city people, those who seemed to have the most money, would be taken away in the limo, perhaps against their will. The others would be left behind, to walk back into the city. Many close-ups, over-the-shoulder shots between the two groups of people. There was also whispering among the foursome as they commented on the various city people's financial prospects.

After spending most of the afternoon under the sun, they moved inside the car, filming through open windows. Keith thought that he had been particularly clever regarding the limo interiors. He had purposefully written that the windows were obscured with paint and travel stickers. This allowed them to film the limo as it sat still, conveniently near the grip truck. By rocking the vehicle slightly and blowing a fan through the hole in the windshield, the illusion of motion was achieved easily. The sound was simple to record and the camerawork, through first one side's windows, then the other, was quick. The Admiral was continuously in motion, spinning his seat one way then another, and the foursome shouted their lines at each other as though they were traveling at high speed in a noisy car.

The work was hot and dusty under a cloudless sky. Keith and Jessica had a few minutes to chat together at lunch each day, but both had work to do before filming restarted. Every day on the desert was twelve hours long. The crew and cast assembled in a Hollywood parking lot at six-thirty in the morning and boarded a bus. With luck, the bus returned to the parking lot at six-thirty in the evening, with tired and sleepy riders. Keith and Jessica could chat on the bus, but usually

Keith spent the time on the script or talking with David about the nuances of filming a particular scene.

As Keith and Jessica rode home together Tuesday night, she asked, "What did you and Angela argue about at lunch? She was really bitchy this afternoon."

"She cut some of my favorite scenes to save money, and I'm still mad about it."

"Well, it must have been more than that the way she was carrying-on with Marge, verbally abusing, as she called them, those ungrateful young pricks, by which I think she meant you."

"She's having a mid-life crisis, trying to regain her youth by screwing anyone under thirty she can snag."

"Not you! I can't imagine you finding much of interest in her old body, I mean, it's ridiculous isn't it?"

"Precisely. How well do you know her? Is this some new phase she's going through?"

"She was getting slow before her operations, but now it's like she's got a new lease on life. I've known her several years, and she's always had a wild streak, going right to the edge, but not quite over it. We sort of complement each other at parties. I'm a quiet moody drunk and she goes insane."

"Someone told me she was a belly-dancer. Have you ever seen her in action?"

"I think so, but I passed out before she really got it on. I heard later that she took off all her clothes and danced on a table, before it collapsed. I remember the hangover more than anything else."

"I'm glad all that's behind you now."

"Thanks, but you're not a miracle worker, and I'm a long way from being cured."

The next two days were devoted to a chase sequence on the desert, which Keith had written as:

Two ancient Marines on a side-car motorcycle and the limo both chase an old garbage truck driven by the clones across the desert. Two clones are in the rear of the garbage truck and they see the motor-cycle and the limo getting closer.

The side-car bike approaches the limo and pulls alongside, trying to pass; Savage yells out his window,

SAVAGE: "Get back you idiots!"

MARINE: "Finders Keepers! We saw them first!"

INSIDE REAR OF TRUCK

Jo has a great idea: she motions to Scott and points to the various large garbage pails in the rear area.

JO: "What's in these things? Let's open them up."

Jo and Scott start to furiously open the garbage pails.

INSIDE THE LIMO
ADMIRAL: (shouting) "Where are they? What's their bearing?"

SAVAGE: (shouting) "In <u>front</u> of us Admi-ral, bearing three-six-zero."

The Admiral quickly swivels around to face the front. We hear submarine sounds ... sonar pings, engine com-mands... The Admiral is reliving his glorious days in World War I.

VIEW THROUGH ADMIRAL'S PERISCOPE
We see through the periscope, the rear of the truck is in the cross-hairs.

SAVAGE "What're they doing Admiral?"

Through the periscope we see the flap on the rear of the truck open as a large barrel of mush is dumped out onto the road.

OUTSIDE
From beside the road we watch as the garbage barrel hits the pavement in slow motion, then sprays mush all over the limo and the motorcycle.

INSIDE LIMO
We see mush fly through the hole in the windshield in front of Savage. Savage is hit in the face with dripping goo ... it is like cold creamed corn. Savage licks his lips and wipes his goggles clean.

SAVAGE: "I know where they got that truck! The Ultra-government Canteen ... so that's where they live."

In actuality, there was very little chasing. Most of the footage was shot from one vehicle or another's perspective, so in almost all the shots only one vehicle was on-camera at a time. The camera was often under-cranked so that the movements would appear to be faster than normal, adding to the excitement. They did various close-ups of the clones in the garbage truck, as two of them in the rear struggled to dump barrels of glop out onto the road, to foil the limo and motorcycle following them. This was matched to interiors of the limo (which was not moving) and interior dialog. The last shot of the day involved a limo interior scene where glop sailed through the hole in the windshield, covering Senator Savage's face as the vehicle spun out of control. It was very tricky to get this right, without hurting the actor. The actual glop was vanilla pudding with food coloring. Jessica had four duplicate wardrobes for Savage, but the scene went so well that only two were ruined.

The most dangerous part of the chase sequence was the crane work. To achieve some of the running shots, a large camera crane drove beside the target vehicle which was in motion. The camera and its operators were on the end of a long boom, which could hang in front or behind a vehicle, raising or lowering to achieve the correct framing. The crane was driven by a highly skilled operator, who maintained his position (while watching for road hazards) with respect to the vehicle being filmed. The boom was moved by two strong grips who could raise or lower it, and rotate it about a central shaft. This is relatively easy on a stage, or on a slow trucking shot like the one in the Abandoned City. However, at forty miles an hour, the force of the wind as well as bumps in the road make this very difficult. Keith had sometimes ridden on a crane's chassis to record sound from the camera position during a chase, and every time he found it a dangerous experience. There were no hand-holds on the flat deck, and he had to be vigilant to see that the counterweight bucket at the back-end of the boom didn't knock him off the crane and onto the road. (the bucket contained fifty-pound leads, which balanced the load at the camera-end. The camera crew moved into and out of their seated positions only with the consent of the grips, who could lock the boom while adjusting the weights.) All of the crane shots were done on the dry-lake, where there was a smooth surface and no traffic. The crane covered glop flying from the truck toward the camera, as well as it hitting the moving limo. Pudding was everywhere by the end of the day.

Wednesday night brought two surprises for Keith and Jessica. The first was that Judge Weyburn had dismissed the lawsuit brought by POBOB. There would be an appeal, but with luck the appeal wouldn't happen until filming was over. Angela's legal team had sent a magnum of French champagne to Keith's house as a reward for Jessica's part in the judgment. Keith wanted to throw it away, but Jessica prevailed on him to save it for the opening-night party, when it would have special significance.

The other surprise happened late at night. Keith awakened to find Jessica sitting on the side of his bed, gently shaking him. He looked up at her body, silhouetted under her pajamas, by a faint light from the hall: what a nice view. "Keith, a strange thing just happened."

Keith returned to asexual reality, "What is it? Are you OK?"

"I just had a dream, or a vision, or some form of contact from the other side while I was sleeping. Did the doctor who attended Kristin and gave her the final shot have a beard, a sort of pointed goatee? Was he thin and old, but with a nice smile?"

"That's exactly what Dr. Mueller looked like. He visited Kristin every day. Why are you asking?"

"He's dying right now, just passing over. He's trying to send a message, to ask you to forgive him. He's sorry that he didn't tell you the truth."

"You're not kidding, this is real?"

"Of course. His spirit said that he had wanted so much to ease her pain, that he hoped he had done the right thing. It was such a strong message, so clear, but only one-way. I couldn't ask him what he meant. It was as though he was apologetic and felt that he might have gone too far. Do you think his mystery injection killed her?"

"I've thought that often, and I'm sure Jim thinks that's part of the problem, part of the reason the hospital is so secretive: they must have found traces of the shot in her blood."

"Wonder what it was. Maybe that explains his words. He said that he has known for a long time that he was dying from cancer and didn't have much time when he visited Kristin, so he went out of his way to help her, to do something special, to go beyond the normal boundaries and legal baloney. But the wording was so peculiar: I could hear so much pain in his voice."

"What exactly did he say?"

"That she had been wronged, horribly wronged, but that he couldn't make it right, so he took her pain away: he was so sad that he could only attack the symptom, not the cause."

"You dreamed all this?"

"Let's leave it alone for awhile. I don't think either of us really wants to know."

"But what if he just confessed? If he did kill her?"

Keith looked up at Jessica's almost beatific face, backlit, nearly invisible in the shadows. "Keith, you know you can't put me on the stand in a courtroom. All we can say is that she passed over with a smile, in the arms of her beloved, saying that she loved you: we can't ask for more on this side. I'm sorry, but it's over."

Keith had a hard time going back to sleep. Logically he knew that Jessica was right, second-guessing a dead doctor was useless, and if he told lawyer-Jim, there would only be pain. Probably the paperwork Keith had signed removed the hospital's liability anyway. Still he wondered if the doctor knew that Kristin would die from the injection, or if she was dying anyway so he wanted to make it easier for her. Damn, there were so many open questions about what had happened.

Jessica had other priorities when she left Keith's side. She returned to her room and sat on the floor of her closet, surrounded by Kristin's clothes and her spirit's presence, and worked very hard to contact Kristin, to ask her what the message meant. Surely Kristin must know, she must understand what really happened to her body. Hours later, daybreak, found Jessica asleep among the shoes, curled in a fetal ball, her tear-stained face peaceful at last after a long hard night.

On Thursday and Friday they filmed more scenes with the limo. Fortunately they were done with all the running and chase shots by Thursday night because the weather changed. On Friday, scattered showers made the lake bed a slick mess, so they filmed on the approach road. The scene involved a clone, John, whose motorcycle had died on a lonely road. He was very surprised when the limo coasted to a stop beside him and offered help. John knew that something was wrong, especially when the Admiral carefully examined John's left hand, measuring it with a small ruler. John realized that the Admiral had two right hands, and began to worry. Judge Julie wrapped a rope around John, screaming that it was her turn to be first. She wanted to play with John's body before the Admiral stated cutting. John fainted with fear.

လာလာ

Friday night Jessica and Keith met David and Spunky at The Silent Movie, an old theater on Fairfax that ran only black and white silent films, for ninety-nine cents a seat. Keith was surprised that both Spunky and David seemed to be high on some kind of drugs. They were too happy, and they kept hugging and kissing and running their hands over each other's bodies. The seats were hard, unpadded, and scratchy music played through old loudspeakers. Few people were in the audience. Tonight the film was THE CABINET OF DOCTOR CALIGARI, a German medical horror film from 1919. David had suggested seeing it because the sets were some of the strangest ever filmed: there were almost no vertical or horizontal lines. Windows were triangular at odd angles. The sets represented the view that a madman might have of the world. Through most of the film, the main character appears to be sane, telling a story about a mad doctor he encountered. In the end, the audience discovers that the main character is mad and that most of the others in the cast are inmates in an asylum.

As they watched the old film in the dark theater, Jessica realized that David and Spunky practically had each other's clothes off. Nothing phony about their activity, they were going all the way right in the seats beside Jessica. Spunky handed Jessica her panties, whispering, "Hold these for me." Jessica shoved them in David's face and turned to Keith as she rose from her seat. "Let's go, right now."

Keith and Jessica left the theater and walked down the street to Kantor's Deli, an all-night restaurant with wonderful food. They had lox, onions, and scrambled eggs, and giggled to each other when they saw a group of men wearing black coats, black beards, and black hats: dead ringers for the Hassidics in their new gas station scene. Then went home in the rain and made a fire in Keith's fireplace. Jessica was wearing a soft white cashmere sweater and a loose black skirt as they sat on the floor in front of the fire. Rain beat on the nineteen-thirties steel-framed windows, but the fire was warm.

"Jessica, remember a few weeks ago when we were in the old school talking about the sex scenes I had written?"

"Yes, that was an interesting tape. Do you still have it? I'd love to reconsider the nuances of the conversations between David and Spunky."

"Sure, we can play it again later if you want, but that day you also asked me if I would tell you about my fantasies concerning you, some day when we were alone together."

"Have you been fantasizing?" she asked as she turned toward him.

Keith moved closer to Jessica. She was beside him, their bodies just touching. "Yes, would you mind if I ran my hands over your soft sweater, if I gently caress your beautiful breasts, if I kiss your lovely soft lips?"

"Please, please try." Keith was surprised at her choice of words, as he kissed her gently. Jessica leaned back and lay down on the floor as he explored her body slowly with his hands. He could feel that something wasn't right. She was going through the motions, kissing him back, but without warmth, without anticipation. She didn't push him away as he stroked her body, but she didn't respond positively either. As he lifted her skirt, he could feel her body tense, so he stopped and pulled back. To his surprise, Jessica took his hand in hers and returned it to her body, pressing it tightly. He could feel her trembling beside him as she held his hand against her body. Then he realized that she was crying.

"Jessica what's wrong? Am I hurting you in some way?"

"Don't stop, please try to do more, help me, help me get over it."

Keith was bewildered and afraid of making a big mistake and of angering her. His natural politeness told him to back-off, that he was involuntarily causing her pain, that this wasn't the night for an adventure. She kissed him and pulled him down on top of her, but it was awkward with her legs tightly together, and she was not only crying but sobbing and shaking with emotion as she held him tightly, her arms around his body.

Keith slowly rolled off, laying by her side, gently stroking her hair. "Jessica, tell me what's wrong, tell me how I can help you."

She turned over onto her stomach, continuing to cry and shudder. "You can't do anything about it. It's not your fault, it happened when I was thirteen. You're so nice, you deserve a real girl, not a frigid emotional cripple."

"We can fix this, we can learn to love each other gradually." As he said this, he rubbed her back gently, then sat up and massaged her shoulders with both hands as he straddled her body. He was mystified.

Jessica pounded the floor with her fists. "Dammit, stop being good to me, I'm not worth the effort."

"Is this why most of your friends are old, safe, sexually-disinterested people? People who would never kiss you or long to feel your naked body pressed close against them?"

"I didn't realize it was so obvious."

"Maybe together we could go to a doctor or a shrink and learn how to."

"How to screw and enjoy it, is that what you want me to learn?"

"Most girls do enjoy it more than boys, or at least that's what I've heard, and you like talking about sex."

"Shut up! I've seen too many shrinks already: they're hopeless, and remind me to stop talking sex with you."

"Want to play the tape again, maybe it will put you in the mood or at least start you thinking about it."

"You've got it so wrong. I want you to kiss my lips, to caress my breasts, to lift my skirt up, to pull my pants down, to ease my legs apart, to climb on top of me and pump my body full of everything you've got. It's just, it's just that I can't help myself, I freeze solid the moment you touch me."

"Is there anything physically wrong, or is it all mental?"

"Mental, I've seen all the docs and they've poked and explored everywhere with their latex hands and sexy smiles."

"Maybe if I found some gloves, you could pretend that I'm a doctor examining you, and relax, then let your body respond naturally."

"If you weren't so sincere, I'd scream. Don't you dare buy any gloves or a white coat. I can tell you positively that you have a very bad idea. You don't know how bad an idea, but a doctor tried that once, and Keith . . ." Jessica started sobbing again.

"Don't talk about it any more tonight Jessica. I've got an idea that may help. Why don't you put on your pajamas, then climb into bed beside me, and sleep with your head on my shoulder. Maybe after many nights side-by-side, our bodies will communicate and your fears will start to fade away."

"I need to warn you, sometimes I have really violent and terrible dreams. That's what happened the night before I came to work drunk. I was up all night, it was so frightening, I screamed and cried, then climbed into the bottle for protection. It's the only thing that works, that relieves the pain, the fears, the horror. Being a medium is a two way street, and the wrong kind of spirits visit me without being called. I may kick and scratch you badly. Sure you want to try sleeping next to me?"

Keith was astonished, and began to see more of the relationship between Jessica and alcohol. "Yes, with all my heart. Nothing can bother you with me beside you."

They curled up in bed. Jessica shuddered violently as she put her head on Keith's shoulder her arm across his chest, and he softly encircled her shoulders with his arm. "Hey Keith,

I can hear your heart beating. It's nice."

"Sleep peacefully, everything will be fine. The spirits don't know you're here. They can't see through my protective aura."

"Bullshit, but I hope you have sweet dreams."

୧ଏ୧ଏ

When Keith awoke in the morning, he was alone. A simple note waited in the kitchen, "I've gone home. Sorry it didn't work out, but we tried. Thanks for everything."

Keith dialed her phone. "Jessica, are you all right? What happened?"

"I need space, I need my own things, go, go find a real girl, I'm not the one for you. Play the song DIFFERENT DRUMMER, it's exactly how I feel now."

"No secrets, right?"

"Right."

"How much have you had to drink since you went home?"

"Shit, only one, well, more like maybe two or three glasses of Scotch. It's nothing. I can handle it."

"If I bought some booze, would you move back here?"

"No, I couldn't drink in front of you, I'd feel terrible. You tried so hard to save me."

"Can I come over and visit you, just sit by your side?"

"Not now, not yet, but you can take me to the Family Brunch tomorrow if you like, maybe around eleven."

"See you then. I miss you so much."

"I miss you too."

Keith felt that his emotions had been stretched back and forth, up and down, in every way imaginable in the past twelve hours. He was wiped out, and ready for a something different. He hadn't lost Jessica, but he didn't have her either, and his cure for her drinking had failed. At least he had some idea of why she drank so much on occasion, and now knew why her friends were mostly old people. He thought that perhaps she was right, she wasn't the girl for him after all, but just a very unusual friend. He missed her as he wandered around the empty house, and noticed that she had left many things behind. He gathered them gently and placed them all neatly in Kristin's room, and wondered who would be its next occupant, or if maybe it would always be empty. Keith took a cold shower, then walked to the Village, to Will Wrights Ice Cream store: he hadn't had a chocolate cone in ages. After that he was going to review the screenplay carefully and get ready to give his best effort to the final two weeks of production.

Sunday morning at the Magic Castle's elaborate brunch, Keith and Jessica sat with Max and Francine. Almost Keith's first words were, "That's a beautiful watch that you sent to Jessica." As the words left his mouth, he realized that this was a stupid way to begin a conversation with an important person, but Max was unperturbed.

"It was nothing compared to the profit I made from her prediction, and I hope to reward her for that one properly at the right time. Get her to tell you about some of the more important times she's helped me. Now, Jessica tells me you're a writer: want to know how to succeed at it?"

Keith was bewildered at the turn the conversation had just taken. "Certainly, but I'm not sure I understand your question."

"Simple, to become a great writer you need the freedom to spend weeks, months, maybe years focused intensely on a project, yet that's impossible if you work for someone nine to five, come home to beer and TV, then spend the weekend

Looking north across the Marina Green toward San Francisco Bay, with Angel Island in the distance.

goofing off. Great writers need something more, they need a source of income that doesn't take time away from their writing."

"That would be nice, but where do they find this source of income?"

"I'm not very bright, I don't like to work hard, and we started with nothing, yet now we have much because we have spent our lives investigating property all over the world. You need to become involved now, so that you can spend the rest of your life doing the things that are important to you, not wasting day after day going nowhere."

Francine added softly with a smile, "Max, you've

worked very hard, and you know as well as I that it's not all a bed of roses. Keith, what Max is trying to say is that he likes you and so he is offering the most valuable thing he has, his advice, to you."

The conversation turned to Kristin and the car that had killed her. Max asked how much money was involved, and volunteered an opinion. "If you want to do something permanent in her memory, and something that will help your writing career, buy a property in her memory. Where was her favorite place in the whole world? Where would she have gone if she could have gone anywhere?"

"She loved San Francisco, especially the Marina Green. As a child she flew kites there often, even in the fog. Whenever we had a chance, we went up to The City and walked on the beach, hiked and flew kites."

"Great location, wonderful view, buy a house across from The Green in her memory."

"But what would I do with the house?"

"Live in it after you get tired of L.A., and rent it out in the mean time. That's excellent investment property, so if nothing else you'll still have the money and more if you decide on a different memorial."

Francine interjected, "My sister lives a few blocks from the Green, on Lyon, so I could tell her to be on the lookout for property that might become available."

"I don't think I could afford such a thing, those houses are expensive."

"Buy it, make the down payment with the car money, and our bank will loan you the rest on easy terms. Besides, the project will keep Francine and her sister busy."

"Jessica, I'll take you up to visit my sister and we can look at all the houses so that you can predict the one that Keith will buy," Francine said.

Jessica smiled, knowing that this was not within her power, but feeling that it was a pleasant thought. Later, as she and Keith sat quietly together by themselves, Jessica said, "You don't have to buy a house, you can do whatever you want with the money."

"I know, but the house idea is good, and I respect his judgment. I see why you like him."

"Then go for it, you need a distraction besides me in your life."

"Can you see our future? Will we live together again?

"I wish I knew. I'm confused, but I'm happy that you're still interested in me in spite of everything."

"Please, take it easy with the booze. If you have bad dreams, or visitations, call me, even in the middle of the night, and I'll come over and help you chase them away. You're better than that, you don't need to hide inside a bottle."

"I'll try, and you, stay away from that Dawn girl and kids like her."

They parted, going to their separate houses, though each longed to be with the other more than they knew.

Seniors Have It Tough

Chapter 8

Shooting & The Crash

Monday morning found the crew back on Stage-9, with different sets. Keith had wanted to shoot the interiors and exteriors of Senior City in Arizona, in a retirement complex like Sun City, but the budget wouldn't permit traveling everyone there and renting an appropriate location. Instead they were re-using sets that others had built, re-writing to adapt to financial reality.

The first scene involved a small medical office in Senior City. The various diplomas and licenses on the walls had prominent green dollar-signs stamped across them. A doctor, wearing a white coat and a headband with an eye-examination disc, was behind the desk. There were jars containing spare human parts on his desk as well as a pile of money which he was counting when Poins, the city-smart clone, entered. The doctor looked like a normal television-commercial drug-doctor, except that a gas-mask dangled from his neck. The mask was attached to a three-foot-long hose, which the doctor twirled and played with casually. In the scene, the doctor interviewed Poins, who had been arrested by the Marines in the old school. Poins was dragged into the doctor's office. The dialog was supposed to begin something like this:

HOSEMAN BRUCE: (as he drags Poins into the office) "I've never seen anything

```
like this one ... seems to have a good
brain in a terrible body. See what you
think before we cut him up for parts.
Maybe we can do a brain transplant into
that golf-pro's carcass we've been hold-
ing." (Bruce exits)

HOSEDOCTOR: "So you really can read;
what's your favorite book?"

POINS: "THINK AND GROW RICH by Napoleon
Hill."

HOSEDOCTOR: (laughs) "Have you ever con-
sidered a medical career?"

POINS: "I'm good at math."

HOSEDOCTOR: (more serious) "That's the
most important part. Maybe we can teach
you how to do a walletectomy. That's my
favorite operation."
```

They were going to start with a master shot and a short camera move that showed the three actors simultaneously. Poins and the Hosedoctor were facing each other across the desk, and the camera would see them talking in a wide establishing shot.

As they started filming, David lost control of the action. Both Poins and the Hosedoctor were having so much fun with the scene that they had made-up many additional funny lines. Every time they ran the scene it became funnier. Angela was annoyed at the actors, who should have learned their lines, then acted them consistently so that close-ups, medium shots and other angles would cut together. However everyone on the set was laughing quietly at the crazy scene, working hard to be silent during the takes. David knew he had solid humor here and didn't want to loose it, but was struggling to figure out how to shoot it. After three passes, each considerably different from the previous one, Keith walked to David.

"It's in the can David, let's get some close-ups of the diplomas and his hose which we can use if we need a cutaway. We don't need coverage, this footage is hilarious as it stands in the wide shot."

"You're probably right. These guys don't need a Director." David turned to the cast and the crew, "OK people, listen-up. We'll do it from the top two more times, so give it your best shot. There won't be any additional coverage so you can say whatever you want. Make it as funny as possible. We'll run this scene as one continuous piece of film without edits."

This was an unusual approach, but one that had been used before, when great actors did their own thing in front of the camera as the crew worked to capture it. Angela smiled, and contrary to her expectations of a mess, this would put them two hours ahead of schedule. George changed the camera movement slightly, in case the actors missed their marks, knowing that he had to get it all down perfectly. The scene length was uncertain, so he asked for a fresh magazine of film. Keith knew that they could run with any of the takes they already had. This was icing on the cake. After two more takes, there was a loud round of applause from the crew, as the actors took bows.

The first scene of the day had been easy and fun, but the rest of the day was difficult. Keith had a gut feeling that although he had rewritten this scene many times, it still didn't ring true. He and David had discussed the scene and reached the conclusion that David would try to make it work, and if it didn't they would slightly extend the adjacent scenes and forget this, doing a plot-patch in a voice-over sound track.

The scene was supposed to show the transvestite

Judge Julie in her bedroom frightening the young clone John so badly that he telephoned back to his friends in the school. Meanwhile, in another room, the inept ancient Marines and Admiral Right-hand were listening to the call and working to trace it so that they could locate the clone's hiding place in the city before John hung up. Julie would become so sexually excited that she attacked John before the call could be traced. The problems were two. First, this scene was supposed to reveal that Julie was a transvestite, a man in woman's clothing. Second, she needed to scare John badly, in a sexual and believable way. The actress was indeed a man, playing a fat tough old woman. But his clothes and makeup were so good that it would be hard to reveal her as a man. Keith's answer was to have her judicial robes fall away, revealing a guy in a heavily padded over-size jock-strap as John fainted. The nearly naked man would be a patchwork of parts and exaggerated black stitch marks, filmed off a mirror on the floor, to give John's perspective of looking straight up at the massive male body towering over him.

By the time David had extracted a believable performance from the two actors, the day was over and everyone was tired from the stress and tension. Keith still didn't know if the scene had worked on film, and spent the night pondering alternate approaches to this piece of the plot.

The next day was cinematically-complex, but not difficult from an acting or directing perspective. It was a large scene of a dance at Senior City with fifty old extras as well as the established old actors and actresses. Much pill-popping, oxygen hoses dangling from the ceiling over the dance floor, silly antics, and fun, which is then interrupted by an urgent alarm. Orson and his I.R.S. Suckers have arrived for a surprise audit! In the midst of all this, several clones escape and rescue Spunky from the operating room just before she is cut-up for parts. Today would show the dance hall, first with all the old people dancing, then later the deserted room as the clones sneaked across it on their way to freedom.

For most of the day, Keith's main task was to play music for the dance through big loudspeakers, in sync with the camera. A recording would be made with a slate so that the editor could initially align the music, which was being played, with the film. The edited film would use a clean recording of the music instead of Keith's scratch track. The music was from the nineteen-thirties, and the dance step was The Balboa, which a male choreographer explained to the large group of old-looking people. It was similar to the Charleston, and allowed much individual variation. As George and the grips and gaffers worked to light the large set, Keith played the music over and over for the cast and the teacher at the other end of the stage.

Jessica walked over to Keith, "C'mon dance with me, I know these steps cold. Don't look so serious, it's a blast: everyone danced this way in the thirties. Let's have some fun, I'll teach you the steps."

Jessica grabbed his hand and before he could object, she was teaching him the basics. They danced by Keith's sound equipment, smiling, amusing themselves, as she taught Keith more advanced steps and turns. The music tempo was fast, the steps somewhat silly but not too hard to learn. To their surprise the choreographer grabbed them and put them in front of the others, "Do what these guys are doing, just follow them, and I'll come around to help you." Some actors caught on immediately, and the choreographer walked around, helping the slower couples. Much laughter and fun for everyone.

David saw them dancing together in front of the cast and walked over with a sly smile. "How about wearing gray wigs and getting in front of the camera for a great two-shot."

"Can we do that legally? What if SAG finds out?"

175

Angela was watching this develop, laughing to herself, thinking of her career in front of the camera and how much she had enjoyed performing. "Do it kids, we can sneak you into SAG, under the emergency clause. Get me a wig too, I'm going to dance with the choreographer, and my card's still paid up."

Keith, as well as probably everyone else on the crew, had occasionally been an unpaid background extra, filling-in when another body was needed, but this was different. He would be front and center, doing steps he had just learned. What had been casual fun was now more serious, but not too serious. He knew that David could cut-away if he screwed-up, so why not appear in your own film. Everyone knew that Alfred Hitchcock appeared in each of his films, so this was not without precedent. Jessica gave Keith a few clothes and a wig, while one of the makeup men applied a gray moustache, a scar, and gray powder to his face. The Still Photographer laughed as he took a picture of Keith in full make-up, wig and headphones, operating his sound gear, and several of Keith dancing with Jessica. In comparison to Keith and Jessica, the choreographer and Angela were really good. The four worked out a simple routine where they would dance as a foursome, then spin and split into two couples. They wouldn't be on the screen long, but it was fun indeed to be on this side of the camera for a change. Jack ran the sound gear while Keith performed. Keith and Jessica enjoyed a very nice day for a change.

That evening they rented a screening Room on another part of the lot to look at a rough cut of the existing footage. There were holes of course, but they had shot two-thirds of the film and the Editor had been busy making a first pass. He was looking for overall comments and opinions. David had been watching dailies and working with the editor every weekend, but Keith hadn't taken time to view much of the film

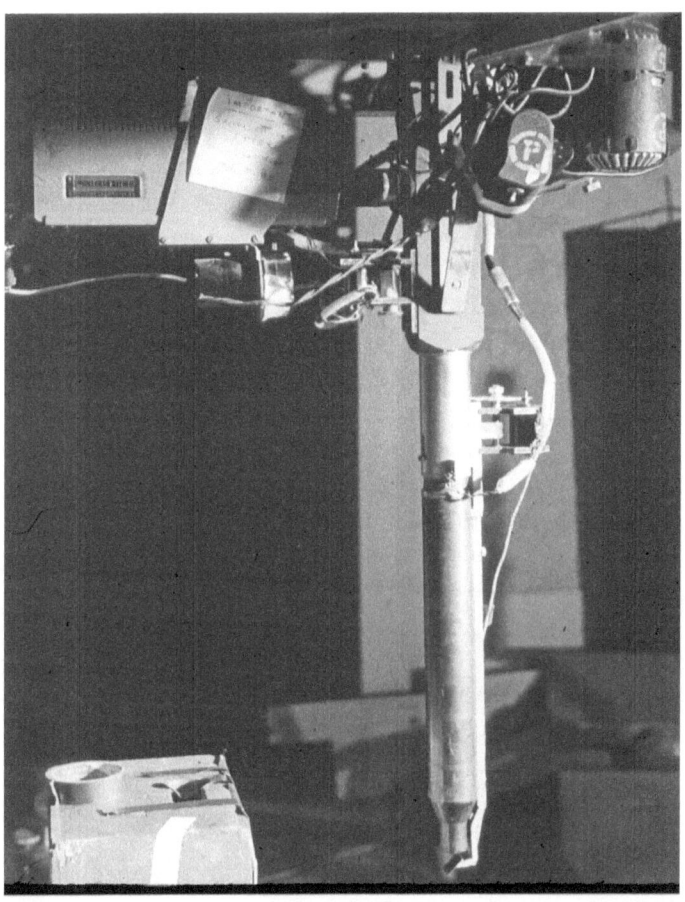

Snorkel Camera, popularized in the seventies by Paul Kenworthy. At the bottom is a small tilting mirror, which is the front of the camera's lens. Several feet above it is a motor to drive the mirror. Further up the tube is a focus motor and a TV camera. Near the top, on the side opposite the TV camera, is a 35mm Arriflex on a flat-bed mount. The vertical tube contains relay lenses. There is also a motor to rotate the whole assembly.

until now. Angela, David, Jessica, Stubby, and George were also invited, as well as one of the doctors who was backing the film. Keith had worried that this was a bad idea, but a quick phone call from the doctor put him at ease. The doc had read the script, thought it very funny, and happened to be in town to do a complex operation. He commented that he wouldn't expect Keith to give him advice in a real operating room, so he wouldn't interfere with their work. The doc arrived with Bernie and they all had many laughs watching a seventy-minute portion of the film.

Afterwards Keith conferred with David and the Editor while the others chatted and said goodbye. Keith noticed that Jessica and the doc were having an involved conversation, but by the time he was finished talking film nuances with the Editor, everyone else was gone. Time to rest. Tomorrow he would call the Editor to find out how their dance routine looked on film.

෧෩෧෩෧

Keith arrived early the next morning, to give himself quiet time to examine the sets and to think about the day's work. The painters were still working the set, putting on the final paint and wallpaper. They often painted late at night and into the early morning, while the construction crews worked in the evenings, tearing down the old and putting up new sets. The painters mixed their own paints with secret recipes, usually involving large amounts of Japan Dryer. It made the paint dry very fast, but the paint wasn't especially durable. That was fine since a set rarely had to maintain its appearance for more than a few days or a month or two at most. The only drawback was that the strong fumes from the fast-dry paint made people feel a bit giddy. More than one painter had fallen from a ladder during late-night paint work.

Snorkel At The Beach, mounted on a large road crane, filming a wrist-watch commercial for a French company. For this footage, the snorkel moved a few inches from the surf-line, discovering watches in the wet glittering sand while the sun set in the background. The grips had to be very careful to control the boom exactly so that the snorkel was not poked into the sand, or soaked by a wave.

Today's work involved a special periscope camera, called the Snorkel. Normally this camera traveled on overhead rails, with various motors to move it across the stage. At the moment its heart was mounted on the end of a camera crane, worked by grips. The camera was at the top of a four-foot long vertical lens. At the bottom of the lens was a small one-inch-square mirror which could be tilted remotely by the camera operator. The operator could also rotate the camera remotely. The tilt and rotate controls were combined into a single joystick. Operating it was similar to the sensation of flying an airplane.

The camera operator flew the camera around the scene while watching a television monitor which showed the same image that the camera saw, (by looking at the image bounced off a pellicle, a thin flat piece of clear glass, inside the lens, near the camera.) The Assistant cameraman sat by another monitor operating the focus control. The camera could focus down to a subject an inch away from the mirror, and all the way out to infinity. This meant many rehearsals to get the moves and focus shifts just right. The key advantage of the periscope camera was that it could travel within inches of a subject, exploring it almost from the viewpoint of a butterfly, but a butterfly that could spin completely around and fly away.

The main drawback to the snorkel camera, which would creep over Savage's and Mary's naked patch-work bodies in this scene, was the amount of light that it needed. The special lens on the camera was permanently set at f/11, but there was additional light loss, making it really a t/18 for exposure purposes. George pushed the film one stop, to make it more sensitive, and underexposed as much of the scene as he dared. Since the scene was supposed to be a dark bedroom, he didn't bother to light anything except interesting parts of their bodies. The rest would be mysterious dark shadows.

Two sets of actors and equipment would be used. Senator Savage and Mary Maker, would lie in bed without their shirts for head close-ups and dialog. This would be done with a normal silent sound camera, but from a low angle simulating that which the periscope provided. This film would be pushed also, so that it looked as close as possible to the periscope film. Then two body-extras, covered with stitch-marks and multi-colored skin would be filmed in sexual ecstasy by the periscope. Intense make-up work, to remove perspiration and maintain the effects, and a very busy time for grips and camera crew, but nothing for either Keith or Jessica to do, except prepare for the following day. In the film business it was not uncommon for crew persons to have hours with nothing to do except wait for other people to finish their work. The minimum that a union person could be hired was half a day, so even on a day with just a few sound takes, a Sound Mixer, a Boom Man, and all their gear would be on the stage looking for something to do. For Keith this was no problem as he could always work on the script, but others would pass the time studying or reading unless they could contribute to the team effort in some way.

The next day they did the Judge-Julie-and-the-virgin-clones sex scene, but Keith didn't talk with Jessica about it. He had learned his lesson and didn't want to offend Jessica or let her tease him about sex either. They both treated the scene as another day in the business, even though it had the potential to be the most sexually-exciting footage in the film.

It seemed to Keith that the intimate part of their life together had passed and now their relationship was mature and more distant. Keith pondered this, wondering why the spark had gone from their relationship. He had the feeling that Jessica was back in the bottle, but so far it wasn't interfering with her work. He didn't ask her about it for he knew that he wouldn't like the answer. Perhaps their relationship was ending with a slow fade to black instead of a turbulent montage.

∞∞∞∞

Friday afternoon everyone worked to set up a night-for-night exterior explosion. The crew was in a remote part of San Bernardino, against the foothills of the Angeles Mountains. This was just within the fifty mile Studio Zone, but probably in the part furthermost from Keith's home. They had several abandoned warehouses and were going to blow a hole in the side of one. Not a giant hole, but one big enough for the clones to run or climb through for their escape. Hired Police and firemen were stationed nearby in case of trouble. This was an expensive, though very exciting, shot. It was footage for the opening credits, a dream sequence where part of Senior City explodes then clones run through the resulting hole and escape onto the desert. Keith would record the sound of the explosion with an old mike since he didn't want to risk damaging a good one if the noise were really loud. There would only be one take, so it was covered from four camera angles, each with a long lens to place it far from danger. Two of the cameras would be running at high speed to capture the explosion in slow-motion. These were Photosonics model 4E, with 1000 foot rolls of film. They would run at four times the normal speed, devouring their film in less than three minutes. (Although these particular cameras could run much faster, up to fifteen times normal speed, George knew from experience that explosions looked best at around four-times normal speed. However, he had once used these cameras at top speed to film a car crashing into a wall and had been quite pleased with the result.) The warehouse wall was lit with a few huge distant arc lights, to simulate moonlight. Everyone relied on George's experience with other explosions to get the exposure and coverage correct.

Their plan called for the clones, in their normal uniform which is like a thin track-suit, to rush through the exploded hole into the night air. The special effects team controlling the explosion was convinced that everything would be safe for the clones and of the correct brightness for George.

Just before they were ready to roll the explosion, Jessica ran to Keith and pulled his arm, "Stop them, stop them right now, do something."

"What, we're ready to roll Jessica."

"No, it's not safe, stop it," she screamed. Keith picked

up a bullhorn and yelled in the direction of David.

"David, stop the scene, don't run it, hold everything."

Jessica was already running to Angela and David who were up on a raised camera platform with George where they could see everything. She scampered up the cold aluminum ladder. "Angela, it's not safe, it'll kill the clones, don't let them do it."

The special effects coordinator, Robert, and George looked at Jessica in bewilderment. Keith climbed up and stood beside her. For a moment the only sound was Jessica's breathing from her fast run, then "Angela, I know, I know it won't work. Double check the explosives, let the clones enter the scene later. This won't work. Don't kill them."

"Who are you? We've done explosions like this thousands of times before. Are you questioning our experience?" Robert asked.

Angela answered for her, "Easy Robert, Jessica sometimes sees the future, and she never makes a mistake. I've seen her do it before, so this is a serious business."

George shouted to the electricians, "Save your arcs."

Herb, Mike and Sy who were visiting with their bimbos, yelled up at the crew, "What the hell's going on up there, we want to see it blow before we leave for dinner."

Keith interjected a compromise, "We can fog the exploded hole, then let the clones run through later with some flickering firelight. Let's pull them out, do the explosion with everyone far away, then move in for a close-up on the hole."

From below, they heard, "Are you guys gonna shoot this or what. We're paying and we want it now."

George had worked with Angela on five films and he had never seen her make a major mistake in judgment. "Your call Angela, this film's not important enough to risk anyone's life over a shot."

"David? Keith? George? Let's do the safe thing, and fake their run-through. I trust Jessica. Robert, I don't know why she sees what she does, or if there's something wrong with the explosives or the old warehouse or the clones' position or what. It'll take ten minutes to clear the set, so there's time to recheck your gear if you want."

David took the bullhorn and called to the clones and the police and firemen, telling them all to come over to the camera platform, which was far from the explosion. He told everyone to clear the set, to get at least as far away as he was. Robert was confident in his work, and waited for everyone to move.

"Hey we can't see anything from way back here. I'm going up to where I was to get a picture with my new camera," Sy complained.

"No Sy, it's not safe, stay back here." Angela warned.

"I've seen fireworks before, and I don't have a long lens like you do, I'm moving up close."

"You've signed a waiver like everyone else on the set, so I can't stop you, but you're making a big mistake. Herb, Mike, you hearing all this, you hearing that I am explicitly warning him to stay back here? I hope your insurance is paid-up," Angela yelled in frustration.

When the Police assured them that everyone except Sy was well-clear of the warehouse area, David yelled, "Strike your arcs," and the scene came to life.

He turned to Robert, "Ready for you?"

After Robert nodded, he shouted, "Roll four cameras and sound." He paused ten seconds to let the high-speed cameras reach full speed, then.

"Action!" Robert hit his switches and there was a tremendous explosion from the warehouse. The wall blew out and the roof sailed up into the air, then came down with a horrendous crash, spewing material and fire in all directions. David let the cameras run as fires started and the dust slowly subsided.

"Cut." Ended the sequence after a very long two minutes. The slomo cameras would be just finishing their film loads when Stubby reached them.

"Holy shit!" was Robert's first comment, followed by "What the hell was in that warehouse wall? It looked clean as a whistle when we inspected it."

The firemen were already spraying down a small brushfire, when Herb noticed that Sy hadn't returned. They found him lying on the ground, his expensive camera smashed into his face by the shockwave from the explosion. The paramedics took him away as the crew moved in for shots of the clones running through the mess. Keith saw Robert hugging Jessica and Angela, crying and thanking them both profusely. Everyone knew how close they had come to disaster. George was wondering how the scene had photographed since the explosion was far brighter and bigger than he had expected.

They did the close-ups of the clones running though the hole as quickly as possible, since everyone was on edge. George ran with them through the fog, hand-holding a camera for several shots. The clones knew how close they had come to death as they were supposed to have been standing inside the smoldering warehouse during the explosion. Within an hour the fire department had all the fires out and the crew was packing-up. The firemen were starting an investigation into the explosion. They had carefully inspected Robert's work and the warehouse beforehand and were very curious, especially since the adjacent warehouses appeared to be identical to the one that had just disintegrated under a small charge of dynamite and a stack of fireworks.

Late that night, Keith went home slowly, thoroughly

wiped-out emotionally. When he had started writing this film, he had never dreamed that it would hurt anyone, or come close to killing his young actors and actresses. He tossed and turned through the night. How could he ever thank Jessica for the lives she had just saved.

Jessica was home, painting furiously, crying occasionally, thinking of the clones, the explosion and what her gifts had done tonight. She could see what might have happened as well as what had actually happened. Both impressions were blended together in abstract paintings, which perhaps only she understood.

მთთთ

On Saturday a somber Keith watched the dailies with George, David, and their editor. The explosion, though overexposed at its peak, was extremely impressive, especially in slow motion, and the shots of the truly-frightened clones were perfect cinematically. He hoped that the clones would have the courage to come to work in the Operating Room scenes which started on Monday. When Keith saw the footage of Jessica and himself dancing, a twinge of longing for her rippled through his heart. He knew that he missed her, but also that the affair was fading out.

Keith spent the day working with David, then went to dinner with Dawn, David and Spunky. As they talked Keith realized that Dawn had much more to offer than her nice body. She was articulate and had a happy laissez faire outlook on life which contrasted sharply to his own morose views. Dawn was enjoying life and not worrying about it. Keith resolved to take a fresh look at his own attitudes as soon as the film was done. As they parted, Keith thanked Dawn for such a pleasant time, for bringing happiness into his life. They shared a warm squirming hug and a long wet kiss goodnight. He realized that their relationship could easily expand, that she was ready and willing to laugh with him and join in all his dreams and activities, to be a ray of sunshine no matter what the world brought. Perhaps she could fill a big piece of his life that had been missing since Kristin's death.

Keith returned home and noticed that his floor furnace had switched itself on for the first time this Autumn. He could smell the dust that had accumulated since March burning off the hot steel surface. The weather was changing, and the rains would soon begin in earnest. He curled up in his favorite chair and reviewed the week's activities over a few glasses of red wine. Although he was tired physically and mentally, he was optimistic: the film was going well, and in his dreams he could begin to imagine it as a big hit. There was certainly nothing else like it on the screen! Involuntarily he laughed out loud and smiled at the prospect. The footage from most days was outstanding in spite of the compromises they had made, and the funny scenes were hilarious. He started to eagerly anticipate the first full-length cut.

ﻩﻩﻩﻩ

Late that night his sleep was interrupted by the sound of someone with a key coming through his front door. As he awoke and regained consciousness, in the moonlight he looked up to see Jessica standing beside his bed, her face and head bandaged, her shadowy clothes in disarray, she was shivering and shaking, crying in pain, a bad dream become reality.

Keith rubbed his eyes, trying to decide if this was true. "Jessica, is that you, what happened?"

Jessica swayed back and forth, her words slurred. "I think maybe a tree jumped in front of my car and smashed it on Mulholland, coming over the top from The Valley. Took a cab from the hospital. Tow-truck left my wreck in your driveway."

Keith sat up in bed quickly. "You look awful, are you all right?"

"Terrible." As she said this, Jessica kicked off her shoes, dropped her coat on the floor and flopped down on top of the covers next to Keith. In the dim light he could see that she was dressed perhaps for a wild party, wearing a provocative, blood stained, thin dress and not much else. Her perfume mingled with emergency room medications and the smell of adhesive bandages. He had never seen her in such clothes, they had no relationship to what he felt he knew of her feelings and he wondered what she had been doing and where.

He turned to her body and ran his fingers through her hair, trying to figure out what was going on, then he tried the one thing he knew that would elicit a response. "Would you like a drink?"

"Got any Scotch or gin? The pain, it's all over. Oh Keith, I've really screwed up this time. You should have seen the cops: they were so pissed when they pulled up my record!"

Keith found a thick wool plaid blanket and gently placed it over Jessica's body, then kissed her lightly on the forehead. Instead of falling asleep, she painfully sat up in bed. "How about that drink: I could really use it just now, then , then you can curl up beside me and we can sleep together, maybe like lovers after a hard night."

Keith thought her words odd, but knew that she couldn't get into further trouble, and realized that this was a time to comfort her any way he could, even though booze was definitely not in her best interest. He returned with a bottle of scotch, two small glasses, and a pitcher of water. "How about scotch and water, maybe half and half?"

Jessica nervously moved around on the bed like a caged and wounded animal, rearranging the blanket that covered her painful body, eager for drink that might ease the pain in both her body and in her mind. "Thanks, cheers." She drank the first glass quickly, her hands shaking, then relaxed as he poured her a second.

"Jessica, just take it easy, we've got all night, no one is chasing you, the spirits can't get you when you're next to me."

"That's crap, as I've told you before, but somehow, I just wish I could stay here beside you forever, but I know I can't, it's not in the cards. It's so sad. I long to reach out to you, to wrap my arms around you, to cry on your shoulder, to make you happy, to take care of you, to be the one you love for eternity."

Keith paused, then asked quietly, his sadness on the surface, "Have you seen the future, that we'll always be apart?"

"No, there's no magic viewing, just reality, it's right here, it's obvious, I'll show you." Jessica pushed the blanket aside, then to Keith's surprise, managed to stand beside the bed, then fighting against the pain, she wavered unsteadily, nearly fell, then pulled her dress up over her head and let it fall to the floor. She lay down on the bed. "See, Keith, here I am, almost naked and ready, ready for you to pounce on top of me and screw me with delight, a real girl friend, just like that damn horny over-sexed teenage Dawn girl."

Keith knew that the reality was different, that if he touched her, if he began to caress the sore and inebriated body beside him, that she would freeze solid. "I know you're not right, that you've had too much to drink. I couldn't, I wouldn't take advantage of you."

Jessica started to cry. "Why not, here, gimme your hands, run them over my body, what's wrong, why won't you love me, am I so old and ugly that you won't even try? It's because you know that I'll freeze as cold as an iceberg if you just touch me. You know that if you just. . ."

She drew her knees up to her chest and started to cry uncontrollably, shaking and sobbing on her pillow, her hands covering her face. Keith desperately wanted to help her, to enfold the damaged and lovely body in his arms, to comfort her and tell her that all would be OK in the morning. But as he watched her sobbing body, he couldn't help but think of tonight's dinner, and the pleasant time he had enjoyed with Dawn: how uncomplicated, how straight forward their relationship had become. Now Jessica was once again intruding, pouring her problems into his life, asking for help that he didn't know how to give. He caressed her head, ran his fingers through her hair where it wasn't under the bandages, and did his best to provide comfort and warmth. "You're beautiful, you just need some sleep, you'll be fine in the morning."

"Bullshit, you don't believe that for a minute. Tomorrow I'll still be frigid, and you'll still be hot for Dawn's body, nothing's going to change that, but Keith, why, why can't it be different?"

Keith poured her another drink. "What happened, why can't you talk about it, why can't you tell me?"

Jessica stopped crying as she heard Keith pouring and started on the drink tentatively, then rolled over and finished it in one swallow. "Oh God, I just want to pass out, please give me another."

As she started to drink more, Keith sensed a subtle change in her voice and continued to gently run his fingers through her hair. "Keith, When I was young, I began to realize that I had some sort of psychic gift, but it was vague and it didn't happen often. Maybe once a month or less I felt something of the future, but no big deal, just interesting dreams and visions.

Childhood was very nice, uncomplicated and filled with a great future. I was smart, rich, and happy, and I miss it very much. I'll show you paintings I've done, trying to go back to before, before it all happened."

She paused, almost panting with fear, "I met this big hairy mystical guy, seemed, at least to me, like he knew all about the supernatural, and he was older, maybe twice or more as old as I was, and he told me that he could tell I was really special. I had just passed through puberty and I didn't have a clue. What a jerk. Before I knew it, I had joined this group of weird people who liked to gather late at night and mumble lots of psychic crap and incantations by firelight. We drank secret potions and they made me feel so strange. What a fool, you'd never believe how stupid."

"Then one night there was a big deal ceremony with torches out in the woods and lots to drink and I didn't realize that I was the star attraction, I was the sacrifice. How could I have been so dumb, I just don't know, but soon I was up on this cold stone alter with no clothes. I could feel the cold stone all though my back and my legs. I was so scared, I can't describe it. There was chanting and excitement and fire and drums and for sure I had been given a loaded drink, then this guy was on top of me and shit, it was terrible. You just can't imagine, these four hooded priests held my arms and legs apart as this big hairy guy showed it into me, and the pain, oh Keith, never, never I don't ever want to go there again." Jessica dissolved into tears shaking and shivering as Keith wrapped his arms around her, covering Jessica with a blanket, his arms, and his own tears.

Then she continued, "The pain was bad, but not as bad as the trial, the courtroom, the judge, the jury, the fancy lawyers and all that crap my parents laid on."

Keith didn't understand, "Wait, what happened, the

191

courtroom?"

"He was tried for raping and corrupting an underage minor, guess who, and sent up the creek for a long time, god the rape was bad, but the trial, it was so painful, so embarrassing, I felt like shit whenever anyone looked at me, yet I was the victim, not the perp!"

"Jessica! Was he locked away forever?"

"Of course not, this is California, and he'll be out soon, on good behavior if you can fucking believe it."

Keith began to see a completely different picture of Jessica, her past, and her motivations. Then he began to have an uneasy feeling, "Where were you tonight Jessica, in your unusual dress?"

"I won't tell, you don't want to be involved, it's none of your, of your, oh shit, I was in Encino if you want to know, at a porn palace, arranging a hit on the asshole the moment he steps out of jail."

"Holy shit, you hired a killer to put him away? Am I now an accomplice?"

"It only cost me ten grand, surprising what the life of a prick is worth. I never told you and you never heard about it, don't forget, you're clean. 'Course the big problem is blackmail afterwards: there's no guarantee that the ten is the last payment. Funny how they prove their work, they asked what piece of his body I wanted to have afterwards, and damn I was tempted to answer, but I didn't."

"Jessica! What about your fancy lawyer and judge friends?"

"They've already had him moved to Mississippi and doubled his sentence, but they can't do much more. Sometimes I can feel his spirit and it's pissed. It's time to play hard ball, and in the words of Hitler, that schmuck's ready for the final solution, he's really got it coming."

"Did you pay the money? Is it a done deal?"

"Ask me in a few months. I'm sorry Keith, not about the perp, but about you and me."

Hours passed as he held her tightly, thinking over what he had just learned. Would she be arrested? Would she ever lead a normal sex life, or would she have children only through artificial insemination or adoption? How could they live a life together as man and wife if she froze when he touched her body? What a beautiful person lay wrapped in his arms, sobbing her wounded drunken body to sleep. Jessica had so many gifts, so much to offer herself and the world, yet her treasures were dissolving, lost in sadness and scars from long ago.

∽∾∽∾

Sunday morning, Keith inspected the wreck in his driveway. Jessica was lucky to be alive. He looked inside and saw that the speedometer was broken, with its needle stuck at seventy. What a waste of a nice car. When he went back inside he saw her struggling to sit-up on her side of the bed.

Jessica had been partially awake for an hour, feeling her surroundings, and once again becoming aware of Kristin's presence. It was hard to imagine, to even describe, just a fleeting sensation, but it seemed that Kristin was so sad, almost as though she was fading away, and that she felt that Jessica was a big disappointment: a wonderful living girl who lost herself in booze and problems instead of in Keith's arms. What a shame. Jessica cried for Kristin, then struggled to sit up and try to do a little better in her memory.

Keith was now beside her asking what he could do to help. What could she say, how could she ease his pain instead of worrying so much about her own. An idea emerged. "Keith, every muscle in my body is sore, I can hardly move my arms and legs."

"Should I take you to a hospital or maybe call someone?"

"No, the quacks said nothing's broken, it's all just stretched and strained: painful, not fatal."

"I'll make breakfast, what would you like?"

"First, did I just dream it, or did I tell you about something that happened last night and a long time ago?"

"A jailed bastard who took advantage of you?"

"Oh shit, well at least now you know, not many people do, I've changed my name since then. You're the first I've told. You're special, special to me."

They paused quietly, sharing a moment, neither knowing what to say. So many feelings just below the surface. Finally Jessica said, "You know more about me than almost anyone else, and well, would you hold me and help me stand up and get the rest of my clothes off? They're covered with god knows what and I can't do it alone."

"I could take you to Angela's if you'd rather have a woman look after you?"

"No, I'm going to be embarrassed enough as it is. You must have realized by now that everyone I know has tried to stop my drinking, and warned me about D.W.I. Angela has already covered for me twice with the cops. Tell you what Keith, if you help me get through this mess, I'll promise to drink no more than you do. I know I can't stop, but maybe I can slow down and have a few drinks with you instead of drinking alone. That's when I really hit it hard."

Together they slowly removed the last of her stained and ruined clothing: the torn stockings, the underwear, some of the loose bloody bandages. As his hands passed over Jessica's bare skin, she shuddered involuntarily, and Keith hesitated to go further. "Please, it's all right, well, you know that it's not at all right, especially after last night, but do it, take everything off and help me onto the john, then into the tub. I feel like such a damn fool, and I know I'm making you feel like a jerk, slowly peeling the clothes off a girl who is useless in bed. Don't worry about hurting me, just treat me like a normal person, don't get lost in my troubles."

"Try to relax kiddo, you've come through a bad night, and I'll recover from the sight of your body."

"Hey, it's not that bad is it?"

"Quite the contrary."

"Good, you'll see plenty of it this week until I get my muscles working again, and the bruises are going to be ugly."

"Just don't run off early in the morning for a shot of booze, promise me?"

"Yes, yes definitely, I'll be here as long as you want me to stay."

As Keith ran the tub for her and put her clothes into the laundry basket, he was struck by the similarity between his actions now and those of taking care of Kristin. For a moment, he flashed back and thought that he was helping Kristin into the tub instead of Jessica. It was fleeting, but so real, he had to catch the side of the tub to keep from falling. Jessica focused deeply into his eyes as a single tear ran down her cheek, "I see what you see Keith, but no, I'm not Kristin, but in so many ways I wish that I were."

Seniors Have It Tough

Chapter 9

Final Week of Production

Monday of the sixth, and final, week of production was back on Stage-9, but with sets that represented the medical complex, the heart of Senior City. Today they would start work in the gas-filled Operating Room. The doctors here could splice almost any part from one body to another, provided the recipient could afford the operation. The operating room was filled with purple medical gas about two feet deep, like a fog layer.

For Keith and David the main cinematic problem was making these scenes funny rather than gruesome. They both laughed for hours when reading the script, but they realized that other people might not find the material as funny as they did, and who knew how their words would translate into film. They were conscious of the fine line between humor and revulsion. If they didn't play this just right, audiences would puke instead of laugh. They were inexperienced, playing with very strong emotions and well-aware of the difficulties.

The Operating Room set was a large room with only one entrance, and that entrance had an air lock. The room could be filled with a heavy purple gas made from a combination of dry ice fog, purple-colored sulfur-smelling smoke from small fireworks, and water-vapor. The stuff smelled terrible but looked authentic. Keith and David decided to use real gas masks and hoses, connected to a supply of fresh air, so that the crew and the actors could breathe normally during the actual shots.

George had experimented with different techniques and finally decided that much of the scene would be a double-exposure, with photography of dense swirling purple gas superimposed over the actual footage shot on stage. (The DX, double-exposure, would be done by an optical house after the editing was finished) He added a special filter to the camera, one which would yield a sharp central image, but soft edges, to further enhance the gassy impression he desired.

Lighting the gas was complex. Small soft purple lights were on the floor, giving the gas extra glow and color, then the rest of the room was hard light, so that there could be dark mysterious shadows. There were several operating tables with overhead lights as well. These harsh lights tended to make the doctors look scary as well as providing illumination for filming.

There was minimal sync dialog to record since there was no way for the audience to see the actor's moving lips in most scenes. As an experiment, Keith put radio mikes on the speaking actors, with the mikes inside the gas masks. He would record a mixture of heavy breathing and dialog, which would help the editor lay in the real words, (which would be recorded separately.) There was a chance that the live dialog-with-breathing might have an interesting acoustic aspect, perhaps representing the way that these doctors really sound when wearing masks.

The normal flow of work was interrupted when a television news crew arrived to interview Angela and Jessica about the explosion and how they had saved the actors' lives last Friday. Word of the averted disaster had leaked, and the publicity team had decided to capitalize on it instead of ignoring it. Jessica, her face bandaged, and her body limping painfully, had no interest in being interviewed on-camera, but cooperated for Keith's sake. Angela told her to pretend that she had been injured by the explosion, while saving the lives of the clones. Not quite the actual story, but they laughed quietly to themselves as they told the reporters what they wanted to hear: "young pretty woman saves lives while being hurt." Good publicity for the film and Jessica became a heroine on the nightly news.

While the interview was being taped, Keith received a phone call from a UCLA hospital Administrator. He warned Keith to stop lawyer-Jim's investigation into Kristin's hospital stay. Keith was bewildered, but remembered Jim's suspicions about the hospital care. Keith had no idea that Jim was causing trouble. The hospital reminded him that he had signed a waiver of all rights in return for no hospital fees. The case was closed, and that was the end of it. As Keith hung-up, he wondered about Jim's activity. He knew that Jim, like all lawyers, was acutely-aware of his billable hours, and that he wouldn't waste a minute investigating something if he didn't expect to profit from it. Jim was no fool, so there must have been something improper in Kristin's care at the hospital. He started to mentally review all that he knew about her activity at the hospital, but was interrupted by Jack, "Keith, are you OK? You look worried, but it's time to roll coverage on the next scene."

They finished the scene, then started to rehearse for the master shot in the gas-filled operating room. Angela's fancy lawyers walked onto the set and sought-out Keith and Angela. Jessica had been talking with Angela, but the lawyers didn't recognize her in working clothes. POBOB was setting-up pickets on the sidewalk outside the studio gate to protest their film. The lawyers wanted Keith to try to talk them out of picketing. Keith wasted an hour talking with the pickets then finally realized that they were all actors and extras hired by the day to make a nuisance of themselves. They had no interest in either POBOB or Keith, but only in the cash they were receiving for a few days of walking on a public sidewalk with big signs.

Keith returned frustrated and annoyed. He had a film to make and yet he couldn't stop worrying about Kristin's medical care. He lost his temper at Angela, apologized, then went off into a corner to eat lunch. Jessica joined him with the news that her car had been towed to a repair shop, so his driveway looked a bit more respectable. She sensed his mood and tried to comfort him, but knew that his worries about Kristin were not something she could solve with a few kind words or a pat on the back.

"Keith, let's talk tonight with Jim, and see if he knows anything specific. Maybe he's just nosing around, hoping to annoy the hospital enough that they'll settle for a fat fee out of court just to get rid of him. Maybe there's nothing wrong at all, except with our legal system?"

Keith smiled, "That's the smartest thing you've said in ages, and I have a feeling that you're exactly right. Let's go to work, this scene is supposed to be one of the funniest in the film, and we both have lots to do." The original scenes that Keith had written were:

```
OPERATING ROOM--SENIOR CITY
     The atmosphere in the operating room
is a blend between the zaniness of a TV
game show and the excitement and tension
of a busy emergency room. A cacophony of
sounds greets us as we enter: we hear doc-
tors yelling, computers talking, and the
unmistakable sound of old-fashioned cash
registers ringing up big sales.

     In the center of the room are six
```

operating tables and four computers. The computers are large box-like devices, about the size of refrigerators. The main thing we notice immediately about the computers is that each has a wide variety of back-lit signs intermittently flashing, and a large money counter. The signs have legends such as: "DEAD ALREADY", "MER-CEDES", "ROLLS ROYCE", "GOOD PIECES", "NOBEL PRIZE", "CAN'T AFFORD IT", "JACK-POT", "GOLD", "SWISS BANK ACCOUNT", "EX-TRA BILLING", ...

To operate a computer, the doctors connect a large cable from the computer to a patient's head to determine the most profitable course of treatment. The computer sounds occasionally resolve into English words and phrases. All medical personnel are covered from head to foot to protect them against the gas. They wear light green gowns, surgical gloves, hoods, and face masks, connected to hoses leading to the ceiling. The personnel wear different colored scarves to designate their function: doctor, nurse, or flunky. All human parts we see are bright purple because of the special gas.

As the scene opens, the first gurney comes flying through the door from the vestibule. We follow the kicking and screaming Rude Old Man, then watch as a thick layer of fog is casually hosed over him. As the gas dissipates, we see that the "patient" is asleep, and that his skin is now purple!

A computer cable is connected to his head. Several doctors and nurses watch

as we hear and see the computer's com-
mentary. The analysis ends with only the
"CAN"T AFFORD IT" sign illuminated, and a
"Bronx Cheer" from the computer. The doctors instantly move to the next work station: we watch as flunkies quickly dump
the unfortunate body down a chute labeled
"FERTILIZER PLANT".

We Cut to the next operating table
where doctors are enjoying better luck.
The computer money counter, a large illuminated flashing sign, is financially ana-
lyzing the patient. The doctors chant
with the computer as it counts:

DOCTORS: "Ten thousand, twenty thousand,
thirty thousand, forty thousand, fifty
thousand, sixty thousand, (pause...) six-
ty-four thousand smackers!"

We hear the sound of a loud cash
register bell and cut to a cash drawer
on the side of the computer as it flies
open. Bloody hands reach in and grab wads
of hundred dollar bills.

We cut to the patient's view, looking up at the medical staff through a wide
angle lens and purple filter. Doctors
begin to "operate", removing all manner
of semihuman parts. (The operation is a
parody rather than a plausible transplant).

FIRST DOCTOR: "Hurry up ... get this
old leg off."

SECOND DOCTOR: "Where's that new saw? I
tee off in fifteen minutes." (We hear a

big electric saw start up)

NURSE: (to flunky) "Hey Burgdorf, bring that third clone over here."

A pair of flunkies rush to one of the clones. They move the clone's table out into the room, and level it as they wheel it over to the operating area. As the clone is brought alongside the operating table, doctors and nurses bustle about with tape measures comparing the sizes of the parts.

DOCTOR: "Hurry up, tape those parts; I haven't got all day."

NURSE: "Relax, you've got the fastest team in the room."

DOCTOR: "But not the richest; let's move!"

NURSE: "Watch it! You almost got my hose!"

DOCTOR: "Then park it. I'm working cash flow, not your air flow."

The doctors work quickly, but then pause to look over to table number four, where chaos has erupted. We follow their looks to the Well Dressed Man on the table.

At table four the computer money counter is in the hundreds of thousands and going strong. Several "MERCEDES" signs are illuminated. The doctors crowd around to watch; we see they are carry-

```
ing assorted bloody parts. Other activ-
ity ceases as the count goes over five
hundred thousand, and all gather about,
chanting and cheering the computer on.
As the total approaches one million dol-
lars, they start to shout. There is a
brief pause, then the "SWISS BANK AC-
COUNT" sign illuminates and pandemonium
reigns. MUSIC changes to "WE'RE IN THE
MONEY", and everyone dances around the
patient and the happy computer. Hundred
dollar bills rain down as the people
throw parts in the air ecstatically.
```

Converting these few pages of words into film required the rest of the day and two hours of overtime. False-bottom baskets overhead dropped fake money onto the scene, but it took time and stepladders to reload them after each shot. Imitation blood was liberally applied to everything. Unfortunately they could only afford two computers, so they were moved around the room and filmed with different colored front panels so that it appeared that there were many. This limited the possible camera angles, and moving the camera around in the fog turned out to be a real pain. Crew people kept loosing things in the fog, and working while wearing masks and air hoses was not easy. How could David talk to the crew and actors from inside his mask, yet when he removed it, he coughed and sputtered? Finally, David directed everything from the top of a stepladder, high above the fog. Angela stayed perched on top one of the set's walls, ten feet off the floor, yelling in all directions. As an odd touch, Keith had filled the control room, which was visible through a large window from the operating room, with a large black and white formal photo of the film crew which was shot on the first day of production. This would just be visible from several camera angles, and most viewers wouldn't notice it, but some would, and they would get a chuckle from it, or so he believed. Keith had much fun playing an old recording of WE'RE IN THE MONEY over and over for the actors and crew.

That night Keith tried to call Jim but was unable to reach him. He left an urgent message on Jim's machine, then helped Jessica get ready for a bath and bed. "I hope you're right, that there's no reason for Jim to investigate."

"We can't do anything about it tonight anyhow. By the way, did you see Marge today? It was like she was a different person, really helpful and nice to me."

"How's Sy?"

"He'll live, but we won't see him for awhile."

"Did Marge know what happened to you Saturday night?"

"Marge, Angela and I talked about it and what I should do now. Guess what they advised?"

"Checking yourself into Betty Ford for the cure?"

"No, they told me to hold onto you with all my strength and never let go no matter what happened."

Keith was surprised at this bit of womanly advice, but not unhappy. "And what about my feelings on the subject?"

"Oh, they assumed I could take care of that."

Keith laughed and eased the rest of Jessica's clothes off. He thought of his conversation with Dawn last weekend and the joys of simple, un-encumbered relationships. Once again, he didn't know if Jessica was teasing him about their future or if she was serious.

"I had a good dinner with David, Dawn and Spunky Saturday night while you were smashing your car. Spunky's a whole lot smarter and much more fun than I realized."

"At least she has a working body."

"It's much more than that. She enjoys life, taking it as it comes, without lots of problems and worries. She and David make a good pair."

"They're both luckier than we are. Maybe you should find yourself a simple girl, someone who only sees the present and who'd squirm in bed with you."

"Maybe, but then that wouldn't be very exciting would it?"

಄಄಄಄

Tuesday found them in the Operating Room again, but for completely different work. In these scenes the doctors are about to cut Spunky apart, but at the last moment she is saved as Poins and John rush into the room wearing Scuba breathing gear. The kids cut the doctors' air hoses, causing mayhem, and rescue Spunky. At one point a Hosedoctor jumps through the control room window, smashing it to bits. For this shot, the window was replaced with one made from clear sugar syrup. This would break with soft rounded edges, so that the pieces wouldn't cut the actor. They only had one fake window, so George covered the break carefully with two cameras.

Keith focused on the complex problems the scene presented for sound recording. Angela wanted to make up time and pushed everyone along. She knew that she must finish the film this week, and the budget was already stretched to the limit. As they rehearsed, Keith and David realized that the scene didn't work, and together struggled to rewrite, then get it moving again. Before they knew it, lunch was called and an exhausted Keith sat down beside Jessica and Angela.

"Jessica, what did that doc have to say, the one you were talking with at the screening? Did he like the cut?" Angela asked.

"Oh, he liked it, but he was talking mostly about surgery and transplants. He said that we had no idea how close our film was to the truth."

"Really, he must have been putting you on," Keith commented.

"No, I don't think so. He said docs are already switching parts around among people, and that soon everything will be transplantable. He's done a lot of experimental stuff with people who are dying in hopeless situations."

Keith was tightly-stretched emotionally, and as Jessica said this he thought of Kristin and how badly she had needed new parts for her damaged body and almost started to cry for her. But his thoughts were interrupted by the clock, it was time to go back to work, and George was calling to him from across the stage.

George had placed a first-surface mirror on an operating table (a delicate mirror with silver on the front side so that it will make perfect reflections: the thick glass was optically-flat and two feet square). The mirror was in the spot where Spunky's head would have been. George had raised his camera up high, then tilted it down, pointed into the mirror. George's view was now exactly the same as Spunky's, looking up at the doctors who were about to operate. "Keith, come up here and look through the viewfinder. See if this is scary enough for you."

The hosedocs gathered around the operating table with their knives and saws and prepared to operate. The view through the camera lens looked up into the hose-faces of the docs, their bloody tools, and the operating light above them, all just as Spunky would have seen it lying on the table if her eyes were open. Even though Keith had written the scene and described this exact shot, when he looked through the lens, his body tensed with fear at the sight. He thought of Kristin and her view of the doctors about to operate. Maybe she had been given a local anesthetic and had seen almost this same scene through her eyes. His body started to sway, his vision clouded with tears, and his breath became shallow and rapid, then he collapsed. Fortunately the Key Grip was right behind Keith, and he easily caught Keith's fall in his powerful arms.

When Keith awoke, he was in his own bed and it was night. Jessica was sleeping beside him. When he moved slightly she woke.

"What happened, what am I doing here?"

"Take it easy. Everything's under control. You've just been working too hard."

"There's nothing wrong with me, I feel fine."

"Then why did you collapse on the stage today and sleep eight hours straight?"

"Damn, people must have thought I've gone nuts."

"They're all your friends, don't worry."

"What did they do?"

"They wanted to call an ambulance, but I stopped it and made them put you on a cot so you could sleep for awhile. Then at the end of the day we brought you home."

Keith felt his sleeve, "What happened to my clothes? Did you take them off?"

"David and Spunky put you to bed, then she helped me. I'd much rather feel your hands on my body than hers."

"I'm so embarrassed. What about this afternoon, who did the sound?"

"Ronny David came in, and he'll finish the film for you. Angela said that from now on, you're just the Writer, so relax for a few days, you've earned it and we're almost done."

"Why didn't you let an ambulance take me to the hospital: maybe there's something wrong with my brain or blood pressure or something?"

"I don't want doctors messing with your body. They might try to get even for Jim's harassment or something. Just a hunch."

"And how are you doing? Sorry I wasn't able to help you get ready for bed tonight."

"I'm getting better. How about a glass of wine before we go back to sleep?"

"Should I, I mean, what if I faint again?"

"I won't let you, so don't even think about it."

"Why not?"

"Because I promised to drink only with you, and an unconscious body can't handle much. If you start to faint I'll tickle your feet to keep you awake."

❧❧❧❧

On Wednesday morning, when Keith returned to the stage, Angela pointed to a chair labeled WRITER. "Glad you're OK. Now sit down and get to work. We've got a lot to cover in our last three days."

Keith dumped his notes on the chair and sought out Ronny, the replacement Sound Mixer, who also happened to be a good friend. Ronny had already read the day's script and was preparing for work. They laughed about the story and how crazy it must have been doing both the sound and the rewrites on such a complex and impoverished production. Keith felt reluctant to give up the sound work but also felt relief that he could now focus all his energies on the script. He knew that Ronny was at least as good as he was, and perhaps better, so there would be no problems with the sound track.

Keith found a cup of coffee then sat down in his folding wooden chair to review the remaining work. He wanted to be sure that the most important scenes, from a story viewpoint, would be covered no matter what happened. First, they needed to finish the Operating Room scenes, where the kids attack the doctors, cutting their hoses and dumping some of them down the chutes to the fertilizer plant. Then he wanted very much to do the scene where Poins hooks two computers together so that they analyze each other, causing both to explode in a shower of money. Keith remembered a scene from the film BRAZIL, where the hero hooks two office mail chutes together, causing the whole city to explode in a shower of bureaucratic paperwork. He hoped people would recognize this as a small version of that scene. After these were out of the way they needed to show Savage and his cohorts fighting the kids in the trashed Operating Room, then the arrival of Orson and his tank-carrying auditors, which allows the kids to escape in the confusion. They had yet to film the various hallway scenes, where kids run one way, the oldies another, followed by Orson. They had two hallway sets, painted different colors, and would hang different pictures on the walls to make it appear that they had many different locations for the chase-on-foot. And he couldn't wait to do the scene where Poins steals a suction machine, then hits the reverse switch and sprays the old people with all manner of pills, coins, medical gear, and clothing.

As Keith worked, he noticed the normal end-of-the-film nervousness among the crew. Everyone had worked hard and a outsider might be tempted to think that the crew would be glad that the project and the long hours of work were drawing to a close. However, Keith knew that the freelance world was exactly like a dating game, with hours of waiting for the right person to call, to offer the next job. Even the best people were unemployed a third of the year, while the worst only dreamed of working again. As the shoot neared completion, the tension of "where are you working next" built. There were clusters of workers who hoped to be hired together as a package. For example, when George received a new assignment, he would ask for his favorite Assistant, his favorite Gaffer, his favorite Grip, and each of these would want his team of friends. When one of these people received an outside offer of work, there was always the question, "If I accept this will I miss a chance to work with George again?" This was a constant problem for all crew people in a freelance world. Potential assignments varied from one-day TV commercials to year-long productions in foreign locations. Once a person said "yes", there was no backing out if a better job were offered if you valued your reputation. There were no written crew contracts except for the most expensive workers (for example, Director, Writer, and perhaps Director of Photography), so a person's word was binding, especially among the small number of people who did most of the hiring.

As Keith pondered this aspect of the film world, he recalled Max's comments about Real Estate and the advantage of having an outside income to allow creative work. Keith realized how valuable such an income would be to carry a person over the lean patches in film work as well. He resolved to talk with Max more often and to gain something of his wisdom.

As different crew people chatted with Keith and asked how the editing was coming, Keith realized for the first time that he had a new and uncommonly serious responsibility to his fellow workers. His efforts as the Writer were more than just a job to them. His work would either make or break the film. The reputations of everyone would be either boosted or blotched depending on its fate. Being associated with a big hit never hurt when looking for work. Each person had given his all for the project, and there was not one on the set who didn't know that this was an unusual movie. There were no bankable actors, not much budget, and both the Writer and Director were unknowns. On top of this, there had been occasional pickets and protests. What would each person say when the "What have you worked on lately?" question arose in a hiring conversation.

Angela's lawyers had visited the set on Monday, and Keith saw them walk onto the stage early on Thursday morning as they were starting to work the hallway chase scenes. POBOB had obtained an injunction from a different judge and was demanding that they stop production immediately.

"Can't you just stall them for two days, we're almost done." Angela pleaded.

"You were supposed to stop Monday, but we maneuvered the paperwork for a few days' delay."

"What happens if we keep working anyway?"

"You or somebody will be in contempt of court, but what that would mean isn't clear, since we've already filed an appeal."

Keith had a brainstorm, "Angela, let's stop shooting for an hour and grab some insurance. We can record all the dialog for the rest of the film, then if we get stopped, we can splice something together to cover the remaining scenes. Maybe George can run up and down the halls with a hand-held camera while we do the recording over in a corner, and we can pretend George is the actual people running. Maybe he can chase some of the people in the halls so they don't have to lip sync."

"That'll look a bit weird, but it's better than nothing and we can hit it quickly."

"You'd better do it Angela, we don't know when the Marshals will be here with the stop-order, but it could be any moment."

"The Guards won't let them enter the stage when the

red lights are on, so as soon as you leave, we'll switch them on permanently for the next two days," Keith added.

Angela pushed the crew hard for the rest of the day, thinking that any moment might be their last shot. When evening came, she served catered food and kept them working for three hours of overtime, in the belief that Government employees would never dream of bothering them at night.

By the time that the Marshals arrived with their paperwork on Friday, the crew was shooting close-ups of details on the computers and other bits and pieces which were nice, but not essential to telling the story. The crew dutifully stopped work, then relaxed and cleaned and packed their gear. Angela had arranged to have a first-class good-bye lunch served on the stage, then dismissed the crew giving everyone the afternoon off with pay.

Keith didn't look at the stack of paper that the enemy had brought, but Angela did then slowly walked over to Keith and David, "Do you two realize what these clowns are trying to do? They want to impound all our footage, lock it up until it can be studied!"

Keith and David almost went into shock.

౿ఎ౿ఎ౿ఎ

After a long Saturday with the film lawyers, Keith and Jessica held a wrap party at Keith's house to celebrate the end of shooting. Keith and Jessica cooked piles of spaghetti and garlic bread, and Angela, George, Dawn, Stubby, Jim, David, Spunky, and many others brought more food and drink. The lawyers' fancy champagne was popped while everyone drank a bit too much, glad that the production was in the can. Everyone had done his or her best and there was a general sense of relief. Many problems lay ahead, both for the film and for each of the people present, but tonight was a time to relax and enjoy the transition to new responsibilities.

Although Keith and Jessica shared many problems, this was a chance to loose themselves in the concerns of other people, to share their successes, worries, and adventures. George and many of his crew people were about to travel to Cuba, via Mexico City, under semi-legal arrangements, to make a period film about the Spanish-American war. Angela was already on the payroll of her next film, a formula action-adventure with bankable stars: her body seemed fully recovered from its operations. Jim was still agitated about Kristin's hospital care, but had just realized that Keith had a much more serious problem: his distribution deal for the film was a disaster: this film, no matter how good it was, might never hit the screen, and hoped-for monies that would provide a little income for David and Keith might already be gone (along with fees due to Jim.) Jim told Keith and David to enjoy the party tonight because it was the last fun they were going to have for a long time: they were to meet him in Bernie's office at nine the next morning.

The party went well, with music, drinks, talking, dancing, and food, late into the night. Around eleven Jessica wondered what had become of Keith and wandered around the house. Out in the back yard, in a little shaded summer house, she found Keith and Dawn making-out, thoroughly enjoying each other's partially-dressed bodies. Instead of walking away, Jessica couldn't help herself, and said to the surprised couple, "How much do you charge per night Dawn? My credit card's fully-loaded, and I'd like to buy Keith some time in your bed?" Before they could say anything, Jessica ran off into the dark, into her room, into her closet, where she curled up on the floor and cried herself to sleep among Kristin's clothes.

Chapter 10

Post-Production

Keith had never paid attention to the distribution side of the film business and now was very worried: what arrangements had SCAM-F made for bringing their package of five films to theaters? He knew that Sy and his associates were not well-informed and began to fear that his film would never be seen by a paying audience, no matter how good it was. Keith and David met Jim at Bernie's office Sunday morning to examine their distribution contract carefully.

Jim turned the pages quickly, heading for the signatures. "Who signed this thing anyway?"

He reached the final page and saw Keith's signature among the others. "My God Keith, why didn't you let me see this before you signed it?"

"What's wrong?"

"Everything, but the main thing is that these guys have dozens of ways to back away from your film and you have no way to get rid of them and look for a better deal. You're screwed!"

Bernie interjected, "Hey, Keith and David were, and still are, completely unknown. Who else would give them a distribution deal on any terms? At least this is signed paper."

"So when have you scheduled the screening? When does the distributor see your film?"

"We won't be finished cutting for months."

"Bullshit, this contract says you must screen it for

these guys within thirty days of the end of production or loose all your rights. You have exactly four weeks left."

"Bernie, why didn't you tell us, we won't have the music or any of the sound mixed by then. It'll be dreadful."

"Keith, don't you dare talk to these guys unless I'm right beside you. And don't sign another contract whatever you do," Jim implored as he went back to reading the fine print.

David and Keith prepared to work day and night with the editor for the next month.

The version of SENIORS that would be shown in theaters would run just under two hours. Theater owners had found that films of this length maximized revenue, in terms of bringing in as many viewers as possible during prime hours, and this length also maximized the sales of over-priced junk food (the profit from which went directly into the theater owners' pockets). The ideal length, one hour and fifty one minutes, (111 minutes) of film, at ninety feet per minute, meant that the final film would be exactly 10,000 feet in length, ten reels, long. In spite of their efforts at economy, Keith and David had shot over sixty thousand feet of film, which was now in need of editing down into the best possible cut. Two-thirds of this total had been printed, so the editor was working with forty thousand feet of print, shrinking it to size. A long task.

Sunday night an exhausted Keith returned home in time for dinner. He hadn't seen Jessica since last night and was worried about her and ashamed of last night with Dawn. He found Jessica painting an abstract view of Houdini, two full glasses of wine beside her chair. He handed a glass to Jessica, "I'm sorry about last night, and Dawn. I'm such a jerk some times."

Jessica smiled and drank, "We make quite a pair. What did she say about my offer? How much will she charge to screw you?"

"I don't know, but I'll be in the editing rooms every night for the next month, we're in deep trouble."

"That's too bad, I was sort of waiting to hear about you and Dawn's body, to maybe enjoy it vicariously."

"I know you're teasing, and the pain you're really feeling deep inside, so let's drop it for now."

"Thanks, any good news?"

"Actually I do have a bit. Jessica, I had an idea while looking at all the piles of film today, an idea about you and your future."

"What sort of idea? Want me to try to imagine the film all put together for you?"

"No, a practical idea. When we see a movie today, every piece of it, every frame on the screen, came from a camera. Most of the cameras were on stages and locations, and some were in labs, aimed at models or animation cels, but they were all cameras. I saw a piece of film last week that came from inside a computer. It was never in a camera. A guy wrote some software and made sketches on an electronic pad, and the film came out the other end of the machine."

"So a geek did it all alone, with no crew, no Angela, no Keith and no Jessica?"

"Well, of course there was some technical help, but what I'm getting at is that you're a phenomenal artist. You can draw imaginary people in the most unusual settings, and I'll bet that with a bit of computer training, you could draw the key pieces of a film into a computer."

"That's just animation, Disney and his friends have done that forever."

"No, what I'm getting at is drawing life-like creatures inside a computer, then pulling in real backgrounds interacting with human actors, doing the whole thing digitally instead of with hundreds of crew people.

"Is that possible? I've never seen anything like that."

"Almost, but maybe just in TV sci-fi now. The quality's not good enough for the big screen, but things are moving fast. You've got the creativity and skill and the tools are getting better all the time."

"They'll always need writers to create stories, even if people like me and the nerds bring them to life. Maybe we can get a package deal and make films while sitting home with computer screens and keyboards."

"That's not so far-fetched. I could help you with the technical stuff if you want to learn."

"I'd like to meet someone who is actually doing it, and see the film you saw. I love drawing and it would be a way to keep working beside you."

☙☙☙

Scarcely a week after the cameras had stopped rolling, Keith received a check from Jim for the sale of the car which had killed Kristin. Jim had deducted twenty percent of the money as his fee, which Keith thought excessive when he learned that Jim had obtained the car by filing the correct paperwork in the right places: one mornings' work for Jim and his Legal Aide.

Jessica and Keith met Max and Francine for dinner as soon as the check arrived. Keith wanted to learn something about investments and wondered what he could do to smarten-up.

Max began, "Keith, the first thing I can tell you is to drop any idea of going to school to learn our business. You're an Engineer, so you know as much math and logic as you'll ever need. I'll give you a list of five or ten books to read, but after absorbing them you need to learn by doing."

Then Francine added, "Yes, you must go up and visit Mabel and walk the neighborhood with her. She'll give you a concentrated introduction to the area where you want to buy Kristin's house. There're only about twenty-five houses on that street, so you can learn all about each one, then narrow your search."

"Francine's exactly right, the secret is focusing your effort onto a location where you are really interested in making a purchase, then learning all you can about the possibilities."

"Max knows the details of every property on Wilshire, from Santa Monica all the way down to Western Avenue. He can tell you who built it, who owns it now, and all the good, bad and hidden details."

"Do you think Jessica and I could drive up and visit her next weekend? We could give Jessica's rebuilt car a shake-down cruise."

After a long weekend in The City with Mabel, Keith and Jessica were saturated with advice and ready to return. Keith had been right about the high prices, but Mabel was confident that she could find something among the houses that directly faced the Marina Green. While walking the area they had not seen one FOR SALE sign, but they had visited a friend of Mabel's who owned one of the houses and the view from inside her house was perfect. Keith was now certain that he would be doing the right thing with Kristin's money.

ℰℐℰℐℰℐ

The date for the legal screening approached quickly as days and nights of work blurred together. Keith slept little, his head full of the details and problems of various scenes and bits of footage that they were patching together to tell the story. Often he went to bed at midnight, his mind still churning.

Today they had been assembling and re-assembling the operating room scenes, trying to ensure that they were funny rather than grim.

His sleep was interrupted by a frightening dream. Keith struggled to escape from the hose-doctors. The doctors were hitting him, scratching, holding his arms, his legs would hardly move. They swatted him with their hoses, starting their bloody power saws. He began to awaken, but the struggle continued. His mind was blurred, confused by the doctors, then he realized that he was home, and that Jessica was screaming, kicking, hitting, scratching him with all her strength. He grabbed her arms in the dark shadows, "Jessica stop it, wake up!", then pushed her away and rolled off the bed onto the floor to escape. In the bathroom he switched on the lights and looked in the mirror at his bloody face and arms. His mind was still not completely functional and he wondered if he had attacked Jessica, thinking she was a hose-doc, or if she had attacked him.

He could see Jessica approaching in the mirror and automatically assumed a defensive position, mentally, not knowing if the struggle would continue. Then he saw that she was awake and as bewildered as he was. "Did I hurt you? I think I dreamed you were a doctor, about to cut me up."

"Oh Keith, his spirit was so mad, it knew, it tried to kill me before it died. Longhair is dead, my goons just nailed him somewhere dark and cold."

სასასა

By seven the next morning Keith was in the editing rooms bringing coffee and fried-egg sandwiches for everyone. He glanced at the familiar poster on the wall which said that an Editor "*. . . is someone who takes out-of-focus, badly-framed,* *and poorly shot footage of people mumbling, bumping into furniture, and forgetting what to say, and turns that footage into a compelling story with lasting value for which the Director will take all the credit.*" (Goodman & McGrath)

The editor was far more than a technician who could quickly splice and scan film. He, or she, was an artist would do his best to make a great movie from the pieces of film scattered about his rooms. The screenplay that Keith had written was only a shorthand outline of the final film. Keith had indicated the contents of the scenes and what the actors were supposed to say and do in each.

David had then taken this outline and used his own skills to control the actors' expressions, the way they smiled or frowned, the way they walked, the way they interpreted Keith's writing. David had also decided how to cover each scene. Normally each scene was shot first from a distance, so that all the action could be seen in one continuous shot. Sometimes the camera would move during this wide shot, and in others it would be steady, watching from a fixed position. Then David would select pieces of the scene to cover from closer positions. Perhaps two actors were talking with each other at some point. A two-shot would show both of them in conversation. If the conversation were important, each actor would get a close-up of his or her dialog and reactions to the other actor, perhaps viewed over the shoulder of the other person. David would select the most dramatic viewpoint for each shot.

George had taken the scene that David directed and selected the exact camera position and lens to use as well as the appropriate lighting for the mood of the scene. An excellent Director of Photography could convert a terrible story into a beautiful painting. The story would still be terrible, but some audiences would come just to see his photography. (The converse was also sometimes true: a wonderful and unusual story could survive almost any technical flaws if it struck a strong emotional chord in audiences.)

Since the film had been shot in the sequence that minimized cost, the editor's first task was to arrange all the pieces in the correct order, and group the shots that belonged to each scene. Then he would put the scenes together one at a time, an artistic, not a mechanical, process. For example, the logical thing to do might be to open a scene with a wide establishing shot so that the audience would immediately understand where the scene was taking place, and who was involved. However, the editor might open instead with a close-up of someone removing a pistol from a pocket. Now the audience was curious: whose pocket? What next? Then if the editor cut to a wide establishing shot involving many people, the audience would be intensely wondering who was going to shoot whom. So, just by arranging the pieces of the scene into a different sequence, the editor could build excitement into the film. As Keith carefully watched his scenes being re-arranged he learned much that he could put into the writing of his next film.

The editor had a wide range of choices in placing the individual splices, and in controlling their effect. In fast-paced action, he could cut quickly from piece of film to the next, but in slower sections he might dissolve one piece of film into the next to make a gentle transition. He could cut in sync with sound effects or dialog and he could also synchronize the cuts in the film with the beat of the music if appropriate, to blend the acoustic and visual experience. Often the editor cut into the next scene's dialog before the current scene's picture was over. Just a slight advance so the viewer would hear the next scene starting before the current scene ended: the technique made the film move faster and appear to be more exciting.

The editor had only one immutable mechanical

constraint: he needed to end each one thousand foot (eleven minute) roll of film with a fade to black, and begin the next roll with a fade in from black. Most movie theaters had a pair of 35mm arc projectors (the old ones had twelve minute carbons which were reloaded for each reel). As the film on one projector ran out, the operator closed a shutter in front of it and opened the shutter in front of the other projector. With skill, as one picture faded to black, the picture from the other projector faded in, starting the next thousand foot roll. The trick was timing this just right. The finished film would have several circles in the upper right hand corner of the print near the end. These were timing marks to tell the projectionist to start the motor on the second projector, and then to changeover to the second projector. Most audiences never notice these odd circles, but they have been in use since the days of silent films.

In some cases, the Director's skill and prestige were such that he almost did the editing himself, with the editor serving as an assistant, to make splices and work to the Director's command. At the other extreme were Directors who were paid only to direct, and who left the project the moment the cameras and money stopped rolling. In the case of SENIORS, David was intensely interested in the editorial work, but was wise enough to know his limitations. He and Keith sat with the editor watching a very skillful person create, offering advice and comments only when appropriate. Keith marveled at how the skills of David, George and the editor breathed life into his simple script.

Keith had seen old editing equipment from the twenties and realized how similar it was to that being used today. Then as now, the prime tool was a Moviola. This machine allowed 35mm film to be viewed at any speed, by pressing a foot pedal. Film could be quickly snapped into the gate and removed for a splice, or to allow another piece to be viewed. The key advantage was that short pieces of film could be swapped in and out quickly, then when the right piece was found it could be spliced into the work print in seconds and the effect viewed. Most Moviolas had two sets of reels, so that sound could be run on the left side, in sync with film on the right side. Short pieces of film weren't on reels, they were loose, hanging on long rows of hooks. The Moviola had a large laundry basket on the back to catch pieces of film of any length that were run through its viewer.

The pieces of film being edited were cut from the dailies that had been printed during production. These pieces, with many rough splices and grease-pencil marks, formed the edited picture. Once the final cut was done, the edited print would be sent to the lab where a Negative Cutter would carefully, while wearing clean white gloves, assemble the correct pieces of original camera negative into rolls that could be printed. (camera negative has unique edge numbers printed on it during manufacture, so the Negative Cutter matches the numbers on the negative to the numbers on the print to conform the negative to the edited film) While the editor had made quick splices with 35mm clear perforated tape, the Negative Cutter made his splices slowly using a hot-splice technique. His splices were strong, permanent, and tiny, fitting between individual frames of film. In this final stage, dissolves, color corrections, and other photographic changes would be made from the original negative. For these reasons the film that the editor was handling, cutting and splicing, could be treated roughly without harm. Its purpose was to guide the Negative Cutter in making the final assembly: an audience would never see it. Unfortunately for this project, the rough cut, filled with crude tape splices and grease pencil marks, would be projected to the first audience. There was no time to conform the negative or color-balance the scenes, let alone to do the optical effects.

Cutting would continue almost until the lights dimmed in the theater.

The sound reels that the editor was handling would be mixed into the final sound track. The sound that Keith had recorded onto one-quarter-inch tape had been copied to 35mm clear film which was coated with magnetic material. This made the sound track fully-compatible with the picture. Both were the same length, both the same width, and they could both be cut and spliced with the same tools and tape. The editor had to be careful to use de-magnetized tools when handling the sound so that pops and gaps were not inadvertently introduced.

Extra bits of sound sometimes came from a Foley stage. This was a recording studio with a screen where the film could be shown. Experts would watch the film while making sound effects which matched the action. Sometimes they would walk in gravel, in sync with an actor walking in gravel on the screen, and other times they would make strange cutting noises or whatever else the film called for while watching it on the screen.

An odd branch of sound recording was creating laugh tracks for TV shows. These tracks mimicked audience laughter. A special machine, a laugh box, was used to make the laughter. It contained perhaps a dozen loops of tape running continuously, with a fader for each. Each loop held a different kind of laughter. An expert would sit with the box, watching the TV show. Whenever the Director pointed, the expert would fade up one or several kinds of laughter, using his judgment to select something appropriate. This was an old art, used in radio for decades, to add life to dry studio recordings. It was so phony that Keith could never listen to a TV or radio comedy without mentally seeing a technician fading laugh tracks in and out, no matter how inane the program material.

Today's task was putting together the chase scene in

the desert. They opened with actors inside the limo yelling that they had just spotted the truck, then they cut to a view through the hole in the windshield of the truck ahead, then to the view through Admiral's periscope of the motorcycle alongside the limo, and so it continued. The fact that they never showed an establishing shot of the whole chase would not be noticed by the audience. Filming the three-vehicle chasing shot had turned out to be too complex, so Angela had dropped it. This was an easy sequence to edit, as they had more good footage than needed to tell the story. However, they had to be careful to cut quickly among the scenes to maintain excitement and tension: holding a shot too long was death in a fast-moving chase. They wanted people in the audience on the edge of their seats, eagerly waiting to see what would happen when the clones shoved the barrel of glop to the rear of the truck and dumped it onto the approaching limo.

ຕາຕາຕາ

On the last day legally permitted they prepared to screen the film to fulfill the distribution contract. Keith would have liked to have rented the posh private screening room at The Beverly Hills Hotel for this event, but they were only able to book time on a mixing stage at Ryder Sound on such short notice. Here the facilities were technically-excellent as far as projection and sound were concerned, but the bare wood floor and informal assortment of comfortable old chairs was not impressive. This was a work environment, not a salesroom. Keith and David had invited Angela, Bernie, Jim, Sy's trio with their girls, and the distributors.

Yesterday the young agent who had found a good film for Senator Savage had called Keith to chat. He was curious about SENIORS since he had seen a piece of it earlier, and was interested in talking with Keith and David about their future plans. Keith explained their frantic rush to complete the edit, and invited the agent to the screening, telling him the story of their dreadful distribution contract and how un-ready they were for a proper presentation. After Keith hung up, he realized that perhaps he had just made a mistake. The agent could be an important future contact and showing him a mess was not the best way to impress him. However, Keith had been comforted by the agent's laughter when he explained the contract. He said that even worse contracts had been signed, and by experienced people who should have known much better.

On the last night they had worked straight-through, adjusting scenes, finding alternate coverage, and doing everything in their power to make the best possible picture. This morning they went onto the mixing stage to do a rough mix of the sound track. Normally this process takes a week or more, as each reel is projected over and over while portions of its sound track are blended together. Music, sound effects, original dialog, and replacement dialog are carefully blended while watching the film on-screen. In a single day, Keith and the sound mixers could only make a rough pass of the whole film, considering that it took two hours just to run it from end to end once. They didn't even have most of the sound effects recorded and the music hadn't been written. However, the sound that they did have was now a workable track, and the absence of tense violins and other music cues gave the picture an unusual acoustic quality. In some ways it was like a film from the early days of talkies, before elaborate music and theater-shaking loud noises became part of most tracks.

Tonight a very nervous Keith, Jessica, David and Spunky put on their best smiles and proper clothes and arrived early to greet their first audience. Fortunately extra chairs had been brought to the stage because uninvited guests appeared. Angela brought Harry, George, and a car-full of friends to act as cheer-leaders, the agent brought two young associates who were in training, and Sy very reluctantly arrived with three doctors from New York who wanted to see what their million dollars had bought.

Jessica elbowed Keith, "Hey, look over there, the rich doc brought your friend, his pretty daughter Carrie."

"She was just curious to see a bit of the film business, she's not someone special, at least to me."

"Well, she's attractive and smart, isn't she?"

"So are you. Let's concentrate on the show."

Keith realized that he was not nearly as nervous as were the financial advisors, Sy, Herb, and Mike, as he was introduced to the doctors.

Carrie smiled at Keith and Jessica, "Great to meet you again, I can't wait to see your film."

Keith answered, "It's just a rough cut, but we have to show it now because of our distribution contract. The sound track's a mess."

"Whatever you've done, I'm sure it's better than the crap the four other projects produced."

Keith was interested: he had almost forgotten about the other four in Bernie's package. "What happened to them?"

"The guys making the porno were arrested in Mexico, the love story jerks ran out of money half way through, and the other two missed their contract dates: you're the only one in the running."

Jessica squeezed Keith's hand and turned to Carrie, "Too bad we didn't have a bit of their money. We could have put it on the screen for your dad and his friends."

Keith and Jim were especially interested in meeting the distributors and learning their plans for the film. When only one person from their group arrived, Keith became worried. It looked like this guy was here just to see if Keith and David were meeting contract obligations and had no interest in the film's aesthetics. Jim quickly ascertained that he was a lawyer who represented the distributors.

David gave a short introductory speech, explaining that they were about to see a very preliminary version of the film, and that it would be covered with grease pencil marks, and would be running without music or most sound effects. People in the business saw this kind of thing often, but David realized that the key people in the audience might have no idea of just how rough this cut would be. At least their room had two projectors so that the film could be run continuously from end to end, unless one of the thousands of splices came loose. The editor was in the projection booth in case that happened.

As the lights went down, Jessica whispered in Keith's ear, "This is a strange group of people. I feel all sorts of good and bad thoughts floating around, but can't make sense out of them."

"Will they like the film?"

"Oh yes, they'll all love it, but there's lots of other stuff going on. We're in for an interesting evening, at least I am sure of that."

After the film, Angela and her team stood up and started a big round of applause and nearly everyone joined in, then friends stood in groups discussing what they had just seen.

The agent came up to Keith and David with a big smile. "It's amazing, and to think you two did that with only a million. Most film-makers couldn't do as well with ten."

"Glad you liked it. Now we need to bring it to the public."

"Don't worry, it's good, very good, so somebody will

distribute it and make a pile of dough."

Harry walked up to the group and talked to Keith, "I loved the sound track as is, without music crapping it up. How many screen credits do you have as a Production Sound Mixer?"

Keith hadn't expected the comment or the question. "Four, counting this one, why do you ask Harry?"

"Four's enough. I'll put you up for membership in the Sound branch of The Academy. They need some new blood with fresh ideas and you could help."

Keith had never considered joining The Academy Of Motion Picture Arts And Sciences. Membership was by invitation only, and consisted mostly of important people who had been in the business forever. These were the people who voted on the Academy Awards, and as a member, he would be one of the small number of people who selected the film with the best sound track for an Oscar each year. Keith vaguely remembered that Harry was a founding cinematographer member, so this was a genuine and most unexpected prize.

"Harry, I don't know what to say, what an honor, thank you very much."

"Go for it Keith, it'll boost your chances as a Writer too, and a recommendation from Harry Smithson is as good as it gets," the agent said with a big smile toward Keith and Harry. Keith knew that the agent was genuinely happy because it would improve Keith's marketability, a thought always uppermost in an agent's mind.

Jessica smiled at Keith, the evening was indeed turning out to be fascinating.

"I want to meet you and David for lunch in a few days, to talk about representation and what we might do for each other. Interested?"

"Of course, and I'm sure David will come too."

Jim nudged Keith and pointed to the other side of the room where an argument among the doctors, the financiers, and the lawyer from the distributors was escalating. Jim, Keith, and Jessica walked over to join them.

"Dammit, I don't care what you and your sleazy associates are proposing, this film's NOT going to be shown to the public," one of the doctors was shouting at the distributor's lawyer.

Keith was shocked. "What do you mean, not shown, it's a great film."

"That's the problem. If you show this, tons of people will come to see it," a doctor answered.

"And before you know it we'll have the public and those jerks in Congress making laws to regulate transplants, foreign research, and all sorts of things," another doctor added.

"But this is just entertainment, it's not true, there's no senior city medical complex, no magic purple gas," Keith pleaded.

"We don't use gas, and most of our experimental work is done in Asia and Africa, not in Arizona, but you've come damn close to the truth, to the future of medicine, and we don't want interference and controls."

"We're almost able to fix all sorts of people who need transplanted parts. But your film and the furor it will engender will set our research back decades," the third doctor added.

Carrie interjected, "But you paid to have this film made, you won't get your money back unless audiences see it."

Her father replied, "That was only money. We're talking about people's lives, the future of medicine."

"There is a way you can stop the film if you want," Jim interjected, as Keith looked on in shock.

"And how's that?" asked the distributor's lawyer.

"I studied the contract carefully, and there's a weird

231

footnote in the fine print on page seven saying that the backers of the film can work on the final cut for up to twenty-five years, provided they pay certain fees to compensate the distributor for delayed revenues. This clause must have been stuck in by the distributor as a way to grab some extra dough if the screening was late."

"Jim, stop it, you're supposed to be on my side," Keith screamed.

"What are the fees? How much cash would it take," the first doctor asked as Jim and Keith glared at each other.

Jim smiled at Keith, "Just be quiet and listen, this is in your interest too." Then he turned to the doctor, "You'd have to cover all the residual production costs, like the re-write fees, deferred salaries, and some other things, and pay the distributor interest on the delayed distribution revenue, but probably a million or two would handle everything."

"We can raise that easily. What happens after twenty-five years?"

"If the film hasn't been distributed, the original royalty owners and those who are entitled to a percentage of the gross, own the negative and can do whatever they want with it."

"Who are these owners?"

"Keith and David are the only ones named in the contract: each has two percent of the gross. The other ninety-six percent is yours. By then medical technology will have moved on, so you could show it without trouble, and maybe collect a big profit."

Keith realized that he would receive almost six hundred thousand dollars if he were compensated for each of his five hundred and twenty one carefully-documented re-write pages as well as his Writer's salary, and David would immediately receive his Director's fees. But this was nothing compared to seeing audiences enjoying his film, laughing and crying, and sharing his thoughts. How could money substitute for the excitement of experiencing your work with an audience? As the conversation progressed into arguments and details, Keith could see that although this was not the reward he had sought, it was perhaps better than what the sleazy distribution lawyer had hoped to negotiate when he had arrived tonight.

Then Keith thought of the POBOB protesters and the gay actor's threat of pickets, and realized that even if they were allowed to screen the film now that the docs were right: this film could cause a lot of trouble.

৩৶৩৶৩৶

Eventually Keith overcame his disappointment. No opening night parties, no sneak previews, no conferences with the music composer, no final sound mix, and no more editing. He did manage to have two sixteen millimeter reversal prints made of the rough-cut before it was locked-away. Someday he could show these to his children, if he ever had any.

A week later, Mabel called with the news that one of the Marina houses, a mock-Tudor with a big lot and a backyard, would be available soon. Keith remembered the house, Jessica's thoughts on how lovely it looked, and Max's comments about decisive action. He told Mabel to buy it, even though he had seen only the front side and had no idea of the interior or its possibilities.

Seniors Have It Tough

Chapter 11

Christmas

On Christmas Eve in Westwood, Keith went for a long solitary walk in the rain, thinking over the past year, very much aware that he might possibly be retracing Kristin's final steps around their neighborhood as his wet feet squished in the cold under the glow of the little streetlights from the twenties. He went as far as Holmby Park, then started to return on Wyton and Loring. At the beginning of his film, Keith had thought that this was his 'big break'. The film would be so great that it would shake the world, but he now realized that he had made just another flick, no big deal on the global stage: more canned entertainment for the masses, if they ever saw it. As he looked at the Christmas decorations in the houses, he saw that there were more important things in life and in his future. Instinctively he realized that he wanted to break free, to play with children and pets, to put his life in order, to close out the year by tying up important loose ends.

He turned and headed quickly home on Warner as the rain tickled his face and ran from his umbrella. As he came down their sidewalk in the glistening rainy light, he paused as he saw Jessica through the living room window, sitting by the fire, reading in the soft light from their little Christmas tree. He gazed at her profile a long time, wondering if she was central to his future, or just a visitor passing through. The flickering firelight blended with the multi-colored red-blue-green-yellow glow from the tree as it illuminated her through the dripping window. It was a perfect and most beautiful image, but perhaps a picture of something unobtainable.

He walked through the front door and went to Jessica. He noticed that she was wearing a blouse and skirt which Kristin had often worn: he smelled Kristin's perfume. She also wore the scarf with his wedding ring that she had worn many weeks ago at Angela's. Even her shoes were a pair from Kristin's closet.

"Jessica, do you need twelve people for a séance, or could just the two of us try to contact someone and visit the spirit world?"

She turned to him and smiled warmly, "We can do it, the number of people doesn't matter, it's the sensitivity and the desire that are important."

"I want to talk with Kristin. I want to ask her what to do with the rest of my life. I know this may hurt you, it may put a knife through your heart, and you can say no, but I must get it out of my system. I want to move forward, to shake the past away. I'll never ask you to do this again."

Jessica wasn't surprised at the request: she had been waiting for it, planning for it, knowing that it would come tonight.

"Turn off the lights and sit beside me on the rug by the fire. I'll do it because you will never rest until you know. Nothing may happen, but her spirit is strong here, I've always felt it when I entered this house, the home where you both lived so happily together. I felt her presence the first time I walked though the front door, the first night we were together here. "

Keith was quite surprised but didn't know how to express his feelings. "You're wearing her clothes and I can smell her perfume, will that help?"

Jessica smiled at his observation, but didn't respond. "Hold my hands and wish that she were here, feel her presence with your whole body, everything. Don't hold back no matter how much it hurts. Open your mind and your heart. Let your emotions flow. I feel her everywhere. This is her spirit home. Tonight I could feel her hands on my body as I dressed."

"What was it like? The touch of her hands?"

"Soft, gentle, warm, quietly talking to me, but not in words."

Tears silently flowed down Keith's cheeks as he imagined Kristin's spirit comforting Jessica like a guardian angel. They held hands tightly in the darkened room as the firelight flickered.

Slowly, as Jessica concentrated he began to feel Kristin nearby, looking at him, smiling. He could almost see her in bright sunlight on the Marina Green with the bridge glowing in the sun. They ran in the fog, bright kites flew above, he could feel the wind tugging on the string they both held tightly as the afternoon breeze freshened. She was wearing the same clothes that Jessica now wore. Her lips weren't moving, but he could see in her eyes and in her lips and face a smile of approval. They were so happy together. He could feel her hands caress his face, he could feel her lips on his. The scene changed and now they were together on a blanket under a perfect blue sky, their bodies entwined. Their clothes had disappeared and they were one in the bright warm light, together forever.

The vision slowly faded. Kristin didn't walk away, she just dissolved very gradually back into a fog as Keith held her tightly.

As Keith slowly awoke from the trance, he realized that Jessica's naked body was in his arms, her head on his shoulder, and that his own clothes were scattered. His face was wet from continuous crying and he now noticed that hours had gone by. The fire was glowing embers. Perhaps a miracle had happened.

As they lay together by the fire's warmth, Jessica told Keith as she hugged him tightly, "I'll tell you a special secret about tonight. I wanted so much to be Kristin, to share my body with you as she did, to openly embrace you with no restraint, that I did everything I could to become her for a little while. I bathed in her bath salts, I put her perfume and powder on my body, and then I felt her warm hands caressing my bare skin, they gently embraced my whole body. She knew and she approved. When I put on her undergarments, when I dressed in the yellow skirt, white blouse, and tennis shoes that she wore the last time you flew kites together in San Francisco, I knew it was going to work. I wanted you so badly that I ached inside. You and I will always be together, and much of our time will be happy. I love you so much."

Keith hugged Jessica silently, not knowing what to make of this revelation. He was so happy, but also was more aware than ever of Jessica's psychic powers. Perhaps she had hypnotized him, suggesting the appearance of Kristin through her clothes and his desire for contact with the other side, kissed him herself, and pulled him to her body while she herself was in a trance pretending to be Kristin. However, she had also been honest with her secret, and no doubt believed that she had seen what she said she saw. Perhaps her trance had been so strong that she had no control over her actions, she literally was Kristin, sharing her body with his.

Keith rose with a smile, knowing now that he had the answer to his future. "Wait right here, I'll be back in a moment."

He returned holding something and sat back down beside Jessica. He held her left hand in his. "I don't know how to tell you how much I love you, it's so strong. May I place this gold ring on your finger? Will you let me take care of you for the rest of our lives, and beyond that, whatever happens?"

Jessica smiled and helped him place Kristin's wedding ring on her hand. "Yes, and I place this ring on your hand: I will be with you always and forever." They embraced again: her frigidity replaced by intense desire.

Spending the rest of his life with Jessica was going to be exciting. What a wife!

Later, as Keith fell asleep and began to snore rhythmically with his arms around Jessica's warm body, she smiled and thought over what had happened. Could she have transformed herself into Kristin and become another person? That didn't seem possible, but at least a part of Kristin had embedded itself in her heart: she could feel it growing warmly. Perhaps Kristin had given her own happiness, her love of Keith, to Jessica, so that she could carry on in Kristin's place? A pleasant thought, but there was something else: it felt as though Kristin was not only passing joy to Jessica, but also a heavy yet unclear responsibility. Jessica accepted it and felt the weight descend upon her without understanding what it might mean. She began to see herself from a new and more serious life-long perspective. She remembered the first time that she had met Keith, and the blurred vision that had rushed through her mind that morning. As she recalled the thoughts, more detail seemed to appear. Children were more distinct now, but she could also feel sharp pain mixed with happiness. She saw the key markers of a whole and complete life pass by as in a slow montage: her birth, their marriage, their children, and their death together. Death, she couldn't see it exactly, but she could feel it, and sense that it would happen far in the future: she knew that they would walk together into the spirit world hand in hand.

လအအအ

The next afternoon, when they arrived at Angela's formal Christmas Day dinner party, Jessica wore a beautiful black velvet gown, with red and green holly trimmings and Keith wore his tux with a Christmas bow-tie. They radiated happiness as they looked into each other's eyes, sticking close together, their bodies always touching, hand-in-hand. Angela noticed their wedding rings as they greeted her.

"Merry Christmas newly-weds, I see Max was right," Angela said as she greeted them.

Keith and Jessica were puzzled. "What do you mean Angela, we haven't told anyone," Keith asked, well-aware that they were not legally married yet, though they were wearing wedding rings.

"Max came by a few days ago and said that someday soon you two would be married, he was sure of it, and he told me to give you this envelope if it happened over the holidays while he was away."

She handed a simple white envelope to Keith and Jessica, who slowly opened it together. Inside was a picture of an old apartment building from the twenties, next to a vacant lot. A large U-shaped white wooden three-story building with green shutters around a courtyard. On the back of the photo was written, "We love you both. Learn by doing, 10520 Wilshire is now your building, treat it with care and it will reward you many times over."

"My god, that's a few blocks from my house," Keith said with amazement at the million dollar gift.

Jessica kissed Keith, and laughed. "And you thought my fancy watch was an expensive present."

"Angela, we're not legally married yet, we can't accept this, I mean, we promised our lives to each other and exchanged rings only last night," Keith said.

"Then you'd better high-tail it to a wedding chapel in Vegas first thing in the morning before Max changes his mind!" Angela hugged both Keith and Jessica, then brought them into the main room, where many friends were gathered by the Christmas tree.

"Ladies and Gentlemen, may I present Mr. and Mrs. Keith Warrington, a beautiful Christmas present for all of us to enjoy."

Keith knew some of the people and Jessica knew most, especially the older ones. David and Spunky rushed up to them as David asked, "Are you really married, I mean, when did this happen?"

"Tomorrow, we only decided last night." Keith replied, very confused at the rushed timetable and at his happiness on both the romantic and financial sides of life.

Jessica added, "Want to come with us to Vegas? We have a sort of private reason for wanting to do it quickly, but I know we really don't have to, it just sounds like a great idea."

Spunky added, "What a lovely Christmas present to give to each other, to give your life to the person you love on Christmas Eve." She held David's hand tightly and looked into his eyes.

As they made the rounds, talking to different people and accepting congratulations, Keith and Jessica were the happiest they had been in many months. They were talking with Angela when a man they didn't know approached. Angela introduced him, "Keith, Jessica, this is Doctor Armstrong: he saved my life just before I started working on your film."

Jessica had a premonition: something was terribly wrong, but she couldn't quite figure it out: her feelings of last night, when Kristin had given her both joy and a heavy responsibility returned. She concentrated hard on the people around her: what was happening, what were these smiling faces hiding: what had Kristin meant?

Keith thought back to his vision of Angela and her scars, lying on her garden couch after their brief encounter, "How did you save Angela's life? She was recovering from a big operation when she started working with us: it was only because of her condition that we could afford her."

"To look at Angela today you'd never know that nine months ago her insides were rotted out through much too much high living. She could barely breathe with those old tobacco lungs and her liver was headed for the graveyard."

Keith hesitatingly asked, "So you replaced her old parts with new ones, just like the doctors in our film?"

"Right in theory, but in reality it was much more complex: it's very hard to find a matching donor, a nearby and recently deceased body with just the right genetics. Sometimes I wish we had a clone farm like the one in your crazy movie. We had almost given up on Angela when we found a good match, but there was only one snag, the donor was still alive, just barely: about to die, but not dead. It was an ethical question. Two people close to death, and we knew we could combine their parts to save one of them. The only way to do it was with two surgical teams, swapping parts between the two bodies, so that the donor would die whole."

Angela added, "Then to everyone's surprise the donor didn't die, but held on for a few weeks."

Jessica interrupted, emotionally blurting out her thoughts as she realized the truth, "Angela got all the good parts and the donor, a beautiful young woman who had come to the hospital to be saved, died instead, her last breath wheezing through Angela's rotten lungs!"

Keith felt his legs begin to slide out from under his body as he fainted to the floor in slow motion. Through her tears, Jessica screamed, "Keith was in love with that girl who fought so hard to stay alive! You stole her life, you killed Kristin!"

---finis---

Seniors Have It Tough

Epilog

Years Later: New Technology

Twenty-five years after they shot SENIORS, Keith and David recovered their film cans from a fireproof vault and took them to Keith and Jessica's house in San Francisco where they would rebuild their movie with modern editorial equipment in preparation for a nationwide release. The truckload of cans contained original negative, the workprint, a multitude of short pieces of print, and many sound rolls.

The first task was copying all of the original negative, sound track, and the existing rough-cut onto digital tape, and then feeding the tape into computerized editing equipment in Keith's living room. They were going to spend their time editing and thinking while a beautiful view of San Francisco Bay and The Marina Green sparkled behind their desks.

Keith and David knew that their original film was out of date stylistically, but marveled at its creativity and originality. Even after all this time and their experiences encompassing much of the cinematic world, they found that the funny scenes were still hilarious, and the plot was still solid and original. No one else had yet done anything like this. They knew that they could re-cut their existing footage to provide the snap and speed demanded by today's audiences, but wanted to add

245

something more.

"Why don't we try to shoot the sex education video which we talked about but never did, then slip it into the film here and there, maybe even in quick flashes as the clones remember the fear it engendered," Keith suggested.

"Flashing it through their brains, just as they are about to disobey its warnings, would be a neat trick if we could make it work," David added.

"And if we make the video really funny we could add some comic-relief to the slower scenes."

"Maybe the oldies who made the sex-education film sometimes think about it too: they know it's bogus, but they had fun making it and smile when they remember playing their parts."

"And think of the explosion escape sequence behind the opening titles. As the kids run away through the night, maybe brief flashes of the video go through their minds adding to their fear?"

"Damn, I wish we had footage of the clones watching the video and conversing about it, to get their frightened reactions."

"Maybe they watch in a dark room, and we see the video over their shoulders and heads: you couldn't tell who's who, and we could do their voices as whispers so people wouldn't hear the differences. We could shoot that part as film, so it would match, and getting uniforms for the clones would be easy. We'd have boys on one side and girls on the other, with occasional across-the-aisle jokes and comments."

"I wonder if we can fake some matching voice-over for the scene where Julie teaches the two clones how to mate with each other. These kids have seen the video, and they must be afraid that what Julie is asking them to do is bad with a capital 'B'."

"She needs to calm their fears somehow, but deep inside, they'll still be afraid. This will be tricky to make believable."

"But it will also be powerful, because we can contrast their fear with what she is demanding, and don't forget that Julie's pretty scary too: remember the look on the girl's face when she saw Julie for the first time: it was unalloyed fear."

"And when Julie took the girl's clothes off, she was petrified."

"The boy nearly fainted as I recall. That's great footage. When we fold in their fear with flashes from the video it'll be stand-out dynamite."

Jessica entered the room carrying a magazine, laughing to herself at their discussion. "Don't you fellows ever change? Over-sexing your film is last year's trick. What you need are digital stuntmen from NaturalMotion. They could leap around the operating room like evil spirits on a rampage, maybe ghosts from the fertilizer plant."

David was puzzled, "What are you talking about, and what's wrong with sex? It's the main attraction in 60% of today's media. Half of internet traffic is porn."

"NaturalMotion is some geeks in Oxford who make realistic digital people who can do anything you can imagine, only they can do it for next to no money, and without actors." Jessica explained.

Keith interrupted her, "Can they make digital characters that exactly match shots we already have? Can they clone our actors from twenty-five years ago so that we can add new scenes?"

"I don't know, but here, you can read this article yourself. They did part of 'THE LORD OF THE RINGS'."
(*"Attack Of The Stuntbots", Oliver Morton, WIRED, January 2004. Page 156*)

"Hey, does it have their phone number. I'll call and ask if their digital bodies do sex scenes," David said in jest.

Jessica was serious however, "This is what Keith and I talked about years ago. Finally the computers and geeks are good enough to really start eliminating film crews. You might pay attention to this, and use it in a project. I'd love to try my hand at making the digital drawings. Perhaps we could do just a little piece, maybe when the suckers are chasing taxpayers, or in the operating room."

Keith and David read the article and continued their discussion for days, blocking out the actual scenes that they would put in the educational video and where these scenes would fall in the final cut. Although the real video might have been an hour of instruction, they only needed five minutes of crucial footage from it, so this was all that they would shoot. They were disappointed that NaturalMotion wasn't really appropriate for this project, but encouraged Jessica to learn all that she could. Perhaps stuntbots could be tried in their next film.

While they worked, Keith often looked over to a corner of the room where his old picture of Kristin sat on a table among pictures of Jessica and their children. He wondered what she would make of their activity to resurrect the story which she had helped write, as they worked in the house which money from her killer's car had bought. Perhaps she really was in Heaven watching them. He often thought of that Christmas Eve years ago when Jessica had contacted Kristin and still wondered if that had been real, if there was another side where the spirits lived after death. Whenever Jessica made contact, it seemed so true, so believable, but perhaps it was actually a form of hypnosis where Jessica, perhaps unconsciously, convinced her partners that contact had been made. There was never any physical evidence of contact, just memories of it in the brains of the participants. Keith had written two films about powerful hypnotists, based in part on Jessica's gifts. She didn't consciously hypnotize people but she could achieve some form of brain to brain communication within her circle during a trance.

Over the years there had been changes in film production driven by technology. Both Keith and David had done a considerable amount of digital editing as the equipment had improved, quickly obsolescing Moviolas and 35mm magnetic sound tracks. But in contrast to editorial work, digital production was a different story. Only one major film, STAR WARS EPISODE 2 -- ATTACK OF THE CLONES, had been shot with electronic cameras. Most other big screen movies were still shot on 35mm film, just as SENIORS had been.

Keith had used electronic cameras, and David was curious about the equipment, though he had never had a chance to try professional quality digital cameras himself. The 'instructional video' which they intended to shoot could be photographed in many ways, all of which would cost about the same, since the primary costs were in talent, sets, and stage rental. They had the time, the budget, and the control to use the approach that would be the most fun. Keith reviewed the choices open to them. The easiest would be to do the 'video' with normal 35mm film and familiar equipment, adding grainy effects to simulate ancient video production. Of course, they could actually shoot it with cheap video cameras, in the manner of THE BLAIR WITCH PROJECT. The most adventuresome approach however, would be to shoot it with the best possible electronic equipment, right on the edge of the state-of-the-art. Keith, as an engineer, loved the newest technology and had little trouble talking David into trying it for this small project.

Keith explained the current situation, and why film was different from electronic production, both technically and aesthetically. "Edison invented motion pictures, and the story is that when George Eastman asked Edison how wide movie film should be, Edison held up his thumb and forefinger indicating a size. Eastman measured the space between Edison's fingers at about one and three-eighths inch. Eastman was selling still cameras which used strips of film two and three-quarters of an inch wide, so he slit his film in half and added edge perforations for Edison's camera mechanism. The resulting film was 35mm wide, and the image area, between the perforations, was 24mm wide by 18mm high. This size standard, set by Eastman and Edison in 1889, is still used today. In 1913 Oscar Barnack, working at the Leitz microscope company, turned a short piece of 35mm movie film sideways, and doubled its image area to make the first Leica 35mm still camera, with an image 36mm by 24mm (first offered for sale in 1923). This remains the format used by almost all 35mm still cameras."

"Today the effective resolution of the best (70mm IMAX) motion picture film is about 4000 horizontal lines. This means that a picture of 4000 equally-spaced black and white lines would just be distinguishable on a theater screen. If more lines were added, the lines would blur into a gray fog. By comparison, home television, in America (NTSC, 1948), has a net resolution of only 330 lines on most sets, and VHS cassettes are even worse, with a resolution of 240 lines. Digital video (1995 standard) with its ever-shrinking little Japanese cameras, has a resolution around 500 lines, so its images are more detailed than the TV that most people watch. At the top of the video world is Sony's CineAlta electronic camera with a resolution of better than 2000 lines. This is the camera used to shoot Lucasfilm's STAR WARS in 2000, and since then it has undergone continuous refinement, approaching 4000 lines today."

"However, resolution is not the reason that the 'video look' is different from the 'film look' in aesthetic terms. Optics and math are another reason. The sensors in the normal little video cameras are very small, one quarter of an inch wide at the low end. This small size necessitates lenses with short focal lengths to obtain normal perspective. At a given f-stop, these lenses have much more depth-of-field (DOF) than the lenses used with large formats, like 35mm film (four times wider image). This means that video shots have more of the scene in focus for a given f-stop. In a movie shot on 35mm film, an actor may be in focus, but the area behind him will be slightly out of focus, providing visual separation and the illusion of depth. The same scene shot with a small-sensor video camera will have much more in focus, and as a result, it will have less aesthetic 'mystery'. CineAlta gets around this by using large sensors and lenses with big apertures to give shallow depth of field. Another reason for an aesthetic difference is dynamic range. Film can see more detail in shadows and in highlights than most video sensors can. The difference in range is about ten-to-one (about 3 or 4 stops). This means that video highlights are often burned-out white and shadows are featureless black, compared to a film of the same scene. CineAlta's electronics have pushed the dynamic range so far that it is almost as good as film for practical purposes. The last reason is skill. When audiences see a feature film, they are seeing images created by a highly-paid cinematographer with a large crew of helpers and fancy lights. But most videos are shot by small crews of less-experienced people who are in a hurry. TV news can be shot by one man on the run, and TV shows are often done in the least expensive manner with flat lighting and near-zero aesthetics."

When Keith paused for breath, David asked, "So we're

251

going first class, with Sony's CineAlta, right? What will be different to me on the set?"

"I'll stop lecturing like an Engineer and tell you what I've found as a user on my little anti-drug films. The Sony is smaller than a big film camera, but it needs large superb lenses with wide apertures to get comparable DOF (Depth of Field), a solid heavy fluid head underneath, and the same kind of lighting equipment we always use, so the total package isn't much different in size or the skill needed to operate it. The digital film is three times as sensitive, so we need one third the amount of light, but the same modeling and control: sets are a bit cooler. George could shoot CineAlta easily given the chance, using his normal lighting and exposure techniques with no changes, and the result would look just as good as his film work. The big differences for you as the Director are three: first, during a shot you can see the actual picture on a monitor if you want; second, after the shot you can review the film in full detail, instant dailies; and third you can try critical special effects right on the stage, to see if they work OK. If you find a problem, you have a chance to fix it immediately. Also CineAlta cameras hold fifty minutes of tape so you can shoot forever, compared to eleven minute film loads.

"And that's how they made digital STAR WARS, right? Same gear and workflow as you use on your short films?"

"Yes, you're going to have a ball with this stuff on the creative side, and as near as I can tell, it costs less overall. But for features, you'll have to convince lots of people in Hollywood who still have all that old camera gear lying around."

"Have you shot anything lately with these cameras?"

"It's not a recommended approach, but I took one of the fancy Sonys and turned up the gain as far as it would go on all three sensors, and achieved sensitivity comparable to ASA-2400 film. Of course it was noisy and grainy, and the

252

dynamic range was stinko, but I needed maximum film speed, and the gritty look was perfect for me: jet black shadows and burned-out highlights. Then I had a mount built to attach my old Leica 50mm f/1.0 Noctilux lens so I could shoot in available darkness from a bit of distance. I put the camera in a black plastic garbage bag on my shoulder and shot Jessica at night, sitting on a bench illuminated only by a streetlight, interviewing runaway kids in the rain over in Oakland by the rail-yard slums. The footage will tear your heart out. Some of those runaways are only ten years old. I wish we could have brought all of them home."

"Do you think your son Edward will ever come back? You've been looking for four years. I wish I could do something to help."

"Want to adopt a runaway, give it a nice foster home?"

"Let's not go there now, but show your film to Spunky when she comes up to see the final cut."

In contrast with the very new electronic cameras, computer-editing technology had been in wide use for at least ten years as costs spiraled down and capability improved. Most theatrical productions still shot 35mm film, and the theater projectors screened 35mm film, but in between everything was now digital. David normally watched digital copies of his film dailies on a laptop computer, and often started arranging the pieces of a scene shot yesterday while he ate lunch today. Once he left the stages and locations, he moved onto serious hardware, computers that held copies of every piece of negative that he had shot, only a mouse click away if he wanted to see them. Having all the footage instantly available allowed him to quickly try different ideas and sequences. The editorial process was at least ten times faster than it had been before.

When digital editing had started, special purpose

computers costing hundreds of thousands of dollars had been needed. Now a high-end personal computer could handle most of the work and there was a range of software from freeware to inexpensive versions of Avid that ran on Windows and Mac workstations. The setup in Keith's living-room was worth less than twenty thousand, yet it could do everything needed for a full-scale theatrical film edit.

As they worked rapidly to re-build their movie on the digital equipment, Keith thought about the original edit, their editor, and all the old equipment and cans of film piled everywhere. He realized that one of the biggest differences was time to think. He and David, on two networked computers, would complete the re-cut in a week or two, without working especially long hours. They knew what they were doing and were familiar with the footage. But in the old editing rooms there were many delays as footage was hunted-down, as reels were rewound by hand, as trim bins were searched for a particular piece of film. During all of these delays they would talk, walk down the hall for coffee, and think about alternate cuts. Now everything happened so fast that it seemed that there was no time for creative consideration. They could of course work slowly with the new equipment if they chose, but by its nature, it encouraged them to work quickly, babbling back and forth as they keyed and clicked scenes together.

"David, we talk about life being too fast now and too easy, but there's something else missing between editing now and back then."

"It's the people Keith. We're alone grinding this stuff out, but in the old days Lynn was cutting while Maury and Potter ran around looking for lost pieces of film and Sandy handled the phones while we interrupted everyone."

"And there was always a visitor or messenger from the lab watching or dropping in to chat. Even though the hours were long, we had so much more time to talk over everything."

"The people are the one reason I keep directing films. I don't need the money or all the other stuff, but I live to walk onto the set and see all my people, my team, ready to do something grand."

"Now a nerd in front of a computer can crank out footage in days that it would take your crew weeks to make."

"I'll never work like that. I'm one of the dinosaurs, with big old cameras, lots of crew people, and swarms of actors and extras."

"But you edit on a computer instead of a Moviola."

"Damn bean-counters don't budget any post-production time. They want revenue as soon as we shoot the last scene."

"Your teams are like the difference between a symphony orchestra with a hundred skilled players under the baton of the conductor and a nerd with a synthesizer and canned rhythm tracks. The parallel is almost exact."

"You're right, and thank god I have enough drop-dead money that I don't have to work those phony reality projects, or the trash the TV people shoot."

David went home for the day, leaving Keith at the editing console working into the night. He struggled to finish the operating room scene, the part of the movie where Spunky's nearly naked purple body is wheeled-in on a gurney to be cut up for parts, just before she is rescued. A typical tense movie sequence which should cut quickly back and forth between Spunky's tormentors and the difficult progress of the rescuers: will they get to the room in time to save her? Will she be saved, and if so, how? The old 'lady on the log headed for the buzz-saw as the hero rides to her rescue' sequence. Keith was confused and couldn't focus on his work, as Jessica approached,

255

looking over his shoulder. "Keith, let David cut this scene, it's too painful for you."

"I can do this, it's just a movie."

"But it's the scene we were about to film when you fainted on stage. It reminds you too much of Kristin in the hospital."

"That was over twenty-five years ago, it doesn't bother me now."

Jessica gently massaged his head as she stood behind him, "It will always bother you; part of you died then, and the wound will never heal."

"That's a bit melodramatic, isn't it? I mean, I'm married to the most wonderful person in the world, so how could I be worried about . . ." he stopped as tears came to his eyes. ". . . Kristin."

Keith shut-down the editing system and stood. "Why don't I ever win these discussions? You're so much better with emotions than I am."

Jessica smiled, " Let's go for a walk."

They wandered in the brisk night air, first along the stone walls at the waterfront watching the sea and dodging spray from errant waves as occasional ship's lights passed, then up to Chestnut Street to their favorite coffee shop for a hot espresso. They loved walking at night, feeling the cold wind, studying reflections off the wet streets and sidewalks, and being together: technology could never replace this.

സെസെ

End Notes & Credits

References:

Dan Ablan. DIGITAL CINEMATOGRAPHY & DIRECTING. Indianapolis: New Riders. 2003.

Alan Dale. Comedy Is A Man In Trouble. University of Minnesota Press. 2000.

John Fauer, A.S.C. SHOOTING DIGITAL VIDEO. Boston: Focal Press. 2001.

Goodman and McGrath. EDITING DIGITAL VIDEO. New York: McGraw Hill. 2003.

Joseph V. Masvelli, A.S.C., 1966. American Cinematographer Manual, Second Edition. Hollywood: American Society of Cinematographers. 1966.

Eric A. Taub. "Shooting Star Wars Bit by Bit", New York Times. May 23, 2002.

Notes in text sequence:

TECHNISCOPE AND ASPECT RATIO

Most films are shot on film that is 35mm wide, about one and a half inches. There are perforations on both sides, so the useful area of each frame is only a inch wide and 3/4 inch high (24mm x 18mm). If great care is taken, these small frames can be projected onto a huge theater screen with acceptable quality. This yields a picture that is three units high by four units wide, the standard from 1900 until perhaps the fifties. The width is 1.3 times the height.

Modern audiences like wide-screen images, where the picture is roughly twice as wide as it is high. To obtain a wide-screen effect, special lenses can be used in both the camera and the projector, to squeeze and unsqueeze a wide image onto normal film. Panavision cameras and similar equipment do this, yielding pictures whose widths are 2.2 times the height. A cheap alternative is to use normal film, but with a half-height (9mm) image. This is called Techniscope, and only half as much film is used because the images are half the height of normal images. The picture width is 2.35 times the height. Normal, non-squeeze, lenses are used, thereby saving more money. Quality suffers since only half as much film area is available to be projected so this alternative is rarely used.

At the other extreme are formats which use film that is seventy millimeters wide (four times the cost, and requiring big cameras), and at the top is 70mm film that is run sideways so that huge images can be recorded at huge expense(Imax).

16MM FILM

When a project is not destined for commercial theatrical release, but is intended for television or educational markets, 16mm film can be used, along with smaller and less costly camera equipment. The resulting small images can be enlarged onto 35mm film for theatrical release but the results are grainy and obviously inferior to work shot on 35mm: the cost is much lower however. Another use for 16mm gear is on expeditions and documentary films where camera weight is a major concern.

TYPEWRITER
Before small computers became available, all writers used either typewriters or handwriting (which was then typed by secretaries). In the seventies offices started using word processors to generate text but these were large machines, fixed in place, not the kind of thing Keith could have moved around easily. The Apple-II computer appeared in the seventies, but it generated half-width, 40-column, pages which were not practical for professional work. Around 1980 the IBM-PC appeared, allowing professional word processing on a personal computer. Soon a portable version, the Compaq 'Luggable' suitcase-size twenty-pound computer appeared, allowing professional writers to use electronic word processors wherever they went.

BREAK-DOWN
Films are written as a succession of scenes, with each new setting being a new scene number. In order to convert the script into an efficient production schedule, so that it can be budgeted and shot, the script is cut apart (symbolically), then re-assembled on a breakdown board. This is an outline of the shooting schedule, with the first day's work on the left, and the last day on the right. Mechanically, it is a folding panel four

feet wide, filled with vertical strips of colored thick paper. Each strip represents one scene, and a normal two hour film might have a few hundred scenes. The strips are gathered into groups, depending on which actors are involved and which locations are to be used for each scene. For example, all the shots on the desert were gathered into one place on the breakdown board, regardless of where the scenes fell in the script. These scenes would all be shot together so that the crew and equipment didn't move needlessly. Similarly, if an expensive big name actress were being used, all her scenes would be grouped together and shot back-to-back so as to maximize the footage that could be gathered in the limited time she offered the project. The placement of scenes on the breakdown board was juggled throughout the project to minimize costs and to recover from changes and unfortunate events like rain, accidents, scratched film, out-of-focus shots. . . .

ACTORS

There were clearly-defined layers of 'talent', actors and actresses, that might be hired. All belonged to SAG, The Screen Actors Guild, which blocked non-SAG actors from domestic films. At the top were stars, people who could command seven figures up-front as well as a percentage of the gross. Dealing with these people was a financial transaction, not an aesthetic consideration. Often the stars themselves were pleasant to work with, as long as things went their way. The next level down was 'bankable actors'. These people were well-known and adding a few of them to the cast might enable the project to borrow money from a bank. These actors and actresses had fan clubs and attracted a fair number of customers to their films. Some had been stars, and others were hoping to become stars. Below this level were competent actors who could do the job, act well, and remember their lines. No trouble to work with, but not box-office draws. These people worked for scale, the minimum union wage, and there were thousands to choose among. Below this level were actors who were either unknown, or known and not desired. There was one level further down, 'extras', who were people without speaking parts who filled out the crowd scenes. They had their own union, SEG, the Screen Extras Guild, which concerned itself with issues such as the provision of free lunches and costumes for their members. Extras made twenty-five dollars a day, and many hoped to become actors. At any moment, over ninety percent of the SEG and SAG membership would not be working on a film; they would be pumping gas, parking cars, waitressing, or doing a thousand other things while waiting for the next casting call.

CHILD ACTORS

Actors over the age of eighteen were treated as adults. When a younger actor was used, the production had to provide a teacher and a portable classroom by law. In addition, the working hours and conditions were specified, making many shoots more expensive than they would have otherwise been. In California the production also had to hire a Welfare Worker whose sole job was to watch the actor and see that she wasn't exploited or treated badly. The teachers and Welfare Workers had to be State-approved, and did not come cheaply. There were also intricate rules concerning how many children, of what ages, a teacher could handle at once etc. These rules were one reason that children were not used unless absolutely necessary, and part of the motivation for some productions to shoot their child scenes in other countries.

UNION CREWS

Most of the theatrical film production work in

Hollywood was controlled by IATSE. Its members were not allowed to work with non-union people, so as long as the best people were in the union, it was nearly impossible for non-union people to work the major projects. Each craft had its own local, and there were rules about minimum crew size and composition. On small projects, far from the major studio lots, a short crew could be used as long as all members were union.

Typical crafts were: Cinematographers and various levels of assistant, Sound mixers and assistants, Grips (a key grip and his helpers) who did everything related to moving the camera and shading light, Gaffers (electricians) who moved and operated the lights, Propmen, Painters, Wardrobe people, Script supervisors, Teamsters (truck drivers), and Craft Service people (janitors). All the Editors and their various helpers and lab people were in an editorial union.

The DGA (Directors Guild) employed all the Directors as well as various levels of Assistants. There is also a Writers Guild (WGA).

A typical production was written by a member of the WGA, directed and managed by DGA people, acted by SAG and SEG talent, and filmed by IATSE crews.

KEITH'S TAPE RECORDER

Keith used a Nagra-IV, essentially the best portable recorder in existence. It was made in Switzerland by Kudelski and recorded the sound track on the full width of quarter-inch tape so as to achieve the best signal-to-noise ratio possible. In addition it recorded a push-pull sync track down the middle of the tape. (This signal was not audible so it didn't affect sound quality.) It's frequency, nominally 60Hz, was proportional to the camera speed, so that the speed of the tape, when played-back, could be exactly matched to the camera speed.

The recorder ran on ten large flashlight batteries and although heavy, it could be carried on a shoulder strap. A stereo version of the recorder was available, and it could be quite useful for recording tracks from two different microphones when the balance was unknown, or when a true stereo sound track was needed.

After Keith recorded the track, the tape was taken to a studio where it was played back at the speed indicated by its sync track. The playback was recorded on clear 35mm film which had been coated with a magnetic stripe. The editor could run this 35mm sound track on his moviola exactly in sync with the picture. Projection booths in most of Hollywood could project the picture while playing the mag-stripe track on a separate machine exactly synchronized to the projector. This kind of equipment was used to view the dailies every morning, as well as rough cuts made by the editor.

GAIN ADJUSTMENT

Keith's main sound mixer task during a take was to adjust the level of the recording for each microphone in use, fading in the currently-speaking actor and fading out the others so as to minimize background noise. The goal was to record strongly enough to almost saturate the tape, to maximize the signal-to-noise ratio of the recording. This minimized the tape hiss which would be heard if he recorded too weak a track. If an actor began to speak too loudly, compared to the rehearsals, Keith would need to quickly turn down the gain to compensate. The process was based on skill, experience, and aesthetic judgment.

In contrast to this, the recorder could be set on 'automatic'. The recorder would then raise and lower the gain itself, to match the speaking level. However this would mean that in between spoken words the recorder would turn up the gain, mistakenly thinking that the actor had become quieter, and so introduce much background noise between words. Then when the actor began to talk again, the first word would be overloaded before the recorder could turn down the gain. Most cheap recorders operate this way, and a careful listener can hear the background noise 'breathe' in and out on recordings made automatically.

This was the situation in 1980. However, by 2006 professional digital recorders with huge dynamic range were available, greatly reducing the need for manual gain adjustment during a shot if only one mike were in use.

FISHER BOOM

Manufactured by J.L.Fisher co, Burbank, CA. This is a telescopic three-wheel microphone boom available in various lengths up to about twenty-nine feet. There is a self-adjusting counterweight at the back end. The wheel axles can be shortened for transport, and the boom can be lowered to reduce its height. A round cranking drum is operated with the right hand to move the mike closer to or away from the operator, while the left hand controls a lever that rotates the mike. A special soft silent mike cable coils and uncoils automatically on pulleys as the boom's length expands and contracts.

RED LIGHTS

On every sound stage, the Sound Mixer, Keith in this case, is given a switch box on a long cord. Normally the box controls the roof-top fans as well as red lights over all stage entrances and a loud buzzer. When Keith sensed that a sound take was almost ready to start he killed the noisy fans, so that they would coast to a stop before shooting began. When the A.D. or Director said "Roll em", he would turn on the red lights and pulse the loud buzzer to warn everyone to be quiet and to keep the doors closed.

VOICE OVER LINES

Lines that an actor speaks when the camera cannot see her lips moving. These can be recorded at any time, and the editor can place them anywhere on the sound track.

LOOPING AND DUBBING

When an actor or actress's speech needs to be re-recorded, the standard practice is to "loop it". Film of the actress speaking the particular lines is spliced into a continuous loop. A matching loop is made from the sound that was recorded during production. Another loop is made with blank tape. The loops and the actress, Editor, and Director go to a special sound studio. Here the film is loaded into a projector and the loops are put on synchronized recorders. The actress stands in front of a movie screen watching herself play the scene and speak the lines over and over. The actress wears headphones and listens to the production sound track. After several passes, she begins working to speak the dialog in sync with the picture and her efforts are recorded. The Director helps her deliver the lines with the desired emphasis and inflection. The Editor listens on headphones to the fresh recording of her voice, and judges how well it matches her lips moving on the film. The track running through the actress's headphones can be changed to the fresh recording so that she can judge how well she is doing. If the lines are complex, or different from those that had been recorded when filming, or the actress finds it difficult to achieve synchronization and the correct delivery, this can take a long time. There are some actors who can never achieve synchronization, and there are others who can do it perfectly after a few tries. This process is also used to "dub" on-camera dialog with foreign sound tracks, though the lip-synchronization is usually poor.

TV COMMERCIALS

These are often shot with large high quality IATSE film crews in a day or two. The reason for this is that the cost of making the commercial, even with the best quality crew, actors, sets, etc is much less than the cost of buying the television airtime. Advertisers want to be sure that the film they show on TV for a few seconds is the best possible representation of their product, so they go to much trouble to produce their commercials.

APPLE BOX

These are special wooden boxes available in standard modular sizes, usually three, six, nine, and twelve inches thick, made from three-quarter inch plywood. The boxes are all approximately one foot by two feet in size. They are strong enough to hold considerable weight and their wood construction allows nails to be used to hold them in place or things to be attached anywhere.

TAROT CARD

There are hundreds of different cards and they are used by some people to tell the future. The practice in Europe is at least 500 years old. There is a Chinese version that is 2500 years old. Many card designs have appeared over the centuries.

COVERAGE

During the actual filming, each scene was covered from different camera positions such as close-ups, wide shots, reactions, over-the-shoulder views of other actors, as well as perhaps with alternate action and dialog. Each set-up usually involved several takes, since the actors' delivery and the crew's skills changed. Even if everything were perfect on the first take, another take would be made immediately in case the negative for the first take was lost or scratched. For these reasons, it was not uncommon to shoot ten times more film than would actually be used in the final release print. 35mm film runs through the camera at ninety feet per minute, and in Keith's day the cost for film and its processing was about a dollar a foot.

OVERNIGHT CLEANERS

Anything can be rented by the day or night in Hollywood. Jessica would have the wardrobe cleaned each night so that the next day's shots would match.

MAGIC CASTLE

The description of the Magic Castle is based on the author's visits in the 1970's: it still exists and today has a website. However, the events described in this book, especially Jessica's psychic séance, are fictional. The piano, Irma, was then as it is described in the text.

WE'RE IN THE MONEY

This song is from "Brother, Can You Spare a Dime," lyrics by Yip Harburg, music by Gorney Harburg (1931). The first few lines are:

"We're in the money, we're in the money;
We've got a lot of what it takes to get along!
We're in the money, the sky is sunny,
Old man Depression you are through, you done us wrong."

FIRST SURFACE MIRROR

Normal mirrors have a silver reflective coating on the

back side so that the coating is protected from damage such as corrosion or scratches. The light goes through the glass, hits the silver, then goes back through the glass and out the front. These two trips through glass can distort an image. In precise optical work a piece of glass is first ground extremely flat, then a reflective coating is applied on the top surface where the light hits it directly. In use, the reflection from the silver is perfect with no chromatic or mechanical distortion, but the mirror must be handled carefully to preserve its qualities.

LIGHT METERS

Cinematographers use meters to measure light intensity and a Viewing Glasses to judge scenes. A Viewing Glass is a dark gray filter (3 stops or more) on a neck strap. It is used by a Cinematographer when looking at a scene to evaluate the contrast. When he first puts the viewing glass over his eye, for perhaps five seconds the scene appears very dark, almost monochromatic, and any unusual highlights can be quickly spotted with practice. After several seconds, his eye will adapt to the low light level and the scene will appear normal, so the effect is lost. Therefore, a viewing glass is only used briefly, except when it is used for viewing clouds or other bright objects.

The standard light meter in Keith's day was a Spectra Professional, which measured the light incident, falling onto, a scene. The cinematographer controlled the incident light rather than the light reflected from the scene because he wanted all the shots in a sequence to appear to have been made under identical lighting conditions so that they would cut together easily. The film sensitivity and the camera shutter speed ($1/48^{th}$ of a second at 24 FPS) were usually fixed so the meter scale could be calibrated directly in f-stops. When the film or shutter were changed, a different slide, a perforated metal plate, was slipped into the meter so that it read f-stops correctly under the new conditions.

FOCUS

The First Assistant Cameraman, who is called a "focus puller" in England, controls the camera focus. Since the camera positions are carefully-rehearsed, and the actors move between fixed marks on the floor, focus distances between subject and camera can be measured exactly. Normally the Assistant places small triangular pieces of tape on the side of the lens for each important part of a shot, so that as the camera or actor moves during a shot, he can control the focus exactly.

CAMERA VIEWFINDERS

On old (pre-1968) Mitchell cameras the entire camera body could move sideways a few inches with respect to the lens. In the right-hand position, a viewfinder is behind the lens so the cameraman can look directly through the lens and see exact framing and focus. When the body is moved to the left position, the camera and film are behind the lens and the viewfinder is useless. This scheme allows a rock steady camera body to operate directly behind an excellent lens without compromise. (Some of these cameras have pulled eight million feet of film and are still running perfectly.) Moving the camera body is called 'racking over'. While actually filming a scene, the cameraman uses a separate viewfinder which is mounted on the left side of the camera, a 'side finder', which is aligned so that it shows about the same coverage as the lens. This only works with fixed-focal-length lenses, but it was quite OK before zoom lenses became popular.

Arriflex cameras have mirrored shutters. While the shutter is closed and the film moves forward one frame, the mirror deflects the lens's image into a viewfinder. Then when

269

the shutter opens, to expose a frame of film, the viewfinder goes black. The result is that the film sees perfectly through the lens half of the time, and the cameraman also sees through the lens, half of the time. The image he sees flickers forty-eight times a second (the mirror is in two segments) , but cinematographers become used to it. This arrangement allows any lens, including zooms, telescopes, and close-up lenses to be used easily, and it reduces the weight and complexity of the camera. The Arriflex was developed in Germany in 1937: Leni Reifenstahl used one for her famous film of the 1938 Berlin Olympics.

In 1968 Mitchell developed a reflex camera of their own, the BNC-R, although Cinema Products Corporation had already been making a pellicle version of the BNC for several years. This camera was, internally, a model NC to which reflex viewing and a sound blimp had been added. The blimp encased the camera so that it operated silently.

FILM REGISTRATION & PULL DOWN

Inside a movie camera the film alternates between moving to the next frame and holding still while an exposure is made. Normal speed is 24 frames a second so a complex and very steady mechanism is required. If the film moves slightly at the beginning or end of the exposure time ($1/48^{th}$ of a second) the image will be slightly blurred. In the theater the image needs to be blown-up from about one inch wide, on the film, to perhaps fifty feet wide on the screen, so movement during exposure is not tolerated. (on cheap films the audience can sometimes see the titles floating up and down, indicating that a crummy camera was used to shoot the titles.)

The best way to hold the film still during an exposure is to poke a pair of precise registration pins through the perforations adjacent to the frame during the exposure. The best way to move the film is to grab it through four perforations so that there is no danger of tearing or enlarging the perforations on the edge of the film. Both of these features have been used on the heavy solid Mitchell cameras for decades.

PROCESSS SHOTS

This refers to camera tricks which allow two or more images to be combined. Still photographers have been doing this since the dawn of photography. In the movie world, it refers to combining two films to produce a composite image. As Harry mentions, a background 'plate', which is film he might have shot from a truck driving through Paris, was rear-projected onto a screen behind actors sitting in an automobile on a stage. When the camera and projector are exactly positioned and electrically synchronized with each other (big three-phase Selsyn motors were used to sync the camera and projector), the effect would be nearly perfect, especially if a wind machine blew the actors' hair, while grips rocked the car back and forth to simulate motion. The cameraman would see the final scene through his lens, and could adjust the foreground lighting for the most realistic effect. The major problems were aesthetic: having the same vanishing point in both the foreground and in the plate, and having the same angle of light in both.

In Keith's day, this was easier to achieve with blue screen photography and color film. The background, and anything that was not supposed to appear in the final composite was painted 'process blue', an intense poster-paint blue that smelled of sulfur. Then the actors, carefully lit so that no blue reflections appeared on their clothing, would act their parts. The lab would erase all the blue from the scene (including, sometimes, the blue in an actor's eyes), and replace it with a different film, perhaps of a distant city, or an explosion, or animation, or photos of outer space. The possibilities were endless, such as Mary Popins flying over London roof-tops, actors fighting giant ants, and spaceships flying through the stars.

Color television, through a similar process called chroma-key, allowed this to be done in real time so that the effect could be seen and adjusted while the scene was being shot.

DOLLIES & HEADS

The large heavy sound cameras could be supported by a heavy tripod, but the support of choice, used whenever possible, was a dolly. This was a wheeled device which could carry a camera as well as its operator(s) silently and very smoothly during a shot. None were motorized, the motive force being supplied by a Grip who could silently push the dolly wherever desired. If the floor were rough, track could be positioned to provide vibrationless travel. Even when movement during a shot was not needed, a dolly provided a convenient camera platform, with seats, that could be easily moved. Most dollies had hydraulic schemes for raising and lowering the camera silently during a shot.

The most popular model, on large stages, was made by the Moviola Company. This 500 pound aluminum device rode silently on four sets of ten-inch pneumatic tires with ball-bearing axles. The wheels were steerable in two different ways. In the normal mode, the rear wheels steered so that the Grip could push the dolly around the stage in a conventional manner. By moving a silent lever, he could switch to crab steering, in which all four wheels steered together. This allowed the dolly to move like a crab, sideways or in any direction desired. The wheels could also be locked in the straight-ahead position for riding on metal track. There was also a brake. Everything moved silently and smoothly: heavy but precise equipment.

The Moviola crab dolly carried a compressor and an

accumulator tank to power the hydraulic boom. The energy stored in the tank allowed the Grip to silently raise and lower the camera on cue during a movement. Any rate of rise or drop could be controlled by valves near the steering handle at the rear of the dolly. The camera seats rose and fell with the camera.

If the camera were light, it could be supported by a fluid head, a spring-loaded hydraulic device like a shock absorber between the camera and the dolly that allowed the operator to move the camera slowly and very smoothly in both pan and tilt directions. Heavy cameras, such as the Mitchell BNCR that George was using, required a strong gear head for support. When using a gear head, the camera was moved in pan and tilt by turning two wheels, one with each hand. Considerable Operator skill was necessary to do this correctly during a complex move, keeping the scene framed exactly in the manner in which it had been rehearsed. Like the dolly, a gear head was a beautifully-made piece of heavy precision equipment, weighing close to a hundred pounds by itself.

On remote locations, smaller dollies, such as the Elemack Spyder could be used. This particular dolly has wheeled legs which can be folded into a range of small configurations.

FILM PROCESSING

The day's film was unloaded and sent to the lab, CFI (Consolidated Film Industries, AKA "Can't Find It"), for overnight processing. At the start of the day, each new steel can of film, either 400 or 1000 feet of Kodak-5254, had been factory-sealed with white tape. An Assistant Cameraman had gone into a darkroom, or put his arms and the film into a black changing bag, opened each can in total darkness, taken the film from the black paper bag which protected it inside the can, then placed the roll of film into a metal camera magazine. Each roll of film was on a yellow core, but there was no reel or side flange to hold the film in place. He had to be careful not to let the film unwind or telescope on its core while manipulating it and threading the magazine in the dark. Mitchell magazines were the easiest to load because the supply and take-up sides opened separately and there was no need to control the amount of leader dangling from the supply side. Arriflex 400-foot geared displacement magazines required more care. In total darkness, just the right amount of film was pulled from the supply side, until the end of the film reached a bump on the side of the magazine, then the end was threaded into the take-up side of the magazine onto an empty core, leaving a perfect loop outside the magazine. The Assistant was expected to get the loop length exactly right, within one perforation, and to do it quickly. At the end of the day, or whenever convenient, after most or all of a roll was exposed, the process was reversed and the exposed film was taken out of the magazine and put back into a black paper bag and into a can. Then each can was wrapped with tape, across a diameter rather than around the edge, to make it clear that the can contained exposed film. The Assistant was very careful to keep each roll's exposure log with its can, so that the lab would know what to do with each roll. All shots were on the log, but the lab would print only the circled takes, at least as far as tomorrow morning's dailies were concerned. After each good take, the Director would say "print it", and both the Sound Mixer and the Assistant Cameraman would circle the take on his log: both used the same self-carboning log sheets.

ARC LIGHTS

Initially, before Edison invented filament lamps, the only electric lights were arcs. An arc light is just a spark between two electrodes. The trick is starting, then maintaining the arc.

To start it burning, the electrodes must be touched together for a moment, then pulled back slightly. If they are pulled back too far, the arc stops. Experienced welders do this all the time as they weld steel, but it's tricky, like learning how to light a match. An arc light wouldn't burn for long if the rods making the arc were fixed in position, because as they disintegrate from the heat their ends move apart. Therefore, at least one electrode must slowly move toward the other if a constant light is desired. (a motor provides this slow movement) Arc streetlamps were developed in the late nineteenth century. They could burn all night by slowly moving very thick rods toward each other.

In the film business there is a desire for at least eleven minutes of operation for everything. This is because a thousand feet of film runs through a camera or projector in eleven minutes (exactly 90 feet per second). For this reason, studio arcs have carbons that burn about twelve minutes when new. The lights used for outdoor night scenes are the largest lights used in the film business. They are called TITANS, and consume twenty-eight kilowatts at full power, 350 amps DC at 80 volts across the arc. (additional power is lost in the massive hot ballast which is in series with the arc, so the generator load is forty-two KW for each TITAN). These heads weigh 261 pounds and the positive carbons are over two feet long. BRUTES are slightly smaller and consume fifteen KW from the generator.

There are two key properties of arc light. The first is that the light comes from a very small pool of glowing plasma, so it can be focused into a sharp beam if desired. This means it can shine quite far. The other key property is that arc light is efficient, converting much of the incoming electricity into light. These two properties are why military searchlights seeking aircraft in WW-2 movies are always big arc lights. (these are now used mostly to attract attention for opening nights and sales.)

GENERATORS, DC

On a large shoot the electric lights consume a great deal of power, easily as much as several homes or a small office building. Motion Picture stages are wired to provide ample power, but locations usually are not. When sufficient power is not available, a truck-mounted generator is used. These are usually sound-proof and as a result they are quite large.

Incandescent lights, the kind of bulbs used at home, can run on either alternating current (AC) or steady direct current (DC). However the large arc lights used on film exteriors can only run on DC which is not available unless huge rectifiers or generators are provided.

INCANDESCENT LIGHTS & STAGE WIRING

These are lights that glow by heating a filament, the same technology that people use at home. Lights for movies come in a range of sizes, all of them large by comparison to home lighting. At home, the largest common size is 100 or 150 watts. Here, the smallest size is a MINI or a MIDGET, both of which accommodated bulbs up to 250 watts. Then comes BABY at 500 or 750 watts, followed by JUNIOR at 1000 or 2000 watts. The JUNIORs are usually called either 1K or 2K, depending on the bulb inside, and sometimes the 2K is called a DEUCE. Next up is SENIOR, at 5000 watts, also called 5K. Biggest is the TENER, also called 10k. All of these use Quartz-iodide bulbs which are expensive, but which are small physically and which maintain their color temperature over their lifetimes. Changing one of these bulbs when it is hot is dangerous, since their envelopes run at a thousand degrees: enough to melt any glove or instantly fry a finger to a crisp. The small lights, up to perhaps 2K, can easily be carried when mounted on wheeled stands. However the 10K, at 117 pounds for just the head, and big, the lens being twenty inches in diameter, is not easily handled manually. Often the 10k is mounted on a wheeled hydraulic base which can raise it high over a set, to simulate bright directional sunlight.

The above are relatively hard lights which can be focused by moving the bulb back and forth with respect to the lens. Soft lights are also used. These are white steel boxes containing one to ten 1000 watt quartz bulbs, each on a separate switch for versatility. The bulbs are hidden so that the light generated by these fixtures comes from diffuse reflections off the white paint. In addition to these, there are many special-purpose lights. All can be rented by the day in almost any quantity desired.

These lights use large amounts of electricity, all supplied at 120 volts, and usually as AC (Alternating Current) from either power lines or portable generators. A large set like the Canteen on Stage 9, could require a peak of seventy kilowatts (a pair of 10Ks and many medium-size lights), which is almost 600 amps. This is as much as three normal houses use, if everything inside were turned on at once. Sets ran hot when all the lights were on, so exhaust fans were important, and most of the lights were turned off as soon as they were not needed.

In Keith's day, wiring to the lights had not changed in perhaps fifty years. The cord from each light ended in a flat three-inch- wide plastic or Micarta paddle plug, with a fat copper electrode on each edge. These were plugged into sockets which could accommodate several narrow plugs side-by-side or one big plug, such as from a 10K. Nothing except caution prevented fingers, nails, or heavy stands from falling into a socket: they were not covered or enclosed. Heavy cables ran from the sockets, and the upstream fuse might blow at 1000 amps on each leg of the incoming power. The cords and lamps were of many vintages, with the oldest using cloth-covered natural rubber cables. The heaviest cables were joined by copper lugs inside wooden splice boxes. Usually a rubber flap was fitted to the sides of the splice boxes, to keep feet and metal objects away from the live copper buss-bars inside. Often connections were made on live circuits to save time, since shutting off power would darken the whole set. There were no fuses on stage, and no ground wires or protective devices of any kind.

RIGGING

EMT, Electro-Metallic Tubing, is the electrical conduit that encloses wiring in almost every public, commercial and industrial building in America. It is steel, silver-colored, thin, and strong. It is available in almost every town and city in ten-foot lengths, and in sizes ranging from a half an inch to four inches in diameter. It is inexpensive and easily worked. Grip trucks usually carried an assortment of EMT to use in the quick construction of temporary structures. Instead of using the proper electrical connectors to join pieces, the normal approach was to cut a piece of EMT to length, then flatten an inch at each end with a few smashes of a hammer. Then a hole would be either punched or drilled through the flat part. The flat ends of various pieces of EMT would be quickly bolted together into almost any structure, from a camera platform a foot long, to a diagonally-braced scaffold twenty feet high. The tubing could be easily cut with either a tubing cutter or a hack saw. Holes could be drilled with air-powered or electric drills. Air power was particularly-convenient, since a tank of dry nitrogen (essentially dry air under high pressure) could be obtained easily at any welding supply store, and it would run a drill for a few hours.

SOUND TRACK AESTHETICS

When sound first came to movies, the track was used to help the picture tell the story, not replace it. Often the picture was made as in the silent era, with the viewer being able to understand the story without the sound: the sound was an extra treat. Music and dialog with an occasional sound effect like a doorbell were the main components of the track. A perfect example is the Dracula film from the early thirties. Minutes pass with no sound at all as the hero wanders around the old castle in Transylvania. There are no tense violins, creepy noises, or exaggerated sound effects and yet the suspense and fear are perfectly portrayed.

The advent of STAR WARS and other loud movies coincided with the development of better sound projection equipment processed through Dolby's electronics and multiple loudspeakers. To a viewer it now seems that each theater is involved in a contest to see which can bring more hearing damage to the members of its audience.

MARINA GREEN

A flat grass-covered park in the middle of the northern edge of San Francisco, adjacent to San Francisco Bay. Before 1906, the Green was a sandy swamp. The whole Marina section of the city was filled in with mud and sand from the Bay then covered with temporary buildings for the Pan Pacific Exposition in 1915. The Green was 'The North Gardens' during the expo. After the expo, all buildings except The Palace Of Fine Arts were torn down and the Marina district became a real estate development. The 'North Gardens' became an air strip for small planes. (There is a monument to flights that originated from it.) After World War Two, the air strip was replaced with grass, creating a large windy open area perfect for games, picnics, and kites. Most days there is at least a sea breeze, and in the summer there can be a strong wind for many days in a row, as central California heats, drawing wind and fog through the Golden Gate.

The two blocks of houses that face the Green are triangular in shape and small in area, and each has ten properties directly facing the view. Each of the other two sides of the triangular blocks are only six properties wide. Lots on the triangular small blocks are odd shapes. The backs of the houses almost touch. Many of the houses are unusual designs, to obtain the most view, regardless of other considerations. Home prices are very high because the view is unrivalled, and impossible to block with new construction.

DISTRIBUTION

While anyone can shoot a film, the big trick is making a film that lots of people pay to see. Only then is there a chance of turning a profit. The steps between editing and theater audiences are called Distribution. In the nineteen twenties and thirties the big film studios bought and built most of the good theaters and operated them as chains showing only their own films. This arrangement made it virtually impossible for films made by independents to obtain theatrical distribution. The big studios claimed that owning a theater chain was essential to their business model. Each studio made many films of varying quality and needed outlets to screen all of them. By owning both studios and theaters, the hits could cover the cost of the duds, and the business as a whole could be very profitable.

Independent film makers and artists attacked this scheme and eventually won Supreme Court judgments that separated the theater chains from the studios after WWII. However, what really ruined the old scheme was television. TV gave rise to new studios and new combinations of artists, agents, and outlets that could compete financially with the old studios. SENIORS could be distributed in many ways, including videotapes, television (domestic and foreign) and theaters (domestic and foreign). Many companies compete to find good films then distribute them at a profit. The distributor's main costs are marketing and making the prints (about $1000 each), as well as shipping them to the theaters. For a nation-wide release, the distributor can easily spend more on advertising than it cost to make the movie. Many financial arrangements are possible and often a film-maker will find that he cannot obtain production financing until he has a distribution deal inked. The risk of making an orphan film that nobody wants is too high for most production financiers.

CINE-ALTA

(Sony HDW-F950) Shoots 24 frames per second without interlace, the same as film cameras, with a choice of exposure times. Native wide-screen 16:9 HD format, with aspect ratio of 1.78:1. Separate red, blue, green sensors. Internal compression ratio of 4.4:1, with an output data rate of 185 Megabits per second. Signal-to-noise ratio best available. Cassette holds 50 minutes of data on half-inch tape. Sensitivity comparable to ASA-300 film. On-shoulder weight, with battery and lens, 17 pounds. Completely adjustable for colorimitry. Adjustable soft-focus and contrast manipulation effects. Can be set to operate as a NTSC or PAL video camera. Records high quality multi-track sound. High detail monochromatic viewfinder or color viewfinder or both. Stop motion capability like a film camera. Cost about $1000/day to rent.

A SAMPLE FILM-DIGITAL-FILM WORKFLOW

After a day's shooting, the 35mm film is developed just as before. However an adequate, but not wonderful, electronic copy of all the negative is made instead of the normal film prints. The electronic copy includes the camera negative's edge numbers, as well as the sound track. This digital copy is moved into a large computer, usually one running editing software from the Avid company. Copies of the digitized film can be carried on small tape cassettes, DVDs and CDs, and viewed anywhere. Once the pictures are inside the Avid machine, editing moves much more quickly than it had in the old days. Any piece of footage can be found with a few mouse clicks. Sequences can be viewed with dissolves and special effects in-place. Different versions can be made and compared. Still photos, animation, and special effects sequences as well as double exposures and all manner of color manipulations can be tried at the keyboard. When the digital edit is complete, the computer prints an Edit Decision List, showing exactly how the original camera negative should be cut for making the final release prints. A Negative Cutter at the lab, working just as he always has, slowly assembles the original negative with hot splices. He watches the digital edit, with all the edge numbers, for reference, while working. The end result on film is exactly the same as it has always been. The only change is that the editing process had been compressed from months to weeks.

AN ALTERNATE WORKFLOW

After the digital editing process, the computer data can be sent directly to a lab which has an ARRI laser machine. It takes the electronic edit and uses it to burn Kodak 5242 35mm internegative film with three lasers, red, blue and green. This interneg is then used normally to make 35mm release prints for theaters. The audience won't see much difference in the prints compared to a pure film release, and this process eliminates the negative cutter and all of his manual splices.

Be Sure To Read
E. Scott Spencer's Other Books:

HAUNTED STEEL ADVENTURES

A bright young man, Matthew, and a posh young woman, Azur, struggle to understand strange psychic phenomena. Matt, a practical Engineer, cannot believe what he sees and feels, while Azur, a snooty English parapsychology expert, thinks she knows all about it. A difficult romance develops as they interact with undead creatures who were Matt's ancestors. These entities are playful one moment and deadly the next, powerful in some ways, surprisingly weak in others, with strong interests in practical jokes and sex. Matt is fascinated by their invisibility, but Azur is afraid they will kill her.

The setting for these adventures is a dilapidated English country house that is falling into the sea. Matt is torn between heartaches over Azur and his fight to install steel beams under the large house before it washes away. He is determined to stop the erosion and restore the house to its former glory, even though bureaucrats are trying to demolish it and build a power plant on the site. Perhaps his weird grandparents can help . . . .perhaps he can somehow win Azur . . . . perhaps the rock under the house won't crush him before he installs enough steel . . . .

Details from both the psychic and the engineering worlds are extensive, and somewhat authentic. A complete but not-overly-technical description of the structural engineering is in an Appendix for those who wish to learn more.

GYPSY WAVES

Kowabunga! Two Stanford students unravel messages ancient ancestors scattered across the planet before the last ice age. An unusual young Gypsy woman and a nerdy, but good-looking guy, use scientific skills to uncover clues that have gone unnoticed for millennia. She's into biotech, genetics, and other people's locks, while he's all math and computers without a clue about girls. Follow them down the tunnels, across the campus, and through secret passages, as they struggle against ignorance and the deadly Alienologists who would rather kill than let the truth be known. Read this book tonight. Tomorrow, amaze your friends with new-found bizarre ideas and strange interpretations of ancient history. Join the excitement as they scam the internet, kill the goons, and break through the wall of unscientific bunk surrounding Egyptology. You'll laugh, cry, and laugh again as their crazy ideas shake your gray cells and dislodge old beliefs about human history.

"He does it again: E. Scott Spencer, author of SENIORS HAVE IT TOUGH, and HAUNTED STEEL ADVENTURES, has written another outrageous adventure combining interesting clever characters, unheard-of situations, and a most surprising ending."